PRAISE FOR LEIGH RIKER

Riker's characters are wonderful. (RT Online Book Reviews)

Ms. Riker is a master of the contemporary...[who entices] the reader with strong characterizations and a multi-layered plot. (The Paperback Forum)

Author Leigh Riker excels at developing characters and situations that are emotionally gripping and intense. (Romantic Times)

Riker again demonstrates her ever-increasing talent as a Women's Fiction novelist. (Romantic Times)

THE GO-TO GIRL

LEIGH RIKER

In memory of my beloved Daisy. Miss you, sweetie.

❧ I ❧

TIFFANY & COMPANY was one of Tess O'Neill's very favorite places to shop.

From a professional standpoint, anyway. Personally, beyond the odd crystal paperweight or silver letter opener, Tess couldn't afford anything the Cincinnati branch store in the Kenwood Towne Centre had to offer. *Breakfast at Tiffany's* wasn't part of her current lifestyle. Neither was lunch today, for that matter. In late morning she was already running behind in her schedule and, worse luck, as a personal shopper she was rapidly running into trouble.

Seated in the store's private viewing room, Tess stared down at her third finger, left hand, as if she'd never seen it before. Like a proverbial bad penny—no, like Tess's persistent memories of her ex-husband—her plain gold wedding band was still there. In almost twenty-five years, and even since their divorce, she hadn't removed it.

"Take it off, Tess." Meredith Walker, her assistant and the third person in the room, slanted her a wicked smile. "I mean, *all off*," she said under her breath. "It's not as if you're still married, and you don't get the chance every day to wear a fifty-thousand dollar diamond ring instead."

Tess tugged again, but her ring didn't budge.

Still, she had real motivation to try again. As Marilyn Monroe had once crooned, "Diamonds are a girl's best friend," and the dazzling, round solitaire set in platinum winked up at Tess from the dark velvet tray on the table. This might be her best chance to see that much polished carbon on her own hand.

Predictably, her mouth began to water. This was a good sign.

She concentrated harder on her client's wish list—the reason she was here. In the past few years Tess had gradually turned her love of retail—or rather a one-time mania for shopping—into a career as everyone's Go-To Girl, which was now the name of her business. *No reasonable request refused* was her motto. *You want it, we'll find it.*

People relied upon her to solve their buying problems, and she wouldn't disappoint Emery Shallowford. For his wedding anniversary the prominent local neurosurgeon wanted to surprise his wife of thirty years with a "significant gift."

Wow, I'll say. Tess gazed at the glittering stone, five carats in all. The brilliant cut flashed like the Aurora Borealis whenever the overhead light in the room shifted, which it was probably programmed to do for effect.

Through the half-open door to the main area of the store she glimpsed several well-dressed women, most likely from the affluent Indian Hill community, one of whom, despite the spring day, was wearing a full-length sable coat. Tess figured if she owned a fur like that—PC or not—she'd think about wearing it too. The scent of Chanel—perfume, not eau de cologne—drifted in her direction. She was definitely out of her element.

This private room with its thick carpet, and gold-framed paintings on the walls, all but shouted high-end, but Tess refused to feel intimidated.

Beside her at the table Merry glanced at the jeweler across from them who wore a classic black suit. "This piece is near-museum quality," the other woman pointed out, which was okay. Emery was paying, Tess reminded herself.

She studied the other, equally expensive gems in the display tray, but they didn't interest her. Only this one did. She felt that familiar surge of euphoria that always gripped her when she discovered the absolutely perfect thing for a client, if not for herself.

"Darn," she muttered, worrying the band Grady O'Neill had slipped on her finger when Tess was nineteen. There'd been no engagement ring then because he couldn't afford one. The quick flash of memory, the intent look in his dark eyes when he met her gaze above this very band, the utter love in his expression then, the smell of candles and old books in the justice of the peace's parlor, tightened her throat. Just in time she pulled herself back from one of her too-frequent fantasies of their bright beginning nearly a quarter century ago, of what might have been, rather than the darker abyss at the end.

Yet like a needed reminder of her failed marriage, her wedding band still wouldn't come off. She twisted one way then the other until her skin felt bruised and her cheeks grew hot.

Grady had probably played poker to win her ring in the first place. But had he won, really? In the end he'd lost Tess. Lost everything. And so had she. Something to remember every time she made another payment on the gargantuan balance on the MasterCard they'd shared.

The jeweler looked concerned. "Is there a problem?"

"A small one...not to make a pun. My ring is a little snug."

Tess tried to blame the weather for her growing discomfort and her obviously swollen finger. Outside the air-conditioned store the day had become much too warm for April. Or were her clothes making her sweat? Her pants from Macy's and cashmere sweater from Dillard's—the latter forty percent off after Christmas—still said winter. The fact that the sweater was a bargain had made the find all the sweeter.

The diamond, *au contraire*, as the elegant saleswoman had pointed out, wasn't cheap by any means—but being a personal shopper had its perks.

If Emery Shallowford liked her choice of the ring, her fifteen percent commission on the sale would go straight into Tess's house fund, bringing her that much closer to buying a place of her own again. Sooner, rather than later, she'd be able —at last—to afford a down payment. This time she wouldn't be diverted from her goal; she wouldn't allow herself to be swayed even by one of her dad's pleas for another loan he would never repay.

Tess glanced from the plain 14K gold band still on her finger to the sparkling solitaire. *I must have it—for Sybil Shallowford.*

Then her gaze landed on Meredith's naked ring finger and her face brightened. "Never mind me. *You* try the diamond."

Merry blinked, her emerald-green eyes wide, obviously surprised that Tess was handing her the assignment. Tess had to bury her own shopping lust for the greater good they might accomplish. By hook or by crook—whatever that meant—they would succeed. Tess always wondered about the actual meaning of such trite sayings, but she wouldn't dwell on it now.

Time was of the essence. Spring was one of her busier seasons, Christmas being the most hectic. She and Merry already had a dozen weddings lined up with bridesmaids' bracelets and groomsmen's cufflinks yet to buy. Mentally she ticked off the rest, recalled from her iPhone's to-do list. Fifteen graduation gifts too, including those for a nursery school or two...

Fortunately, Merry got the message. Taking a deep breath, she ran her fingers through her short, spiked red hair, plucked the solitaire from the velvet tray, and shoved it on her finger.

The jeweler hummed in approval. Finally. From various angles Merry and Tess too admired the play of light through the stone. It twinkled and flashed in a full spectrum of colors that even outshone Merry's outfit, a pair of chartreuse satin pants and a purple empire-waisted top that to Tess looked like a maternity dress. So far Tess had had no luck upgrading Merry's fashion look for business hours, but she smiled at her now. On the diamond, they agreed.

"This is the one," they both said at once.

"No question," Merry added. "Mrs. Shallowford should love it."

Tess beamed. "What's not to love?"

"Excellent." The jeweler rose from her chair. She scooped up the velvet-lined tray from the table then held out a hand to Merry for the chosen ring. "Once Dr. Shallowford approves, I think the appropriate gift wrap will be gray and white embossed paper with silver ribbon—and of course our signature blue box."

Merry gasped. "Tess, I can't get it off!"

Her pulse stalled in alarm. "Sure you can. Give it a twist."

"Let me help," the jeweler said, setting the tray down without looking at it. She fumbled open the drawer in the table then extracted—what? Soap? A can of WD-40? A pair of tin snips? Tess didn't look to see. She steadied Merry's wrist while Merry pulled at the ring.

"Your finger's longer, Tess, more slender than mine," she said. "This is the wrong size for me but I didn't think..."

The jeweler twitched. "Ladies, please."

"Ladies," Tess muttered. "At my age that seems worse than 'ma'am.'"

The next few moments were a blur of activity. Her perfectly made-up face flushed, the jeweler squirted Merry's fingers with some liquid, tried to spin the band and at the same time ease it off, but it held tight. Finally she summoned a manager who apparently had his own bag of tricks for removing an expensive ring from a woman's hand.

Tess barely saw what they were doing. Not only did the two people block her view of Merry, Tess felt torn between her concern for the costly diamond, and Merry's bruised skin, and Tess's own inclination to hoot with laughter at the very irony in the situation. Merry had given her far too much grief over Grady's wedding band. Now it was payback time. A little voice inside her head wanted to shout, *Gotcha*. Not a very attractive quality, but there it was. Tess was only human.

When they were finally out the curved double doors that resembled a bank vault and on the sidewalk, *sans* diamond, Tess gave a tension-relieving snort she could no longer suppress. The jeweler had promised to deliver the ring by courier to Emery Shallowford that afternoon for his approval. *All's well that ends well,* Tess hoped.

"Don't you dare make fun of me," Merry warned her, stomping off toward the parking garage where they'd left Tess's car. "You didn't do any better."

"That's exactly what's funny."

"Ha-ha." Merry whirled around. "Know what I think about *your* ring?"

Tess groaned inwardly. She could guess what was coming. Meredith hadn't forgotten what started all this, and on that topic she could be relentless. Now she had even better motivation.

"I think you still care for Grady." Merry paused. "I mean, he's a hunk, I'll give him that—"

Tess cut her off. "He's also a compulsive gambler. I should know. I'm still paying off the debt from our marriage, but I learned my lesson."

"I don't think so. That ring of yours is a symbol," Merry insisted. "No wonder you can't enjoy your 'new life.'"

Tess bristled. "I enjoy it. I'm fine by myself. Almost. It will take me another few years to become financially solvent again—thanks in part to Grady—and in the meantime I'm not looking for another man."

"Well, you should be."

Tess might have said the same about Merry's current boyfriend, but she bit her tongue not to say so and hurt Merry's feelings. For some reason Merry was crazy about the less than desirable Frank although in Tess's opinion she gave too much without getting anything from him in return. "Once burned, twice shy," she said instead. "In my case you had to be there."

Tess marched into the parking garage, her ignition key ready, as if to protect herself from some attack. If the ring was a symbol, as Merry said, it had a sobering purpose. Tess didn't intend to make the same mistake again.

Still, maybe the real question was: How to forget Grady?

I n retrospect Tess preferred to blame her ring problem on the ten pounds she had gained since she left Grady four years ago. Since she'd *had* to leave Grady to save her sanity. Their final divorce decree, on top of too many years of his plummeting downhill, and dragging Tess with him, hadn't quite killed her, but eighteen months later she still had raw places on her heart that hadn't healed—and of course that extra weight on her one-time more slender hips.

She was driving up Montgomery Road toward home at five-thirty when she spied a small child too near the busy street. Tess did a double take. Once a mother, always a mother, and Tess felt her maternal instincts kick in. The road was hardly equal to the task of handling rush hour traffic, and so close to it was certainly no place for a child to stand. The little girl was holding a cardboard box with a homemade sign that Tess couldn't read from a distance.

Abruptly she braked, pulling over in the northbound lane beside the trendy strip mall across from Don Diego's Mexican restaurant.

Horns honked all around her. Tess flipped on her hazard lights, steered her used Toyota off onto the grass, flung open her door, and practically fell out into the road in her haste to reach the girl before some impatient driver hit her. A blast of now-cooler air struck her face. Enticing aromas from the nearby restaurant blended with the scents of gasoline, motor oil, and rubber tires.

"Sweetheart," she started to say, "watch out—"

But sudden fear flashed in the little girl's eyes. "I'm not allowed to talk to strangers," she said, an odd comment when she obviously hoped to peddle something to people she didn't know.

Tess frowned. Why would the child's mother allow her to risk her safety in such a dangerous spot? Most likely, she didn't know where her small daughter was right now.

"I think we can make an exception," Tess said.

Gently, with a soothing tone of voice, she guided the girl farther off the busy road into a strip mall's parking lot where the cardboard box the child carried finally caught Tess's full attention. It was moving. Squirming.

She heard a soft mewing sound.

Free Kittens, read the clumsy letters scrawled on the box, and with an inner groan Tess, a world-class soft touch for anyone in a jam, especially a child, knew she should run the other way.

Instead, teetering in her heeled boots as they sank into the scanty grass that edged the street, she couldn't help giving in to curiosity. She lifted one flap of the box to peer inside— and felt her heart melt like a double dip of Graeter's black raspberry ice cream in a Cincinnati summer's humid heat.

"Oh, dear," she murmured to the tiny wriggling bodies, their brand-new scent rising to her nostrils like the sweet-smelling innocence of a baby's skin.

Apparently someone's cat had given birth not long ago to an unexpected litter that now needed homes. The traffic whizzed past with the occasional blast of a horn as if warning her not to get involved. What was wrong with people? Some-one, preferably the girl's mother, should call the local animal shelter. But would the kittens be adopted then or condemned to...? Tess couldn't finish the thought.

Two pairs of beautiful blue eyes stared at her in obvious appeal. Two chubby, longhaired, cream and brown bodies scrambled toward the light, eager to be free. Afraid for their safety now as well as the little girl's, Tess nudged them back into the box then secured the lid.

"Poor babies," she cooed, tapping the carton. "You'll be fine. Some kind person will come along in no time. You'll see," she tried to tell herself, too. "Who can resist a cuddly ball of fur?" she added, trying to allay her fears for their fate.

Before the words had left her mouth, the child's eyes lit with what could only be hope. "You want 'em, lady?"

There was that *lady* again. This time Tess didn't mind it.

"Are they yours?" she asked.

The girl's head bobbed up and down. "Yep. All mine. My brother's just a baby and my mom has too much to do already. She says we can't keep 'em."

Tess suppressed a smile. She had to admire the child's ingenuity in trying to find homes for them, as if she were running a lemonade stand on a quiet side street, and her concern for the tiny kittens touched Tess's heart. The girl looked older than Dilly, Tess's four-year-old granddaughter, maybe six or seven, but she was still a child. Dressed in a light sweater and jeans, she shivered in the chill air at sundown, and Tess hoped she hadn't strayed too far from home. In fact, there was an apartment complex a block away.

"How old are they?"

"Jus' a few months." Her mouth turned down. "Their mama got lost."

"Oh, dear," Tess said again.

Her stomach, and her willpower, plunged to her boots.

She looked at her feet then studied the small salad dressing stain on her pants from a fast-food lunch with Meredith after their visit to Tiffany's.

What would Tess do with a kitten?

Still...she played devil's advocate. Maybe if she had a pet instead of coming home each night to the echo of her own footsteps in the foyer, she might feel not as, well, lonely or over-burdened by other people's problems, but less...unsettled.

Cats were more independent than dogs, weren't they? Less clingy. This might be one way to move on with her life, to bury any lingering feelings for Grady. To stop worrying quite so much about her son and his wife, or about Merry and Frank. Intrigued by the prospect, she gazed down into the girl's hopeful brown eyes.

In her mind she could see Dilly's elfin face instead, her classic rosebud mouth and gray-green eyes, the color Tess had given her from the family gene pool. Her granddaughter didn't have Tess's chestnut hair, but her fine, silky blond might darken over time.

She would love a kitten to play with. "She's a dilly all right."

"Who're you talking about?" the little girl asked.

"Someone just like you," she answered. "'Diligence,'" she said Dilly's full name. "I...can only take one," she heard herself say before she realized she'd actually made the decision to save a life.

The twilight had dimmed to what the French called *l'heure bleu*. A car door slammed nearby in the parking lot. Someone emerged from Snooty Fox, an upscale consignment shop across the way, and a woman breezed out the door of the nearby bakery, the stomach-growling aroma of cinnamon buns and fresh bread wafting through the almost-night air.

The little girl tore back the lid on the box, grabbed up both kittens, and thrust them at Tess. "They're brother and sister. One would be all alone—and cry. You gotta take 'em both."

"Oh, dear," Tess said for the third time. The sudden warmth of twin furry bodies filled her arms, the empty place in her heart. That's all it took. That, and the pressure of the kittens against her ever-present wedding band.

"These two have no idea what they're getting into," she told the girl.

But Tess wondered: Would the reverse prove to be true?

S till pondering the question, Tess dumped her briefcase onto the table in her foyer. She rented a modest frame house in the middle of a Cincinnati suburb called Lakeview. After leaving the Montgomery Road shopping area, she'd driven the little girl to the nearby apartment where she lived with her mother, a single mom. A very worried mom by the time Tess brought her daughter home. In her own house— well, technically, her landlord's—she looked around for a place to put the cardboard box with her new roommates inside.

Now what? Tess had no experience in caring for animals.

Years ago her father had been too busy destroying their family to find time or room for a pet, her mother too exhausted. Later Tess had been preoccupied with Grady's own tumble down a hole playing five-card stud while she tried to maintain some sense of normality for their son. She hadn't been able to take on yet another responsibility.

Well, look at me. Now, it seemed, she had two of them, and they would learn together. Just as she'd learned when her son was a newborn baby.

Full of fresh purpose, Tess headed for the refrigerator.

She poured cold milk into a saucer then warmed the liquid in the microwave. Testing with a finger, she swirled the milk to make sure it wasn't too hot in spots then, satisfied, set it on the floor before she released the cream-and-brown, long-haired kittens—part Himalayan, the girl's mother had told her—from their cardboard prison.

Like kids let out of school, they scampered across the ceramic tile floor, spilling over Tess's booted feet and making her laugh. Delighted to see them lapping up every drop of milk as if she had produced a gourmet meal, she felt good about her unexpected decision to save them.

Tempted to pour herself some milk too and cut a big slice from the apple pie on the counter, she could empathize with the kittens' simple pleasure.

Their audible purring warmed her spirit as effectively as the milk must soothe their tummies. Yet that wasn't solid food. So Tess opened a can of tuna fish for them. No wonder they were hungry; they were like growing children, something she knew a little about. How hard could this be? Tomorrow she'd find the nearest pet store, purchase some gaily decorated feed bowls and a few toys with catnip inside. Didn't all cats like catnip?

Feeling good now about her new pets and the Shallowford diamond, she drifted out to the foyer to pick up her mail.

The house had been built in the 1950s, and had one of those old-fashioned slots in the front door, which would produce a definite draft in winter. Would it be too cold for the kittens?

Tess heard a crash from the kitchen.

She rushed back down the hall. Another step, then her boots met the resistance of a tacky floor, and broken glass crunched under her feet.

The two kittens had finished their milk and still wore little white mustaches like ads for the Dairy Council. Left to themselves for a few minutes, they'd licked clean the tuna fish bowl then discovered "dessert." The pie that had been sitting on the counter lay splat on the floor, fruit and crust everywhere, the ovenware plate in pieces. The cats hunkered in the middle of the feast, their fur clumped with sticky apple juice.

Tess shooed them away and cleaned up the mess. Was this attack of altruism on her part another bad decision, like her marriage to Grady? Hours later, as she tried to fall asleep in her bed, she was still resisting the thought. If only things could have ended as happily as she and Grady had begun...

"*Second thoughts?*" *Grady asked.*

But Tess had never been happier in her life. On the front porch of their first real home together, she looped her arms around Grady's neck. He smiled down at her, his dark eyes warm and loving.

"None," she assured him. "This mortgage is a new concept, though. I'm used to paying rent on our little apartment. Just think, every time we make a payment this place will be that much closer to being all ours. The house, the yard, even the maple trees." Tess grinned. "We're homeowners, Grady."

"Our little piece of paradise."

The small white Cape Cod-style bungalow wasn't exactly a dream. It had sagging shutters, wooden floors that needed sanding then a fresh coat of polyurethane, and a tiny upstairs bathroom with a leak in the ceiling, which probably meant paying for a new roof.

Tess didn't care. They were young, with energy and love to spare, if not cold cash. She and Grady could do much of the work themselves. For the first time in her twenty-two years she didn't have to fear being evicted as she had when living with her parents. She didn't have to rely on her father coming up with the rent—or not, as had often been the case. She didn't have to lie awake listening to her mother weep or, almost as bad, argue with Larry.

Instead, Grady was her hero.

They were married, responsible adults who could care for themselves, and with an almost-two-year-old child. "I can't wait to see Ethan's face when he toddles into his very own room tonight. Mom said she'd drive him home—isn't that the loveliest word, Grady—whenever we want. I just need to call her."

"Later," he said then swung her up into his embrace, hitched her higher in his strong, sun-browned arms. His beautiful brown eyes darkened. "In the meantime I'm sure we can find something to do."

"Well—" Tess paused to prolong her growing anticipation "—I guess we could make sure his room is ready. That is, if you can carry me upstairs."

He gave a mock groan. "Let me see if I can get you through this doorway first and over the threshold."

He was joking, of course. Grady loved to tease her. Tess loved to let him. When he bent his head to kiss her, the thrill she felt at the warm touch of his mouth ran through her body, along every nerve end, straight into Tess's heart. She couldn't wait to get him alone for the first time in their new bed.

"I love you," she whispered against his lips.

"Not as much as you're going to love me in the next five minutes." His tone turned husky with desire. "I love you, too, babe. Don't ever forget that..."

. . .

I f only she could forget. Yet Tess clung stubbornly to her memories of happiness, still wishing nothing had changed.

Feeling hot and restless, she jerked awake. After cleaning up the kittens too, she'd spent several hours at her computer, but the usual Internet sites she visited hadn't turned up any new housing choices. At least none in her price range. Finally, she had fallen into bed then into a light sleep, only to hear an insistent bell chiming now in the distance, as if to announce the winner of some prizefight.

Was she dreaming again? Her mouth seemed to be full of...fur. When she opened her eyes, two small bodies were draped around her neck and over her face, half smothering her. Her lips felt glued together and she smelled apples, as if she had been tarred and feathered with fruit.

She sighed. Before she'd tucked the cats in for the night, with her help they'd taken their first bath, but obviously not all of the pie had washed out of their coats. It wasn't easy, she'd discovered, to bathe a cat. And two at once was impossible. They seemed to have a thousand legs each, a million razor-sharp claws flashing as if they were chefs at Benihana. Then there'd been the session with the blow dryer. Having narrowly escaped serious injury, she wasn't eager to try again anytime soon

"Yecch," she murmured, picking fine hairs from her mouth.

The bell rang once more. Someone was at her door. Alarm swept through her.

"I'm coming," she called, though whoever stood on her porch couldn't possibly hear her. A police officer bearing terrible news?

Heart thumping, she pried the two kittens off her goose-down comforter, and hurriedly placed them on the spare pillow on the carpet that she'd fixed for their bed. They obviously preferred to sleep with her, but that was a little too much closeness even for Tess.

And to think, only that morning she'd felt mostly satisfied with her new existence, with this temporary home, and with the careful way in which she ran The Go-To Girl. In her work she had involvement with other people without the risk of an intimate relationship. Grady, on the other hand, had risked everything on a turn of the cards.

She shut the cats in the bedroom then hurried along the hall toward the foyer with the kittens' outraged cries pursuing her.

Were they already missing her? She doubted that. They might look sweet, but the kittens had the devil in them.

Besides, thanks to her, they also had each other.

Tess took a quick peek through the security viewfinder then reeled back. No uniformed cop stood at her door, thank heaven, but the man she recognized all too well standing there didn't ease her mind or the frantic race of her heart.

She shut her eyes to block his image: thick, dark hair, warm brown gaze...

When Tess opened her eyes, he was still there, like the embodiment of all her fantasies. *Grady.*

"What do you want?" she asked through the closed door. If he'd come straight from some poker game...

"Well, finally. I've been ringing this bell for ten minutes. I was about to perform a B & E by climbing through your window." But he didn't sound angry. Even now she couldn't quite close out the need in his all-too-familiar voice, or...was that worry she heard? "Open up, Tess. I have something to tell you."

Tess worried the snug gold band on her finger. A mother's instant vision of a car wreck, a plane crash, a home invasion, blood and guns, flashed through her brain. Their son. His wife, who was like a daughter to her. And no, it couldn't be Dilly...it was after midnight. Dilly would be safe in her bed. Still, Tess couldn't help asking. "*What's wrong?*"

Through the peephole she stole a second look at Grady. His hair looked furrowed, as if he'd been raking his hand through it, as he always did when agitated, often with her.

She had her hand on the deadbolt a second before he said, "Let me in, Theresa."

When the chips were down, even her ex knew he could count on her.

2

"DON'T CALL ME THERESA." Nevertheless, Tess flung open the door, letting in a burst of the cool spring night breeze and the enticing scent of Grady. Her full view of him didn't do her usual determination to keep her distance any good. Neither did her newest If Only earlier that night, starring Grady. Even his use of an old nickname (Tess was just plain Tess) didn't cause her to shut him out.

For an instant even her fears for their family were eclipsed by the sight of him, the man she'd been married to for twenty-one years. His black leather bomber jacket, looking soft as butter, only enhanced his broad shoulders and deep chest. Solid muscle, Tess remembered, like the not-quite concealed bulge of his biceps under the jacket and the long, hard line of his jeans-clad thighs.

In the flesh, standing in her doorway, he smelled of wood smoke and...was that lemon? Worse for her, he looked remarkably good, fine enough for even Tess to want to jump his bones again, but Grady obviously hadn't come to her house at this time of night with romance in mind, and her instinctive fears came back with a vengeance.

"Please. Tell me no one died," she said.

"Nobody's...dead. At least there's that." When he stepped past her, Tess's knees turned to jelly, not entirely from relief. In the foyer Grady took off his shoes then left them by the door. The simple action, his long-time habit after work when they were married, sent her heart tumbling. So much for her new determination to look toward her future, not back.

Suddenly the narrow hall felt way too small. Even the ceiling seemed to drop, pushing down on her as if she were ham & melted cheese in a panini. Grady sucked the very air from every inch of her rented house. Shoes on or off, he didn't belong here. In her life now.

Tell it to my hormones.

Tess drew herself up, her gaze fixed on his face. And felt her stomach take a swift dive toward her bare feet.

Grady still had the best mouth, generous, quick to smile and to charm, with that little upturn at the corners that she was such a sucker for.

Oh, no, you don't. You're not getting to me again.

She crossed her arms, hiding her breasts under her thin nightie. But of course Grady's gaze followed the motion, and his eyes darkened.

The fact that he didn't grin surprised Tess but only for a second. Their mutual love of their son Ethan, his wife Chloe, and little Dilly was their one true meeting ground these days. He was always shaken by family events. Something was really wrong, or he wouldn't be here.

"Grady, what's happened?"

Without answering, he walked around her and on into the living room. He took off his jacket then dropped onto a deep-upholstered chair. "Take it easy. No one's hurt, but unfortunately Chloe seems to be missing. Have you seen her?"

"*Missing?*" Tess felt like a talkative parrot. Her daughter-in-law had disappeared? "You mean...*kidnapped?*"

He said, "No, nothing like that. Sometime this afternoon she left Ethan a note on their kitchen table saying she 'needs time to think,' took Dilly—and disappeared. When he got home Ethan found the house empty. Said it was a real weird feeling. Apparently, he never saw this coming."

"They've separated?" She couldn't envision the possibility. Grady sent her a look, as if to remind Tess she had left him, too. "There must be some other explanation," she tried again. "Maybe one of her parents is sick and she had to go home—"

Grady frowned. "Ethan is supposed to be her home now, Tess. Her folks are still in Florida." Chloe's parents were snowbirds who spent the winter there. "We didn't want to worry them. It's too soon, anyway. Chloe's only been gone a few hours. The cops won't call her a missing person until late tomorrow."

Cops? Tess sank onto the sofa. If her knees had felt like gelatin before, it hadn't set. Because of Chloe her joints were liquid now. Unfolding her arms, she didn't bother to cover her breasts against Grady's penetrating gaze.

Their daughter-in-law could be a bit, well, unfocused, and she had a tendency to be clumsy; but even so, she was a dedicated homebody. Chloe loved to fuss with her plants, to decorate the house on a shoestring budget, to cook at holiday time for the whole family even when she almost always scorched something or served the turkey half-raw. And Chloe was a terrific mother. She and Ethan had bought their first house only last year—an irony for Tess, who was still saving for her own down payment. Grady was right. Why would Chloe abandon her home now with Ethan? Where could she have gone?

"What about...my dad? He and Chloe are pretty good friends. She never seems to see the worst in him." But then, Larry always saved that for Tess.

"Couldn't reach him. We'll try again in the morning."

"Knowing Larry, he's probably at the casino across the river in Newport, but that also means Chloe probably isn't at his place. If she was, she would have answered his phone, don't you think?"

Grady shrugged. "Yesterday I would have said yes. Tonight I'm not sure what she might do. Avoid us all, maybe. She didn't answer her cell either."

Tess couldn't help it. Horrific visions filled her mind all over again. There'd been so many stories lately in the news about women who vanished from their homes and were found murdered, or women who couldn't take it anymore, whatever *it* might be, who didn't just run away but snapped and hurt themselves or their children.

Grady sensed where her thoughts were going. "Chloe would never harm Dilly. You know that."

"She loves Ethan, too," Tess agreed. "I can't imagine..." Although of course she could. She'd been cursed with a too-fertile imagination. And Grady knew her as well as she knew him.

"Tess, the one thing I do feel—deep in my gut—is that Chloe and Dilly are safe. Frankly, it's Ethan I'm worried about. I finally poured him into bed after a couple of beers and told him I'd take care of this. Find out what I could."

He raked a hand through his already-rumpled hair, thick and glossy. At forty-six, Grady hadn't lost his hair like so many men his age. He was still in his prime. "I've already called her friends," he told Tess. "The last one mentioned that Chloe looked a little ragged at lunch the other day, like she hadn't been sleeping well. Her friend was sure something was wrong, but Chloe wouldn't talk, she said."

Tess had the most peculiar feeling, as if she and Grady still lived together, were still married, and discussing Ethan, some growing-up problem rather than his adult relationship with his wife. Tess thought a moment. "I did notice some tension between Chloe and Ethan when I sat for Dilly while they went to that wedding in Columbus a few weeks ago, but...no, she didn't confide in me either."

For a long moment they stared at each other. A million bytes of memory whizzed through the computer of Tess's mind. Family dinners, Christmas, Dilly's fourth birthday party and the lopsided cake Chloe had baked.

Finally, Grady said, "Ethan doesn't have a clue what's wrong. Leave it to a woman," he added, which made Tess bristle.

"Don't you dare take Ethan's side without hearing what Chloe has to say."

Grady spread his hands. "Hey, I'm a guy. That's what we do. Besides, I'm a father and Ethan's employer. It's not as if he's running around on Chloe, spending money they don't have. Where would he find the time? The only thing he does is work."

Tess couldn't stop the thought. Grady had found plenty of time to squander money they didn't have.

"It's certainly not Chloe's fault," she said. "She may be vague at times, and I know she has these little mishaps now and then—"

"Every day," Grady acknowledged. "But that's no reason for her to split."

Tess agreed, but then... "Grady, I love Ethan, too, with all my heart, but as a *woman*—" she repeated his word "—I wonder. Maybe Chloe simply wrote the whole truth in her note, and a short break is all she needs. Marriage, as I learned the hard way, can be a difficult proposition."

"Hell, yes." He half smiled. "If I'd ever figured out what was on *your* mind maybe we wouldn't have gotten div—"

"Oh, please. You know why I left—"

Tess didn't finish. A sudden yowl had gone up from her

bedroom through the closed door, and Grady jerked upright in his chair. "What's that noise?"

"My cats."

"Cats?" he echoed, but Tess was already on her feet. Apparently as a mother she'd somehow failed Chloe and Ethan. But what a terrible kitty parent she was, too. "I've adopted twins. And at the moment I imagine they've had too much time alone."

Half relieved to change the subject, because it never paid to discuss their divorce, she hurried down the hall to open the bedroom door, her new babies erupting from the room like rockets then flying over her bare feet again. Life wouldn't be dull with them in the house. But her smile drowned as quickly as it had surfaced.

With their slice-and-dice claws scrambling across the wood floor, the kittens dashed into the hall. Their cries had turned to hisses, snarls, and deep-throated growls, the larger of the two kittens sounding to Tess like an enraged lion. Dazed, she watched them disappear around the corner.

Fighting? If they were brother and sister, then sibling rivalry wasn't limited to humans.

"What the hell?" she heard Grady say.

By the time Tess reached the living room doorway the cats were rolling on her carpet at Grady's feet, talons flashing, teeth bared, their tiny bodies entangled in one ball of furious fur until Tess couldn't tell them apart. "Oh no," she said, standing in the doorway.

Grady shot to his feet. "I hate cats," he murmured, but Tess sensed he was angry with her for the thoughtless remark she'd made about their marriage.

"I'm sorry, but you can hate them later. Right now, help me."

The larger of the two kittens opened his jaws, his teeth

bearing down on the nape of the other cat's neck. Grady danced to avoid the roiling mass of cream and brown that flipped and flopped across his sock feet then around her living room like a pair of whirling dervishes. Their mingled cries, ever louder and more primal, sounded to Tess like Tasmanian Devils.

"Grady, I'll take the little one," she said. "You grab the big boy."

He cursed under his breath but did as she asked.

Grady snatched the male kitten by the scruff of his neck and pried him off the female, clearly the victim in Tess's view. She watched with one hand clapped over her mouth, the other wrapped around Little Girl's still-full belly.

At least the caterwauling had ceased. But then with a grunt Grady dropped Big Boy like an unwanted rock at one of his construction sites. The kitten twisted in mid-air but landed right side up on Grady's foot.

Right through the cotton sock Big Boy's knife-sharp claws punctured skin. Grady shouted a four-letter word as he nudged the offender and a chubby fur ball shot past Tess like a stone from a slingshot. Before the cat reached the floor of the hall Grady's sock was splotched with red. Big Boy never slowed down.

Tess set down Little Girl then hurried to him. "Grady, I'm so sorry."

"You should be."

"I can't imagine what got into them," she said, gently pushing him back into a chair. Tess wasn't quite telling the truth; she could all too easily envision another kitty disaster, if not what caused it. The two cats had vanished into the kitchen where God only knew what they might discover to eat, or do, next.

Leaning toward Grady, she peeled off his sock. The angry holes along his instep made her wince. "This looks painful."

"Only when I laugh." He gave her a thin smile. "I told you I don't like cats."

"Evidently the feeling is mutual."

"I gotta hand it to you, Tess, they're better than a pair of Dobermans."

"You think I sicced them on you?"

He arched one eyebrow. "The thought did cross my mind."

I n the next instant Grady was alone.

"Let me get something," Tess had said, and headed for the bathroom.

He watched the familiar twitch of her hips, the sway of her shoulders in that determined stride—a determination to escape him? Her sleek brown hair swung just above the collar of her prim nightgown, and although he couldn't see her eyes he remembered their changeable greens and grays. Right now he was betting on a deep forest green, and a flash of heat swept through him. Her breasts would be moving too with that soft little jiggle he loved.

He almost smiled.

In spite of his pain Grady knew an opportunity when he saw one. Gritting his teeth, he struggled up out of the chair to follow her. She was shutting the medicine cabinet door, holding a first-aid kit, when he came up behind her, his reflection joining hers in the mirror. Preoccupied with her apparent guilt over the unexpected accident, she probably hadn't heard him limp down the hall.

In the small room he stood close, crowding her a little, reminded of many such better moments during their marriage.

Grady's lower body tightened. How many times had they shared such intimacy while getting ready for a family gathering or a party? On more than one occasion they hadn't gone at all; on more than a few they'd shown up late with smiles of satisfaction on their faces to the knowing amusement of their friends. "You should sit down," she told him now, a flush on her cheeks. Had Tess guessed at the poignant memories that flooded his mind? Sensed the growing evidence of his desire for her? She looked away from their images in the glass. "Take off your sock."

"You already took it off, Nurse Ratched." Eyeing the item she pulled from the kit, he thumped over to sit on the toilet lid with a grunt of pain. "Just get some soap and water. Can I trust you not to scald me?"

"You need an antiseptic."

"Never my drug of choice." He nodded at the bottle of peroxide in her hand. "Your mother's not the only one who used that stuff. So did mine. Froths all over the place."

"It may look nasty, but it doesn't really hurt."

"You're not the one that monster just tried to kill." He inspected his left foot propped over his right knee. "See *why* I'm not a cat lover?"

"But they're usually so..." Tess trailed off, as if she wasn't sure exactly what they were. "They'll be fine once they settle in."

"Bully for them. What about me?"

He was teasing, one of Grady's favorite pastimes with Tess. But he was also, on another level, serious. From the moment he'd met her, he had wanted Tess in his life. Their divorce, a mistake in Grady's view, hadn't changed that. But Tess couldn't seem to get past his formerly bad behavior.

"You are not settling in," she said, her tone thick. "Once I clean this puncture wound, you can be on your way."

"Again."

Grady suppressed an inner sigh. If someone dealt him a bad hand, metaphorically speaking, he simply waited for the next one. Since Tess had left him, he'd managed to haul himself out of a virtual debtors' prison, hadn't he, and—like her—start all over again? But the fact that he and Ethan were making real progress in Grady's construction business didn't seem to register with Tess. Like his persistent efforts to win her back.

With utter concentration she focused on his foot. Long and lean with well-defined tendons and veins, it boasted an elegant arch that embarrassed Grady but that any woman in four-inch heels would envy. He might not be the brightest bulb in the pack, but he liked to think he was all man, all over.

"Like what you see, Tess?"

The question hit home. Looking shocked by the sultry tone of his voice, she met his gaze. How could she help but see the glint of obvious need in his eyes?

He heard her breath catch. "I always liked what I saw," she confessed, pouring peroxide over his wound. "After a while I just didn't care for the rest."

He hissed at the first sting of the antiseptic then glanced away. "Gee, let me guess. You must mean my gambling."

Her mouth tightened, forming little white brackets at the corners of her lips. "I mean the business you lost, the reputation you ruined, the credit you destroyed, and the house the bank foreclosed on—*our* house at the time."

Grady's desire sizzled out as if someone had poured water on a campfire.

"You're never gonna let me live that down, are you."

Without answering, she sent him a look then patted his foot with a piece of gauze. Losing the house, he knew, had been the last straw for Tess. Grady didn't play cards these days, or anything else, but by nature he was still a gambler. So when he'd seen the surge of renewed interest in her eyes, a little voice inside him had said, "Go for it."

When Tess dropped the soiled gauze in the waste basket, the motion drew his gaze to her wedding band. "Everyone deserves a second chance, Tess. Even me."

"Apparently Ethan agrees with you."

She had thrown a hissy fit when she learned about Grady hiring their son. Ethan and Chloe and Dilly depended upon Ethan's income. What would happen, Tess would be thinking, if Grady's business failed again? Next time, she'd be sure, he would take down Ethan, too.

"I hope you don't disappoint him," she murmured.

Grady stood up. "You mean disappoint *you*. Gimme a break. I'll always be a recovering gambler, but I'm okay. Ask Ethan. We signed two new contracts just last week. Pretty soon we'll have more business than we can handle." A bad choice of words.

Tess rolled her eyes. "That's what I'm afraid of."

Her lack of trust shot through him like a nail from a gun. "Oh, I get it. Once I put my hands on some real money again, I'll head right down with your father to that casino and piss it away? That what you think of me, *Theresa?*" Again, she couldn't seem to answer. With a light touch he tilted her chin until she had to look into his gaze or shut her eyes. "I'm not the bad guy here, Tess. Maybe I was, once, but I've changed."

She pressed her lips tight. "Don't you dare make me cry. We're done, Grady. It doesn't matter now."

"Hell, yes it does. It matters to me. How can I prove that to you?" Before she could form a reply, if she would have, he raised her face another notch, so near her features blurred. She wouldn't be about to cry if she didn't care. A little. The realization encouraged him, made him bold. "Everybody makes mistakes—"

"Some bigger than others," she tried to tell him.

"Yeah, and I made some whoppers. But I'm different now —the new and improved Grady O'Neill—except for *this*." His mouth lowered toward hers before she could pull away. "Still the same."

In a heartbeat Tess was breathing fast, too. Afraid? Or tempted? Grady chose to believe the latter.

But then she stared at the ceramic tile wall over his shoulder and said, "This is hardly the place for a clumsy seduction."

"Nothing clumsy about it. Feels right to me." He moved closer still, less than an inch away, then almost nothing, freezing Tess in place like a startled woodchuck in the yard. His lips, slightly parted, hovered above her mouth, daring her to close the small remaining gap. "Haven't you heard? After a divorce, the most common sex partner is the ex spouse."

"Grady, no."

In the next second he would have kissed her. But then he made another of his famous errors where Tess was concerned. With a teasing look, he said, "Can't help myself. You're the one. You always were."

And Tess stiffened.

Grady knew better than to ante up again. He threw in his cards. For now.

Despite the hammering of her heart, and the fresh regret that swept along her veins, Tess stepped back. The dangerous moment had shattered, and she was still in one piece. Barely. She wanted to say something, but when she opened her mouth, nothing came out. The words merely echoed in her mind. *I can't trust you. I can't take another chance.*

Even Grady's expensive-looking black bomber jacket wasn't proof that he was different; for all she knew, his changes were temporary, and he'd won the jacket playing poker. Even if he had turned his life around in some ways, as Ethan and other people kept telling her, there was no guarantee he wouldn't throw it away again on a hand of five-card stud.

Her father—not exactly the world's best role model—had come home often enough with some undeserved booty of a similar type. A camel's hair sports coat, a pair of tickets to a Super Bowl, a weekend at a time share—that is, Larry came home flush when he didn't get his pockets turned inside out. He still did.

And he was always promising to change.

Now that her mom was gone, Larry made his false promises to Tess.

Both Larry and Grady were charmers, and Tess had left her childhood home with one only to marry another. What this said about her ability to choose men, she didn't care to examine.

Certainly she couldn't live through the financial and emotional fallout again. She didn't dare trust Grady even for one kiss, a ploy she was far too old to fall for, though Tess had to admit he still had a way about him.

"You want a bandage?" she asked, her face turned away.

"No, thanks. *Saint* Theresa."

Before she could blink Grady was out the bathroom door and down the hall. Half wanting to apologize, Tess trailed him to the front door where he had already put on his leather jacket and was pulling on his damp, now-pink sock.

"I better go," he said, addressing his shoe. "I'll keep you informed about Chloe. I hope you'll do the same for me." As if he doubted she would.

Ouch.

Tess almost called him back, but nothing would be gained by another apology for simply trying to protect herself.

"I am not your St. Theresa—" she began, but in a flash he slammed out the door, taking another little piece of her heart that Tess couldn't afford to lose.

. . .

S till preoccupied with thoughts of last night, Tess rushed around the one-room office on Fields Ertel Road that housed The Go-To Girl. As if to escape herself, in a flurry she gathered files, grabbed another cup of coffee from the urn between her station and Meredith's then hurried back to her desk.

Bright sun shafted across its mahogany-veneered surface, highlighting the stack of multi-colored file folders for current projects. Depending on how you looked at it, the size of the pile was either daunting or satisfying. Or it would have been the latter if Tess didn't still feel so unhinged by Grady's visit last night and, equally important, by Chloe's mysterious disappearance.

To make matters worse, this morning Meredith was pouting. She stayed at her desk, fielding phone calls and scheduling appointments, but not even her latest outfit—a long blue paisley skirt and hot pink spandex top worn with dangly pink crystal earrings—could lift her spirits.

Because Merry wasn't talking, Tess supposed Frank must be responsible. Merry had been trying to set aside vacation time, avoiding the worst of the spring and summer wedding onslaught at work, but not one of the dates she suggested had appealed to Frank. Big surprise. Tess wanted to urge Merry to get away on her own instead, but unless she was asked she wouldn't offer her opinion. She'd tried that before.

When Merry finally looked up from the day's to-do list to express her concern for Chloe, Tess was surprised to see her emerge from her mood. "I can't believe Chloe is lost," Merry murmured.

"Not lost, missing. She never said anything to you?"

Merry shook her head, but her spiky red hair didn't move.

"Chloe and I are friends—just like you and me. Do we tell each other everything?"

"Mostly," Tess admitted, remembering the incident at Tiffany's. Which of course had led to that night's If Only, and then to Grady, whom she hadn't mentioned this morning. How had she come *that* close to a kiss with her ex-husband? She could still imagine his mouth closing that last inch between them, the zing of reaction that would race from his lips to hers at that first light, testing touch then straight to the business parts of her anatomy.

She refocused her thoughts on Chloe. "On my way to work I called everyone else I could think of, but no one has seen her. I'm really worried."

What if Chloe vanished with Dilly and never came back? What if someone harmed them? Chloe could be naïve, even gullible.

Merry picked up some papers. "Chloe doesn't always plug in to what's going on," she said at last, "but she's tougher than she knows. Whatever's wrong, once she has that time to think, she'll be okay, Tess."

Merry didn't sound that confident. Tess knew she was worried, too, but there was no more to be done except to make the same calls she'd already made later again today, and a dreaded one to the cops. That would make Tess's fears seem all too real. "For now, I don't know what else to do." Except fret. And try to erase her newest stubborn fantasy—and Grady—from her memory banks. Why did he have to be so darned attractive?

Her latest If Only hadn't been just a foolish fantasy of what might have been. It was a real memory, and her awareness of Grady was pretty normal, wasn't it? Most divorced women must wonder how life might have turned out if a partner hadn't taken a turn for the worse, but paying off massive debt because she owed a spouse's share of Grady's gambling bills and others wasn't her idea of a marriage. Right now, though, Tess's daydreams shouldn't matter.

She re-crossed her legs under her desk. And focused on a stack of client information cards, jotting notes and shuffling projects according to priority, dividing them with Merry as she went. The Winfield wedding was two weeks from Saturday. Merry had offered to pick up the bride's pearl earrings, her gift from the groom, and Tess retrieved that file for her then picked up another.

"I'll deal with the Nelson party," she said with a smile she didn't quite feel. It made her think of Dilly. "Getting a pony for your fifth birthday is pretty heady stuff. I'm praying for sun. I'd hate to see that adorable Shetland and its spiffy new saddle soaked in a rainstorm. Which reminds me: I have to call the stable to make sure the pony passed its vet check." She rooted through the papers on her desk. "What did I do with that trainer's number?"

Merry passed her a business card. "Here, and what about the Eggleston bash?"

Tess plowed through another pile until she found that folder. "Someone needs to check on all those engraved silver swans. Can you believe? Over a hundred of them as favors." She laid the file on her stack. Probably because of Tess's distracted state, Merry had already taken more than her share. "The question is what are those little statues good for? You know how much they cost. If only Mrs. Eggleston had taken our suggestions instead. But she didn't. I wonder why she hired us." Tess sighed, knowing the customer was always right, even when, in this case, Clara Eggleston was wrong. "However, we do aim to please."

Merry grimaced at the tower of folders. "I know there's a method to our madness but, really, Tess, this is getting crazy."

She was right, but Tess had started out in business buying items for her friends. Then the word of mouth had spread, and now she had almost too much work. "Why complain? Business is good." Tess had done some late night calculations after Grady left. Unless business fell off after summer, and if her father didn't beg for money, she could be *that* close to making her down payment on a house before Christmas.

"Business is great, but we need more space," Merry insisted. "Maybe a third person to help."

A small wave of fresh anxiety rolled along Tess's spine. They did need more room and she wanted to expand, but she couldn't seem to make the decision. "I'll give you a raise instead. A small one."

Merry glanced at the ceiling. "We outgrew this place six months ago. I know the location's great, we're right in the midst of retail heaven, and although the traffic's awful here, it's good for business. Isn't there a larger suite for rent nearby? A bigger sign, with a new design to catch the eye, would be nice too."

"Not today, please."

Merry's tone softened. "I'm sorry to bring this up when you're worried about Chloe, but you know we're barely holding on here with the two of us. There are only so many hours in the day—or night. Frank was in a real mood because I didn't cook dinner yesterday. Just think about it, okay?"

"Maybe in August," Tess said, her stomach tightening another notch. "The idea of a bigger overhead alone scares me. You're talking more expenses, phone lines, furniture, increased cleaning costs..."

"Sometimes you have to spend money to make money." Her gaze slid to Tess's ring finger. "A little risk would be good for your future."

When the phone rang Tess grabbed it like a lifeline. She didn't want to discuss taking risks, even for The Go-To Girl, right now. She sure didn't want to talk about Grady either, but to her even greater dismay the caller was her dad, and

Tess felt suddenly trapped. The spring meet at Turfway had ended, but there was always horse racing from other tracks for him to bet on.

Tess didn't give him a chance to explain the reason for his phone call. "Sorry, Dad. I'm broke until next week." The conversation continued, mostly from Larry's side, for another few minutes, but in the end he won, as he always did with her, and Tess agreed to raid her ATM once more on his behalf.

She was already re-juggling her finances in her mind when she hung up, feeling deflated as she always did with Larry.

"Another bail-out?" Merry asked. "He's such a user."

Tess shrugged. "He always makes me feel bad, but I can't stand to watch him suffer. He needs a roof over his head, good food, clothes on his back—"

"A job would help." Merry should know. Frank spent half his time collecting unemployment benefits, which had become his career.

"Dad hasn't been himself since Mom died." Larry had lost Tess's mom after a series of strokes the same year Tess finally left Grady. For a while she'd felt truly overwhelmed, struggling with the end of her marriage and starting a new business, helping Chloe and Ethan set up their first household together and care for Dilly when she wasn't driving Larry and her mother to doctors or visiting the hospital. She'd sat with him in those last days, held his hand when her mother slipped away. "At seventy it's hard for him to get a job."

"And then there's Grady..."

Merry never missed a chance to bring him up. "Yes, and I know we have a family crisis at the moment, but I can't talk about this anymore."

Tess made herself even busier for the rest of the day. Not only did that keep her mind off Chloe, but if she worked a little harder, she could take some pressure off Merry and avoid taking that risk just yet. Her job would also keep her from dwelling on Grady.

But at four o'clock Meredith left to pick up the bridal pearls, and Tess called the same numbers she'd called that morning without success. None of Chloe's friends had talked to her. In desperation, against her better judgment, Tess phoned Grady. "Have you or Ethan heard from Chloe?"

"Not a word."

More bad news. "How's your foot?" she asked, not knowing what else to say that wouldn't make both of them feel worse.

"Sore, but I'll live. As for another part of my body—"

Tess flinched. No way would she discuss that almost-kiss last night. "What? I can't hear you." In the background at the other end of the line something clanked and whirred and someone yelled, "Clear!" before Tess heard a huge crash.

"We're stripping a site before new construction starts," Grady said. "Ethan's holding up today, barely. Maybe I'll come over to your office when I'm done here and we can brainstorm."

Her pulse jumped. "No, don't bother. I'm almost through for the day. On my way home I can meet Ethan at the police station to file a report."

Grady didn't respond and his freshly wounded silence spoke volumes. When Tess hung up, she heard a car door slam outside the office. A second later a child's voice called out. Dilly? Before Tess could react, her door flew open. A small whirlwind dashed in. And to her vast relief, Tess saw her concern, and Grady's, for Chloe was no longer necessary, at least not in a physical sense. "Grammy! I'm here!" Dilly shouted and flung herself at Tess.

"Goodness, sweetie, so you are." Every cell in Tess's body gave thanks. She held Dilly tight, stroking the silk of her hair, inhaling the scents of little girl and peppermint. When Dilly briefly drew back, Tess saw her dear face and a truly stunning lavender ruffled skirt with a matching print top. Dilly loved fashion. "I'm so glad to see you, baby." *Where on earth have you been?*

"We stayed at a mo—ho—tel," Dilly reported, arms around Tess's neck. "It was fun except Mommy was cry—"

"Dilly, stop choking your grandmother." Chloe stepped in right behind her and shut the door with what sounded to Tess like a guilty *thunk*. Unfortunately, she also closed the hem of her man-tailored shirt in the door. Tess heard the sound of ripping cloth as Chloe struggled to free it. She didn't meet Tess's gaze.

Chloe's wrinkled shirt and jeans, her uncombed pale blond hair and utter lack of makeup spoke for themselves. She'd spent a rough night. Good thing she was a natural beauty. Still, Dilly had spoken the truth. Chloe's dazed blue eyes were rimmed with red. She had obviously been crying.

"I'm sorry, Tess. I didn't know where else to go," she said, her voice husky with tears. "I know I should have called but I couldn't. I suppose you've talked to Grady." Clearly, she didn't want to mention Ethan.

"Yes, and your father-in-law is as upset as the rest of us."

"I'm so sorry," Chloe said again. "I didn't mean to cause any trouble, but I thought...I can't afford a second night in a hotel. I was kind of hoping Dilly and I could stay with you for a while. I can't go...home."

Tess's relieved heart turned over. Of course she wouldn't turn poor Chloe away, and the chance to spend time with Dilly always appealed. Tess was everyone's Go-To Girl, not only in business.

But what did she know about possibly saving someone else's marriage?

✤ 3 ✤

"WATCH OUT, GRAMMY!"

Dilly flashed by Tess in a blur, the two kittens in hot pursuit. Big Boy, as she called him for want of a better name, skidded around the kitchen corner and barreled into the front hall. In mid flight Little Girl sidestepped some invisible obstacle, her back arched high, legs stiff as pokers, eyes fully dilated.

"Ah, the thrill of the chase," Tess murmured, barely rescuing the dinner plate she'd been scraping into the trash. A hint of a wry smile crossed her lips. How had her orderly, reconstructed life been turned upside down in such a short time? First the cats had come to live with her, then Dilly and Chloe. Had it been only a week since they'd showed up at her office?

The scent of burnt meat filled Tess's nostrils. Chloe, standing next to her, had offered to make dinner tonight, but her beef stew hadn't turned out the way she planned—which made her the only one who was surprised. Why did it trouble Tess that they'd eaten sandwiches from the corner deli for supper? Again? Or that earlier, Chloe had destroyed Tess's one cashmere sweater by putting it in the dryer?

Lately, love Chloe and Dilly though she did, there wasn't enough room in the house for Tess. There weren't enough hours in her day. Enough sleep time.

Her half smile at Dilly's shriek of laughter and the kittens' antics abruptly died as she heard a crash, twice into the front door, then claws scrabbling across the floor again. Another body, Dilly's obviously, had slammed against the wooden banister with a loud "oomph."

With her heart in her throat, Tess ran to help before Chloe could turn away from the sink. Tess dropped to her knees beside Dilly, hearing an ominous crackling sound from her own joints.

"Dilly, sweetheart, are you okay?"

"She's fine," Chloe said, brave words from a woman who appeared to be permanently on the verge of tears.

Still, Chloe had come to Tess for help, and she did have the most experience as a mother and grandmother. She probed Dilly's slender form for broken bones then checked her small skull for bumps, her touch making Dilly giggle. For good measure she gazed into Dilly's eyes. They looked equal and reactive, if she remembered the terms right from some TV trauma show. No harm done. She should be thankful for that, at least.

She should be able to breathe past the constriction in her chest.

"I didn't want to squish the kitties," Dilly explained, her gray-green eyes wide with innocence, as if she hadn't been part of the mischief. "I grabbed the railing to stop me so I wouldn't run them over."

"Very good thinking."

Tess patted Dilly's blond hair then stood with a sigh.

When she turned around to make sure the cats were okay, they were gone.

"They're hiding," Dilly said. "So you and Mommy won't yell at them."

"Believe me, it does no good." With a reassuring smile she didn't quite feel, she steered Dilly up the stairs. "Chloe, I'll start Dilly's bath then put her to bed."

"And read me a story?"

Tess took a breath. "Just one tonight. Grammy's worn out."

"Because you're old?"

"Dilly!" Chloe leaned against the kitchen doorframe, looking as if her last ounce of strength had been spent. Tess knew exactly how she felt. "Your grandmother is not old."

"Uh-huh. She's older than me."

The logic didn't escape Tess. "You're too young to understand," she said, "but in a few years—well, more than a few—trust me, you'll realize that age is just a state of mind." Right now she felt roughly a century old, not forty-four.

Chloe tried to rescue her. "Tess, I know you're tired too. I can handle Dilly's bath and story."

"I'm sure you can." Not entirely sure, but... "Why don't you finish the dishes instead? And put on a fresh pot of coffee? We could both use some caffeine. Once Dilly's settled I need to talk to you."

Unfortunately, when Tess came back down the stairs, she was still pondering how to bring up the subject of Ethan. She hadn't dared to broach the topic before—and cause Chloe more tears. Then as she hit the last step, Tess gasped. Ethan himself was staring at her through the front door sidelight.

"Acckkk!" she said, a hand pressed to her heart.

Ethan swept inside, smelling of healthy male and the lingering scents of fast food, which had obviously been his dinner.

"Hey, Mom. Didn't mean to scare you."

Tess felt a rush of maternal love for her only child. "Almost anything would scare me right now." She hugged him tight. Ethan had grown into a handsome man, a good man who, as far as she knew, and Grady had said, never strayed from the straight and narrow.

No one needed to steer him. Ethan was always too hard on himself. In his opinion the worst thing he'd done in his twenty-five years was to get Chloe pregnant before they married. Not the wisest course, as Tess well knew, but no worse these days than any number of Hollywood celebrities and everyday people who didn't bother to marry.

Ethan closed the door and lowered his voice. "Is Chloe around?"

"I'm not sure it would be a good idea just yet to—"

Chloe materialized from the living room. And froze.

Ethan's smile for Tess turned into a frown. "Give us a few minutes, Mom?"

"Of course." Tess had the feeling she'd stayed too long at a bad party. "I'm already gone."

"No, stay, Tess. I have nothing to say to you, Ethan," Chloe told him.

Tess reached for both of their hands and intertwined them. Chloe's fingers felt icy cold; Ethan's burned like fire. "Chloe, please listen to each other. Whatever's wrong, you and Ethan can work it out." *I'll be here if you need me.*

"A man's mother is always right," he said, which Tess doubted would help his cause. "I'm a perfectly sane, reasonable man."

Chloe planted her hands on her hips. "That's a matter open to interpretation—"

"For God's sake, I'm..." he hesitated. "...I'm from Cincin*nati*!"

His odd statement didn't sit well with Chloe. "What possible difference does that make?"

Ethan flung up both hands. "You think it doesn't? Sure, fine. Let's make a great start here then, why don't we?" The picture of a baffled male, he marched into the living room with Chloe trailing in his wake.

What to do? Tess was the Go-To Girl, the one who should have all the answers—except for herself. She was staring after them, mentally wringing her hands, when Ethan closed the French doors to the hall and flipped the blinds, shutting her out.

With the growing fear that they'd end up drawing blood, she went out to the kitchen. Trying to ignore the burnt stew smell in the air, she slumped down at the center island. She had just laid her head on the cool granite surface when the telephone rang. Tess snatched up the cordless. Too tired to care, she didn't bother to check the caller ID. "Please tell me this is 555-JOKE calling. I could use a laugh."

"That bad, huh?"

The deep rumble of Grady's voice sliced through her like a stiletto, and Tess couldn't help the swift flash of memory from a week ago in her bathroom. "Worse than you can imagine," she said, a night in which everything had gone wrong. But look on the bright side. Temporarily satisfied with the latest "loan" from Tess's bank account, at least Larry hadn't called again. And she hadn't seen the kittens since their pile-up at the front door.

They were quite safe from Tess. But how safe was she from Grady?

"You seen Ethan?" he asked.

"He's here." She cocked an ear, listening for the sounds of a quarrel from the living room but heard nothing. "He just showed up, unannounced."

"Maybe he got tired of Chloe hanging up on him when he calls your place."

"Umm," she said. "But the last thing I need is shock and awe in my living room." She imagined Grady in his favorite chair in front of the TV. "I do hope you're enjoying your peaceful apartment—all by yourself."

She could hear his quick smile. "Who says I'm by myself?"

A quick, unwelcome bolt of desire ran through Tess. "And you think I'd care if you aren't?"

He hesitated, his tone more serious when he said, "You have nobody to blame but yourself, you know. Maybe you shouldn't have been so quick to take in Chloe. Now Ethan has to chase her halfway across Cincinnati to talk sense to her." Another pause. "How's Dilly?"

"Holding her own. Bless her heart. She must feel confused, though, by all the adult drama in the air."

"This can't be good for her, Tess," Grady agreed. "Why don't you pack her stuff and Chloe's then send them home?"

Her teeth clenched. "Hey, I'm on the front lines here."

"So what are we going to do about it?"

She couldn't let Grady come too close. It was dangerous, this family meeting ground they had, a bond that, unlike their marriage, would never be broken. Maybe if she lost her ten extra pounds, she could get her wedding ring off, as Merry kept urging her to do, and move forward with The Go-To Girl. In the meantime she hadn't seen him since the Nurse Ratched incident, but even talking on the phone threatened her resolve to avoid him for her own good.

"*We're* not doing anything." She poised a finger over the End button. "I'll think of something. 'Bye, Grady."

"Wait," he said, laughing, as if he sensed her retreat into self-protection mode. "You haven't even asked tonight about my poor foot."

After learning the puncture wound seemed to be healing

slowly, and glad to hear he was on the mend, Tess finally hung up. With Grady, she seldom knew whether to laugh or cry.

She never got the chance to decide. Tess heard a sudden shout, then the sound of an object breaking, probably against the wall that the living room shared with her kitchen. She put a hand to her throat. Oh, please, not her Murano glass vase from the mantel.

Before she could rise from her stool, Ethan stormed out into the hall, yanked open the front door then slammed it behind him hard enough to rattle the windows. Tess heard Chloe weeping in noisy, gulping sobs. From upstairs Dilly called out, "Grammy?" in a plaintive tone.

Tess hurried to comfort her before going to Chloe, but as she took a first step the kittens reappeared like specters from the underworld, dust bunnies clinging to their feet. They must have hidden under her bed. One chased the other over Tess's shoes then up the side of a cabinet—which Tess wouldn't have thought possible. Big Boy misjudged the jump from there to the curtains at the window over the sink. The distance from the glass pane to the counter wasn't enough to right his body as he fell. Limbs flailing, he landed ker-splash in the now-cool, dirty dishwater Chloe had used to scrub pans. A grease puddle floated on the surface, adhering to the kitten's fur like Crazy Glue. With a yowl Little Girl plunked into the makeshift pool, too, her cry enough to curdle the lumpy gravy in Chloe's burnt beef stew.

"You and me both," Tess muttered to the wailing cats.

They would need another bath. She fished them out of the sink, her day now a complete failure.

G rady never liked to admit defeat.

Sure, he'd fouled out with Tess. Twice. Once in her bathroom, and tonight on the phone. He was hitting o for 2 but he wouldn't give up. He didn't want Ethan to throw in the towel with Chloe either. "If I were you," he told Ethan, "which I'm not, I'd put an end to this."

Ethan's eyes widened. "*Divorce* Chloe?"

"I don't believe in divorce. It was your mother who kicked me out."

"No," Ethan said mildly, "it was the sheriff. After we lost the house."

Ethan had shown up at Grady's apartment seething after his run-in with Chloe at Tess's place, but more than that, Grady could see, he was hurt. He had no doubt Ethan loved Chloe. "You need to make a pre-emptive strike. Bring her home. The longer she stays with your mother, the worse the situation will get."

"And how would I do that? Like some cave man?" Ethan's expression turned mulish. He consulted the display on his ever-present iPhone. "This isn't Mom's fault."

Ethan was always quick to defend Tess. Grady sometimes wondered if he would be as fast to stick up for him.

"Doesn't have to be her fault." He twisted off the caps on two longnecks and handed one to Ethan. "Not that Tess hasn't played a part in this." The two men flopped onto the recliners in what Grady called his TV room.

Picking his words, he stared for a few moments at the screen. In the tenth inning the Reds were still tied with Boston. "I can tell you she's busy making nice with Chloe right now and spoiling Dilly. On top of that, she works too hard to keep that business of hers going."

Ethan made a scoffing noise, as if he'd seen right through Grady. "What, Dad? You hope she fails then comes crawling back to you? Boy, never mind me and Chloe. You two are a pair."

Grady picked at the damp label on his sweating beer

bottle. The trouble with having a grown kid was that he knew his parents too well.

"Wish we still were," Grady muttered. He had this big hole inside him that no one but Tess could fill.

"Me too," Ethan said.

They exchanged looks, and for a second he and Ethan were completely in synch. A couple of befuddled males who had to stick together until they figured things out. He pointed his bottle at Ethan. "Know something? You are a classic case. The kid whose parents screwed up and made him their mediator. Don't go there, Ethan. It's a lose-lose situation."

He hadn't forgotten the night at Tess's house, those crazy cats of hers, or the punctures on his foot that he'd lied to her about. They were still red and painful, more than he might expect of such small wounds. Unlike the huge emotional scars from his marriage to Tess. There ought to be some kind of tetanus shot for that.

"You love Mom." Ethan took a long swallow of beer. "There's always hope."

Grady frowned. "Not when she holds all the cards. What's the real deal with you and Chloe?"

"You're asking me? From the minute I opened my mouth tonight, she was all over me. I still don't know what I did. Or didn't do."

A sense of sadness settled over Grady. Not just about Tess. He'd had high hopes for his son and Chloe. He didn't want them to make the same mistakes he and Tess had. Or rather, *he* had. The worst part? He couldn't blame her for not wanting anything to do with him now. He'd given her a rough time. He wasn't ready to permanently lay down his hand, so to speak, and quit the game as if he were still playing poker, but things didn't look promising. For Ethan either.

"Maybe you should put that college education to use instead of working with me."

"You think Chloe's unhappy about my job?"

He shrugged. "You've got a business degree, Ethan." Grady set his beer aside. The stuff was making him feel morose. Or was it the damn baseball game, which the Reds seemed determined to lose? They were playing like sleepwalkers, which they might well be. At this rate, the game could go on all night. Or, maybe he wasn't being fair, and he felt bad because of his bumbling attempts to win back Tess's trust. "I don't want you to end up like I have," he told Ethan. "I've stumbled around for too many years. Take the rest of my family, for instance."

"Uncle Brice and Uncle Logan?"

Yeah, and Grady still felt edgy after his brothers' most recent call earlier tonight. Brice the Banker. Logan the Lawyer.

"Hey, Grady," Brice had said. "How's the nail and hammer business?"

Both he and Logan had laughed. Comedians.

"You on a conference call?" Grady had to say something without letting them know they were getting to him. He hoped to sound halfway intelligent for a change.

"Conference? Guess you could call it that. Bet you don't have much use for high-tech stuff."

"You'd be surprised," Grady muttered.

"We're on speaker, both in New York tonight," Logan said. "Brice's bank has season tickets for the Yankees. Too bad you couldn't join us, but on short notice the airfare would have been a killer. No sense sending you back into bankruptcy."

Grady tensed. "Yeah, and my pickup's in the shop. Otherwise I could drive, meet you guys in Manhattan for a couple of beers."

Brice obviously couldn't believe Grady's low-brow taste. "Nah, we're having dinner right now at Ambrosia, usually a two-month wait for reservations. But you know how it is— pull a few strings—or, wait. No, you don't."

After another few minutes of chatter about Brice's new Lexus and Logan's three-bedroom condo in Vail, Grady had grunted, "Gotta go."

"Take it easy, man. Don't get carried away with that nail gun." Brice laughed at his own joke. "I hear they can shoot one of those things right through your brain."

"Hell," Logan said, "there's nothing between his ears to stop a nail."

Hours later, Grady's trigger finger still twitched. It had taken everything in him not to throw his cell phone across the room.

"Yep," he said now to Ethan. "A banker and a lawyer." Two superstars. "Your uncles have more smarts in their little fingers than I do in my whole head. Early on I knew I was destined—doomed—to make my living with my brawn, not my brain."

"That's not true, Dad."

Grady shook his head. He knew better. He'd always been the dumb one, the jock, the loser forever playing catch-up with his brothers, or trying to. The guy who'd picked the wrong cards, anted up anyway, and lost the pot. If he was smarter, he'd know how to win back Tess.

Ethan bristled. "Dad, you're smarter than they are in lots of ways. There's nothing wrong with construction," he said, shooting another surreptitious glance at his phone. With Ethan, it was either that or his iPad. "I'll dope out this trouble with Chloe somehow—and you will too with Mom."

From the TV Grady heard the crack of a bat. He sat up straight in his chair. The Reds' hitter had slammed one over the fence to break the tie. Finally. "Maybe you're right. The game's not over yet." He didn't mean baseball. "We men have to stick together. All we need is a plan."

T ess liked working with other women.

She and Meredith usually got along without a blink of conflict. They'd been together long enough to be able to finish each other's sentences like old married people, and on most issues they agreed, often without words. Except in two cases. As usual Grady was one exception, Merry's current boyfriend the other.

Tess had taken refuge at her desk behind a pile of projects all morning, hoping to resist the urge to dwell on her problems. Trying to deal with Merry's increasingly despondent mood, figure out Chloe's situation with Ethan, forget Grady—somehow—and learn to cope with the two kittens she'd adopted had become more than another full-time job.

Then there was her father. Always. His last call still echoed in her mind. That newest loan. But now, Tess reminded herself, wasn't the time to focus on Larry or her own frustrations. If there was a solution there, she hadn't found it yet. When she heard another shaken sigh from the other desk, she almost welcomed the distraction except that Merry had both hands covering her eyes.

Tess said gently, "You might as well tell me."

"Frank," came a muffled cry from behind her fingers. Tess counted a ring on each of them, even her thumbs.

"He forgot your birthday."

"You were the only one who remembered! Thanks again for that gorgeous scarf. You know how I love sparkly stuff." Merry dropped her hands into the lap of her shiny gold skirt and gazed at Tess in absolute misery. "What am I going to do? He treats me as if I'm totally invisible."

"Ah," Tess said, "how could I forget? The Reds played last night."

"All night." Merry's ringed hands fluttered in the air as if to wave away the event. "I used to think he had ADD, but Frank never blinked through the *whole* game. He had the remote clutched in his fist from the first pitch until the team finally won in overtime as if regular play wasn't long enough. And then he watched the post-game shows. *All* of them. I swear I'm tempted to take the batteries out of that thing and throw them away."

"He probably has a spare remote." Tess considered the uncomfortable suspicion that Frank also had a problem, not unlike Grady's. "He's not putting money on the games, is he?"

"I don't know."

"You should talk to him, Merry."

"I've tried. You know I have. What else can I say?"

Tess picked her words carefully. "I don't mean to sound harsh, but if Frank won't listen or try to change and take more notice of you, then maybe you need to look for a different relationship."

"Oh, right. Coming from you..." Merry didn't continue.

Tess frowned, and deliberately missed the obvious point. "I haven't watched a game with Grady in ten years. I hate baseball."

She fought the urge to fidget. Maybe her dislike stemmed from all those Little League games of Ethan's and the many practices she'd attended solo in Grady's absence. Over time Tess had become unpopular with the other team mothers who seemed to consider her a threat to their own marriages. They'd shunned her, really, convinced that Tess was a single mom on the make. At one post-season picnic, several of the dads too had expressed surprise that she was actually married. Grady's awkward attempt to fit in at the lone occasion he'd shown up for—long after he was needed to help coach the fledgling team—had only made things worse.

Now Tess felt obligated to defend herself. Her gaze homed in on her wedding ring. Her finger still looked faintly pink from all that tugging and twisting in the private showroom at Tiffany's.

"I know you had a point when you said in effect that I should put this in a drawer and start dating again, but it's not as if I invite Grady to Sunday dinner every week."

Over my dead body. The near-kiss with him in her bathroom had been an aberration, a one-time chance she hadn't dared to take. And never would.

"You invited him for last Thanksgiving." Merry began ticking off the dates on her fingers. "And Christmas. And then, remember, on his birthday."

Tess flushed. "Ethan wouldn't hear of Grady spending those holidays by himself. To keep the peace, I had to invite him."

"You use Ethan as your excuse."

Tess's pulse thumped. "Do I look to you like a self-destructive person?"

Merry made a show of sizing her up. "Sometimes," she finally said.

"Meredith, we were talking about Frank. I really think you and he need to confront this issue. How long have you lived together?" As if she didn't know. Tess had helped them carry boxes on moving day. Her back had hurt afterward for a month.

"Three years."

"In *your* house," Tess said. "What does he contribute?"

"We share some of the bills—utilities, repairs..."

"Well, that's something. But you pay the mortgage. And you need to know: Is he interested in this relationship, or is Frank using you to limit his own expenses?" On a roll, she

took a deep breath. "It's time that man fished or cut bait...
whatever that means. Remember, he saved enough by living
with you to buy himself that surround sound system and a
new DVR. What did *you* get last Christmas?"

Merry shrugged. "One of those neat slicer-things they
advertise on HSN. It can julienne potatoes and carrots and
cut a whole onion in one swipe."

"Amazing." Tess rolled her eyes. "See what I mean? That
gadget should have been a big, showy diamond." She looked
pointedly at Merry's hand bedecked with costume jewelry. "A
real one, like Sybil Shallowford's."

"Speaking of which..." Merry had fixed her gaze on the
front window. Following her eyes, Tess saw a large man move
past the glass then the doorknob turned and in walked Call-
Me-Emery Shallowford.

His neurosurgeon's ego matched his considerable size.

Tess's heart sank.

Oh, no. He must have heard about her embarrassment at
Tiffany's.

She had to admit Emery cut an impressive figure. His big
frame was the perfect coat hanger for his obviously expensive
suit. Armani, she guessed from the drape and quality of the
silk. Emery had a full head of thick, graying brown hair and a
pair of laser-sharp gray eyes. His tasteful tie and yellow shirt
had been carefully chosen—not by her.

"Ladies, I would have come by sooner, except the hospital's been a madhouse. But here I am. I have to say—" He
broke off, and Tess steeled herself for his next words. Instead,
Emery announced, "Thanks to you, a few nights ago I, well, I
got lucky as a pig in clover."

Tess blinked. "Lucky?"

He grinned, showing his blinding white teeth. "Sybil loved
your ring."

"Her ring."

"Whatever. Right choice, Terry," he said, beaming.

She forced a smile. "It's Tess, actually."

Emery ignored that. "Our anniversary was like the Arabian Nights. Like some harem, or a paradise with, what is it, dozens of women?"

Tess cleared her throat. Emery might be a well-respected surgeon with a super-sharp focus, but he had more than a few remaining rough edges. She didn't need to know about his sex life. "I'm glad your *wife* liked the ring."

His chest puffed out. "*Liked* it? I'm lucky to be able to walk." He must have seen Merry's eyes, so wide that she looked like a doll with a too-big gaze. "Sorry," he muttered, "but a man likes to feel appreciated, and you two really did the trick."

"That's our *business*." In which Tess met all kinds. "And about Tiffany's," she began, deciding to pre-empt any problem before Emery mentioned it.

"Oh. That. The clerk there wasn't quite sure what to make of you." He laughed. "I set her straight, though. 'Course she got me on the phone while Sybil and I were still in bed and I couldn't have been in a better mood."

Tess inwardly groaned. "I get the picture. Thank you, Emery. I'm glad you—and she—reached an understanding."

"You and I understand each other, too." He looked her over and Tess waited, wondering if she imagined the too-friendly tone of his voice. Clearly, he had something more in mind. "Good-looking woman like you needs a man."

"I had one. Past tense."

"That ex-husband of yours didn't know how lucky he was." Emery knew Grady and, as with Tess, the two men shared an equally bad history in business. "Time to look toward the future, Terry. What do you say? Let's talk. I'll buy you lunch."

The invitation didn't quite surprise her. Behind his back

Merry studied the ceiling. Was he asking Tess for a date? What a nerve he had.

"Sorry, but I—" Tess started to say she had her weekly appointment with the fashion buyer at Macy's and had no time for lunch, but Emery didn't wait.

"I insist. This is personal. You had a bad experience with that husband of yours." He named a restaurant near the Aronoff Center for the Arts. "Meet me at one o'clock. By then the lunch crowd will be nearly gone. We'll get a booth for privacy. Discretion," he added, "is a big part of my character."

Her lips tightened. So, apparently, was infidelity. Poor Sybil Shallowford. And here, Tess had thought she'd gotten a reprieve about Tiffany's. Did she dare tell him off? And risk being blackballed all over Cincinnati? Or could she find some graceful way to refuse his invitation? Tactfully, if possible. She didn't get a chance.

Emery nodded at Merry, who hadn't been included in the lunch, then headed out the door toward his gleaming, new top-of-the-line Jaguar in the parking lot.

"Oh, brother," Tess muttered. Things just kept getting worse.

"Was that guy actually hitting on you?"

"Sure sounded like it."

Merry rolled her eyes. "Frank and I have our problems. But, Tess, cheating? And Shallowford must think he looks like Mr. Exactly Right."

$\gg$ 4 $\ll$

"KNOW WHAT, Dill? Let's be super heroes today."

Chloe, as usual, was whistling in the wind, but she believed in putting a good face on things. With Dilly at her heels she buzzed down the stairs, barely skimming each step, like a carpenter bee hovering over its territory on Tess's wooden deck. This wasn't her area of expertise—as if she had one.

Tess's home wasn't hers to clean or to take care of. Still, she felt bad about the ruined beef stew, even worse about Tess's now-child sized cashmere sweater. And then there was the shattered vase. She wanted to make up for her own clumsiness, the drama and ineptitude that seemed to follow her through life like a reminder of her father's constant criticisms.

Stop bumping into things, Chloe. Watch where you're going.

You should have finished college, Chloe.

Make something of yourself, Chloe.

Sometimes it seemed she'd spent all of her twenty-five years trying to live up to his impossible expectations while Chloe remained stubbornly imperfect.

As if to prove the point, at the bottom of the steps she tripped over her own feet. Chloe clutched the railing to steady herself. *And for my next trick...* She had already disappointed Tess, but inept or not it was Chloe's responsibility to correct the situation. To try, anyway. Ethan was another matter. If she even thought about him this morning, she'd fall apart again.

"Can we wear super hero capes?" Dilly followed her into the kitchen where Chloe whisked clean plates from the dishwasher. She moved too fast, fumbled one in her haste then grabbed for it—and missed.

The accident seemed to happen in slow motion, as most did, and she watched in horror as the china fell then smashed into pieces on the ceramic tile floor. Holding up a hand, she managed to signal Dilly out of harm's way. "Stay back, baby. You'll get hurt."

With wide eyes, Dilly surveyed the damage. "You broke it."

"Yes, I did."

"Last time at our house you broke Grammy's turkey."

Chloe groaned inwardly. "We're not supposed to talk about that, remember?"

The expensive platter with a turkey hand-painted on its surface had been Tess's first anniversary gift to Chloe and Ethan, handed down from her mother and grandmother before her, meant to be used for special occasions, especially Thanksgiving. Chloe had received the family treasure with awe, a symbol of O'Neill acceptance into the family. Then she'd betrayed that trust. She'd never known how to tell Tess it was gone. So she hadn't. It was a wonder no one had ever mentioned its absence.

Chloe had a growing list of precious objects that no longer existed in her own cabinets and on her shelves. Whenever she could, on Ethan's computer she scoured the Internet looking, hoping, to find a replacement for Tess's platter before anyone noticed it was missing. She squirreled away extra cash from her weekly budget to pay for it. Ethan didn't have to know that either. So far, the turkey platter hadn't shown up on eBay or Craig's List. The china pattern had long ago been retired so the item wasn't easy to find.

A familiar queasy feeling clutched at her stomach.

Sometimes she wondered why Ethan had married her.

Maybe she'd done him a favor by moving out, except that because of her hurried packing she and Dilly were already running out of clothes suitable to the changing season. If they stayed much longer, until summer, Dilly would need a whole new wardrobe. She grew so fast. And how would Chloe pay for that?

More evidence that her father was right about her.

From behind a kitchen stool, Dilly watched her retrieve the broom and dustpan from Tess's utility closet then sweep up the broken pieces of china and dump them into the trashcan.

"Are you hiding them like the kitties hid from Grammy? Will she be mad?"

Chloe gnawed at her lip. "No, of course she won't."

"Will you tell her?"

At the frank question she turned to find Dilly's solemn gaze on her. *Is this a test?* Chloe didn't want to flunk that too, or worse, give her daughter the impression that she was a sneak. Had she done that already about the platter?

"When the time is right," she told Dilly. "I broke it. *I'll* tell her."

Being a good mom might be Chloe's only skill. She didn't want to blow that, too. Ethan was always telling her how great a parent she was—how loving—but these days he didn't seem to see the rest of her.

Unlike Chloe, Ethan was so totally competent, like his

mom, that it was scary. He was devoted to his job—focused now on that more than on their home life—and of course he had satisfying work while she did not. Except for Dilly, the most awesome accomplishment of her otherwise under-achieving life.

What could she do, really, with half a college degree? Sell china—heaven forbid—at Dillard's and lose most of her pay to replacement costs for all the breakage she might cause? Ethan would probably just laugh and tell her it was nothing. How many women, he might ask, would relish the chance to smash a little crockery now and then? Good therapy, he'd say.

The thought of Ethan made her eyes fill. He didn't understand why she'd left home. But then, neither did Chloe.

She wouldn't tell Ethan that he reminded her these days of her dad. The Big Surgeon. The man who was rarely home, and never quite there for her when he was, the imposing physician who always "diagnosed" Chloe—at five, ten, twenty —and found her prognosis to be less than hopeful. Unlike him, Ethan had never yelled, except the other night, but...

"Don't feel sad, Mommy." Dilly took the empty dustpan and broom from her hands and put them back in the closet. "Grammy and I will take care of you."

"Oh my God." With the hoarse words Chloe swept her up into a hard hug. Even a four-year-old child could see her klutziness. "It's my job to take care of you, baby."

"Grammy too?"

"Well, sometime," she said. "If she ever needs me."

Chloe drew back. She doubted that. Tess was her opposite, always in control, ever ready to step in to solve a problem. Look how she'd taken Chloe into her house without any hesitation, but just see how Chloe had repaid her kindness. The stew, the sweater, the vase, now the shattered plate, and it was only ten o'clock in the morning. The day had just begun.

She straightened her shoulders, even more determined to prove her worth to Tess.

"Here's our plan: we'll dust and vacuum for Grammy today. Save her some work. How's that?" Sounded simple enough. "Maybe after we finish, we'll order take-out to surprise her for dinner."

"Pizza?"

She smiled. "Your favorite."

"Grammy likes it, too." When Chloe raised an eyebrow, Dilly nodded, her twin blond ponytails bobbing. "She does, Mommy."

Chloe sent her a stronger look. Her baby's gaze slid away.

"Well, she *says* she does."

"Diligence O'Neill, what did we decide about making up stories about other people that aren't true?"

Her expression mulish—just like Ethan—Dilly tried to dig a toe of her sneaker into the tile floor. "It's not good."

"Not unless you're a writer," Chloe told her. "Which you might be someday, or a movie producer, maybe even a great actress." Dilly had a natural talent there, which made Chloe struggle not to smile while she delivered the rest of her lecture. "For now, the truth is absolutely essential. At all times. Do you understand, young lady?"

"Yes, ma'am."

Chloe wished she could take her own advice. Tell Ethan how she felt. And she would. As soon as she figured that out herself.

Dilly was still trying to comprehend truth telling. "What's as-sential?"

"Necessary. Important."

"Like me," Dilly said. Her daughter had more self-confidence than Chloe.

"Totally, one hundred percent important."

Dilly grinned. "'Cause you love me bunches? Even when I fib?"

"Don't push it," Chloe said and ruffled her hair. "More than bunches. More than anyone else in the world."

"Even Daddy?"

That stopped her. Oh, no. Dilly must have heard their quarrel in Tess's living room. Another mistake on Chloe's part. "I love you both," she murmured. When she reached into the fridge for the orange juice container, her hand shook. But to her relief, in typical four-year-old fashion, Chloe had already moved on.

"Can we play super heroes now?"

Chloe had a change of heart. Still shaken about Ethan, she wasn't ready to put on a cape, or to pick up a dust rag, for that matter. "Tell you what," she said as Tess's two cats streaked through the kitchen. "Let's save being super heroes till after lunch, okay? Dusting too. We'll have a snack now then play with the kitties. How does that sound?"

"Yes!"

Chloe could manage that much. There'd be plenty of time later to help Tess—or break up the place.

A s soon as she walked into the restaurant at one-fifteen, Tess spied Emery Shallowford in a corner booth—and wished she could turn around and run. Before the hostess had a chance to ask if she could seat her, Tess waved a hand in Emery's direction.

"I see my party right there, thanks." Party being the operative word if, as Tess had feared, Emery actually propositioned her somehow.

She couldn't wait to give him a piece of her mind, except she hadn't quite decided what to say. All the way from Fields Ertel Road to the downtown restaurant, she'd rehearsed without ever feeling satisfied. She needed to be careful but still get her message across. Risking The Go-To Girl's future, and her own, would be disaster. She had to do this right.

Merry, of course, had tried to stop her.

"So, the guy's a jerk. He's not alone. Stand him up, Tess. Stay here. We have to buy for the Jensen housewarming party."

Tess might have stood Emery up, but she couldn't afford the slight. Instead, she had re-scheduled her meeting with the buyer at Macy's, which almost never happened. Tess rarely short-changed her vendors. But Emery had powerful friends, colleagues who might also hire Tess someday.

He glanced up from his menu. "You're late," he said.

"Sorry," though she'd deliberately stalled for time. "Traffic was heavy."

Tess slid into the booth on the opposite side, as far away from him as she could get. All at once the privacy he'd wanted didn't seem like a bad idea. She didn't want anyone else to overhear them. If, on the other hand, he tried to scoot closer, to touch her, she wouldn't be responsible for what happened. Screaming seemed a good option.

Ironically, Tess had first met Emery because of Grady. At his lowest point, Grady had failed to complete some patio work on the Shallowford house, and Tess had stepped in to try to smooth over the bad feelings. To this day Emery and Grady remained enemies, but for the past few years Emery had sent Tess Valentine's Day cards, which he claimed he did for all the women in his life but which might have been a clue to his intentions now, and last Christmas he had hired her to find gifts for all of his associates.

Until this morning she'd assumed he simply felt sorry for her—not a position she cared to be in either.

He took a swallow from a stubby glass crammed with ice and some pale liquid that looked like Scotch. Drinking, in mid-day? He said, "I was afraid you wouldn't show up. I was beginning to feel disappointed." He pushed a second menu toward her. "Let's order. I'm hungry."

"I'm not staying. I came by to tell you—"

"Terry, I know you're busy. Seems to me, though, you can spare me a little time. That diamond for Sybil cost half the earth. Your fee alone—"

Tess took a deep breath. He was playing the money card.

"I'm well aware of that. I did as you asked, according to your budget, for my commission and hourly rate. I also—" She broke off. How could she say this? Tess was on the verge of leaving the restaurant.

With a frown Emery leaned back against the booth.

"You seem angry. What's the problem?"

Tess gathered herself. "Doctor Shallowford. I appreciate your business—really—and I hope there won't be hard feelings, but I make it a policy never to see clients outside the office...that is, unless we shop together—which, of course, is still work. From my perspective."

"Wait a minute." His frown gradually became a smile. His gaze followed hers to his half-empty glass. "I see. To clear the air here, first of all I'm drinking cream soda. And you think I asked you to lunch expecting a quickie afterward?"

Tess remained silent. Mortified. She felt her cheeks heat. "My assistant got the same impression. I realize this may be standard in, um, some circles, but not in mine. I'm divorced, as you know, and thus 'available,' some might think, but I actually lead a quiet, very private life. I'm not interested."

Emery's smile grew into a full-fledged grin.

Did she sound vain? It wasn't as if Tess considered herself to be a knockout. But since she'd started The Go-To Girl, she had been propositioned a few times, which was always awkward. Those fumbling seductions, even Grady's recent, more skilled one, reminded her of all the reasons she preferred to be alone. But she'd never had a man laugh in her face.

Tess started to rise. "I'm sure you must find this amusing—"

"I sure as hell do." He reached out, hauling Tess back into her seat. "Sit down. I think we have a few things to straighten out." Before he began, their waiter appeared. "We'll both have the special," Emery said. "Make it fast, will you? I'm doing surgery this afternoon and I could eat a moose."

"Yes, sir, Dr. Shallowford."

He waited until they were alone again. "Didn't you hear a word I said this morning? About Sybil?"

Tess cleared her throat. "I understand you had an interesting anniversary celebration." Her face was flaming. Had she been wrong? Then what *did* he want?

"Sybil and I have been married for thirty years."

"Yes. I remember. That's why you bought the ring."

"I'm aware that I have a tendency to colorful speech. I grew up in Kentucky," he said as if that explained everything. "Where I come from, we speak our minds, whether that's socially acceptable or not. I am the bane of Sybil's existence."

Tess had to laugh. "Kentucky is a beautiful state," she murmured.

"And I'm proud to be her native son. I was raised there among plain, honest people, went away to college—the first in my family to do so— then borrowed my way through med school and I've made my folks proud. But I'm still a country boy at heart. Talk like one, walk like one, don't worry much about what comes out of my mouth." He paused. "Have you met Sybil?"

"Once," Tess said, feeling more chagrined. Their unhappy meeting had concerned Grady and that unfinished patio. And as a socialite Sybil knew everyone in town, although Tess had also found her to be a rather fluffy-minded person. Still, like Emery, she had potentially valuable contacts too.

"Wonderful woman. Best thing I ever did was marry her. And since I urged her to find work that would, well, keep her busy now that our girls are grown, she seems happy again." He hesitated. "I have never once cheated on her. I'm not about to begin now. Not that there haven't been opportunities," he said. "Some of those young nurses—"

She rolled her eyes. "Don't spoil it. I was just starting to really like you."

Emery grinned again, showing all those pearly whites lined up like ivory keys on a piano. "I like you too, Terry."

She sighed. Okay, fine. Let him call her by the wrong name.

"Tell me more about yourself," he said, lounging in his seat again.

Surprised by his interest, and still embarrassed by her mistaken impression of their lunch date, Tess gave him the barest details. But Emery was very good at drawing people out and, somehow, she ended up including her father in the story. Then, because Emery already knew about Grady, she didn't need to dwell on him, but instead expressed her concern for Ethan's job at his company.

"I can't help but feel afraid for my son and his family," she finished. "I know exactly how painful it is to live with—or depend on—a gambler."

"The divorce damaged you," Emery concluded. "*That's* what I meant earlier. You definitely need someone else." His sharp gaze assessed her until Tess wanted to squirm. "I don't mean myself," Emery added, "to put your mind at ease. How about I look around for you? At the hospital too? There are some eligible M.D.s there, even a few administrators who might suit you."

Tess paused. "Thanks, but no. The only thing I care about right now is finding a house I can afford to buy."

He stared down at his napkin. "My wife is a Realtor. That's what keeps her occupied and happy. Maybe she can help."

Tess didn't care for his attitude about women but didn't comment. It was Sybil Shallowford's place to rein him in, not hers.

Again, he hesitated. "There is one thing you can do for me," he began then didn't continue. Clearly, this was the real reason for their luncheon, but he waited until their entrees had been served. "Don't tell Sybil."

"Excuse me?"

"Don't tell her I hired you to buy the danged ring. She thinks I picked it out myself—that I love her so much I knew exactly what she'd like," he said, studying the fish on his plate. He picked up his fork. "But for the past few weeks I've been up to my red-neck ass in blood and guts at that hospital." Tess winced at the graphic image before he went on, "Didn't have a free second to go shopping. Wouldn't matter to Sybil. If she ever—*ever*—learns another woman chose that pricey stone, my sorry butt will be in the street or at least out of our bedroom."

"I did choose that ring," Tess pointed out.

"Sybil is a prideful woman. By now she has boasted to all her friends, including the other wives in the hospital auxiliary, that I'm the best man in the world. Their husbands pale by comparison, believe me, but she also has a jealous nature." He lowered his voice, his gaze scanning the room. "Do you get what I'm saying?"

Tess made a zipping motion. "My lips are sealed."

With a satisfied expression he dug into his food. "I knew I could count on you, Terry."

"Some of my other clients prefer the same sort of anonymity," Tess agreed.

For long moments there was silence. She jammed a forkful of garlic mashed potatoes in her mouth to prevent a smile. Emery had his rough spots, but he seemed nice enough, even if some of his views of women were more than outdated. He wouldn't risk breaking his wife's heart. How about that?

"Tell me something else." Emery's plate was already clean, and his gaze had homed in on Tess's ring finger. "Since you're divorced from that scoundrel—"

"For a year and a half," she admitted.

"How come you still wear his wedding band?"

D riving across town to the office after lunch, Tess thought she knew the answer. Her mother had never divorced Tess's dad, not in the worst days of their marriage when they'd lived in a series of cheap apartments and ramshackle rented houses. Her mom had died without ever owning a home. Or feeling secure.

Her mother's devotion—or her foolhardiness?—made Tess feel guilty about Grady. As if she should have tried harder, hung on longer, made one more attempt to change him.

But she had tried. She really had.

If only...

T *ess lay in the big bed she shared with Grady, waiting for him to come back to her from Ethan's room. Even at ten years old their son had a tendency to pick up every germ that came along, and this sudden bout of flu had him chilled and feverish. They'd taken turns caring for him, and Ethan had finally fallen asleep. Grady had gone to check on him.*

When he slipped in beside her again, she drew him close.

"He's really better?"

"Temp's almost normal, I think. He's over the worst of it." Grady wrapped his strong arms around her, nuzzled the side of her neck. His lips brushed over her skin, and in spite of the long night they'd shared —or maybe because they had shared—Tess opened herself to him.

Grady's hands at her breasts, his mouth on her from lips to nipples to the soft skin of her belly and, finally—oh God, yes—at the very heart of her drove Tess wild. With every year, his lovemaking got better and better.

"I'm so glad you're mine," she whispered, taking him in until she felt filled with his love for her, with her love for him. "Don't ever leave me, Grady. I promise, I won't leave you."

"I'm here, Tess Trueheart," he murmured as if they were two halves of one whole. "I'm right here."

W hen she finally reached home after work, Tess was still caught up in her poignant remembrance of what might have been. To be fair to herself, she'd stayed with Grady after that night for another ten years. She tried to think now of her luncheon with Emery, but her bittersweet trip down memory lane and his question about Grady's ring kept coming back too.

Tess prayed Sybil never learned the truth about her anniversary diamond. But then, how would she? Tess was sworn to secrecy. Merry would be too as soon as Tess got to work tomorrow, and Emery, as he'd said in parting, "would have my tongue pulled out" before he uttered a word.

Then all thought died—like that oh-so-pleasant If Only she'd enjoyed on the way home—as Tess pulled into her driveway. Her father was sitting on her front steps. Lost in the past, she hadn't noticed Larry's car parked along the opposite curb.

Tess felt a familiar twist of anxiety deep inside. This couldn't be good. And with that, she had to admit, the memory she'd just entertained about Grady wasn't either. It wasn't even true. In fact, it was all false. In reality he hadn't been there with her. He hadn't come home that long-ago night until dawn. She'd cared for a sick Ethan by herself, and her remembrance was just another fantasy after all.

By then their first years in the house she loved had seemed like another lifetime, with another two people who had once loved each other. Everything had changed except for those sagging shutters she could never quite find money in the budget to replace; the scarred wooden floors she'd always planned to strip and refinish; that leak in the bathroom ceiling repaired with shingle patches on the roof that still needed to be completely redone.

At that point Grady had played poker nearly every night —and probably some days when Tess assumed he was at work.

Where have you been? she'd asked when he finally came home that night.

Don't nag, Tess. I'm wiped out. He'd sounded just like Larry.

And Tess had sounded like her mother. *How are we going to pay the doctor? The mortgage is due, Grady. I've already maxed out all our credit cards...*

Tess blinked. With her blurred gaze fixed on Larry now, she took her time getting out of the car, gathering her briefcase and a small bag of groceries from a stop on her way home. As she went up the walk, to her dismay she noticed Chloe's car was missing from the drive. She and Dilly must have gone to the park or to run some errand or maybe they had gone home to Ethan. In any case that left Tess alone to face her father who couldn't have picked a worse time to visit when her memories of Grady and their failed marriage were all too fresh again.

"Hey, Dad," she said with a faint smile as he reached out to take the bag from her.

"Hey, yourself, sugar-pie."

Tess's heart sank at his too-hearty tone. He definitely wanted something. She fumbled in her purse for her door key. "What's on your mind?"

Without explaining the reason for his visit, Larry trailed her inside.

Total silence greeted them, and the back of Tess's neck prickled. Where were the kittens? Normally they met her at the door with friendly meows in the obvious hope that she would feed them. They had increasingly voracious appetites and never missed a meal. Or, for that matter, the chance to startle Tess with a sideways leap, soft paws wrapped around her leg before they glanced off and both cats ran, full of mischief, for the kitchen.

Larry of course didn't notice their absence. He didn't know she had pets. He went straight through the front hall, thumped the bag down on the center island, then proceeded to unpack and shelve everything for her. A plastic-wrapped container of chicken went into the fridge. "Well?" Tess said.

He turned around, his dark puppy-dog eyes downcast.

"I need some money."

Big surprise. "What for, Dad? It hasn't been that long since I emptied an ATM for you."

He shrugged. "I owe a guy in Dayton."

"How much this time?"

"More than I got." He pulled his pants pockets inside out, with a small, wry grin that failed to charm Tess as he probably intended to do.

She noted his lips had thinned and bore lines underneath from the years when he'd been a smoker. But for all his other faults Larry took pride in his appearance, as if that was all he had left.

He kept himself trim and fit, and in spite of the fact that he probably didn't have a dime to his name, he still wore his one good suit, neatly pressed, whenever he came to call on her. His personal banker. As always, his white shirt looked clean and crisp; his slightly loosened tie appeared to be silk. He'd likely been waiting on her front porch for some time, and his still unlined forehead bore a faint sprinkling of perspiration, but she had to hand it to him.

To the casual observer he would seem to be a winner.

The realization made Tess feel even sadder than she did about today's If Only and Grady. "How much?" she said again.

He stalled. "You're not going to invite me for dinner first?"

"Chloe and Dilly are staying with me." As if there wasn't a fourth chair at her table.

"Why?" he asked.

She cleared her throat, not eager to tell Larry her troubles. "Chloe decided to visit for a few days. She'll be back soon," she said, although Chloe hadn't left a note on the counter or the fridge. "Sorry, there isn't enough chicken."

She looked around again. Surely the cats smelled fresh poultry. Little Girl was something of an addict. By now she should be perched on the counter hoping for a snack. *Where were they?*

Larry prowled the kitchen. "You'd think with your mother gone, you and I would get closer."

Tess's pulse skipped. *Here we go.* "I have a long memory, Dad."

"Well, see, that's one of your problems, sugar-pie. You oughta let go of that before it eats you alive. How's Grady?" he said without missing a beat.

Larry had disapproved of their divorce. He liked Grady. Of course he did; they shared a passion for poker.

"I wouldn't know," she said.

"Saw his truck across town the other day. Him and Ethan. They didn't see me or I'd know for myself how he is."

"He's probably avoiding you." The words weren't out of her mouth before Tess wished she could take them back. "Sorry," she said again, ashamed of herself. He always brought out the worst in her.

Larry dropped onto a stool at the center island and stared at his hands. Clean, with no age spots, they were long-fingered. Tess had always envied them—until she'd realized one day that she'd gotten those very hands from him in a smaller, more feminine version.

Finally, he looked up. "I'm in some trouble, Tess."

"I figured." *Again. Why am I not surprised?* Exasperation and sorrow spiraled up from her suddenly uneasy stomach into her throat.

"I owe the guy in Dayton twelve hundred bucks."

Tess shook her head. Too many bad memories flashed through her mind of her father, then Grady. Except Grady stuck to one game while Larry had no preferences. The horses, the slots, cards... "Dad. You promised...you've been playing poker, haven't you?"

"It was a good game. I was winning big—"

Tess threw up her hands. "Until you lost. It's the same as Vegas or Atlantic City or one of those Indian casinos. Don't you get it? The house always wins."

"This was a private game. Just me and three other guys."

"And that makes it different? They could be gangsters. They probably are. And don't you dare tell me the cards were marked. I've heard that one before. Big or small, the result is the same. You lose." She whirled away from him toward the refrigerator. She took out the chicken, slapped the package onto the counter and hunted for a knife. "*I* lose," she muttered, fighting back tears.

"Tess, I know you're upset with me—"

She gritted the words. "Can you blame me?"

Looking contrite, pulling out the charm, he waited a moment then said, "Help your old dad out here, huh?"

"Great. Just great." Tess tossed the chicken pieces into a skillet then dumped in barbecue sauce from a bottle and set the pan on simmer. "I have half a mind to just tell you no. Larry—"

"What would your mother say?" he asked in a wounded tone.

Tess heaved a breath. At the stove she counted to forty. Ten could never ease the sense of loss she felt. Merry was right. Her father was the biggest manipulator she knew— except, of course, for Grady during the worst of his gambling days.

Just give me a few more bucks. I'll make it up to you when I get paid.

I won't be late tonight, Tess. It's a quick game...

I feel lucky.

She told herself to forget Grady, as Emery would advise. His eyes, his smile, and his whiskey-smooth voice. But this was Larry, and in spite of everything Tess worried about him. He was her only other family except for Ethan, Chloe, and Dilly.

She couldn't say no. He was right. Neither would her mother.

Without Mom, he's alone now, she told herself. *It's the least I can do.*

Just one more time...

The old litany was automatic. With a defeated sigh she walked past him to the small desk built into a recess of the kitchen. "I must be the biggest sucker on the face of the earth." She drew out her checkbook. "This means I can't pay down my MasterCard this month. Or add to my house fund."

Emery's diamond ring money helped, but she was still short of her goal. Even shorter now.

Larry screeched back his stool. He stood behind her, his hands settling on her shoulders. "I know, Tess. Thanks. I won't ask again."

Yes, you will. Blinking, she didn't know what she would have said next. The front door had banged against the wall and Dilly raced in, already talking a mile a minute.

"Grammy! Mommy broke a dish before we could play super heroes. I helped clean up the mess, but Big Boy stepped on some glass and hurt his foot. We had to take the kitties to the *doctor*—"

"Dilly, sweetheart, slow down." Tess glanced at Chloe, behind her.

"Don't ask," she said. And gave Larry a little wave.

"—and then the bet—"

"Vet, Dilly."

"—the *vet* had to dig the teeny pieces out of Big Boy's paw. He was *bleeding.* Some got on my shirt." She pulled the fabric away from her tummy to show Tess the damage. Proudly, Tess thought. "That's 'cause I picked him up too fast. But he didn't scratch me, Grammy." She gave the duffle bag in Chloe's grasp a fond look over her shoulder. From inside the makeshift carrier Tess heard the familiar cries of the two kittens. "The doctor said they have fleas. He put powder all over 'em." Tess shuddered, hoping her carpets weren't filled with bugs as Dilly rushed on, "And while we were there, Mommy said both the kitties should get their shots, too. She paid for 'em 'cause she broke your plate."

Tess smiled. "Thank you, Chloe. For the shots, not the dish."

"It's the least I could do. I missed seeing those shards of glass."

Impatiently, Dilly tugged at Tess's shirt.

"Then you wanna know what else happened?"

Tess smiled. Dilly's stories were always elaborate. "I can't wait."

"When we left the vet place, we got pizza. Only when Mommy turned the corner too fast, the boxes fell on the floor in the car. So, guess what?" Dilly finished. "We don't have any dinner."

"Good thing I didn't know your plan."

Dilly sniffed the air. "Hey. I smell somethin' good."

"The chicken won't take long." Tess finished writing the check. She handed it to Larry just as Chloe let the cats out of the bag, so to speak. "That was quite an adventure," Tess told Dilly. She turned toward her father who had suddenly yelped.

The kittens were already climbing his pants legs. They'd never met a stranger. Except for Grady. Neither had Dilly.

"Great-grandpa Larry!" she said, hugging him around the waist.

"Stay for dinner," Tess said, for the first time matching his smile. "The more the merrier. If there's not enough chicken, we'll make sandwiches."

She didn't have to lay down the law to him right this minute.

She had divorced Grady, but she couldn't divorce her dad.

⚛ 5 ⚛

LARRY WENT HOME after dinner with Tess's check tucked in his pocket. In her experience the money had been a mere down payment on what he actually owed "some guy in Dayton." Too bad that, like a character in *The Godfather*, she couldn't refuse Larry's "offer."

Worse, she could only hope his creditor didn't belong to the Mafia.

When the taillights of Larry's aging VW disappeared in the night, she turned back into the house to face Chloe. They'd never found a chance to talk before or after she and Ethan quarreled, and if Tess couldn't deal with her father she would try with Chloe now.

Not quite to Tess's surprise, Chloe lay curled on the living room sofa, the two kittens sprawled along her side. Their limbs were so entwined, their cream and brown coats so similar, Tess couldn't tell where Little Girl began and Big Boy ended. Taking a breath for courage, she walked into the room. The cats startled awake, ears perked, eyes wide.

"It's not p-l-a-y time," Tess informed their hopeful blue-eyed expressions. If she actually said the word, those two would scamper to find the nearest toy and wouldn't take no for an answer. "Cat treats in your bowls," she told them. "Chloe and I need to discuss something."

Tess had hoped the kittens would be good company, and they certainly made her laugh, but within seconds the sweet-looking duo could take over any scene. If she let them stay in the room, Chloe would focus on them not Tess. Chloe and Dilly had an affinity for her new pets that Tess could only admire. Of course, they hadn't been here when Big Boy tore a chunk out of Grady's foot.

She took another breath. In spite of the enticement of a snack, the kittens stayed put. Upstairs, thank goodness, Dilly was sound asleep. Tess had put her to bed, exhausted after an earlier play session with the cats.

Tess put on her best smile. "Chloe, I love having you and Dilly here. That goes without saying. But staying with me hasn't really been a rest for you, has it? You're obviously unhappy. What about Ethan? Your home? Whatever the problem may be, this interlude can't be good for your marriage."

Idly, Chloe stroked the two cats, which for some reason hadn't moved. Tess could hear them purr like fine-tuned Formula One engines. Her voice trembled. "Ethan doesn't need me."

"Oh, that can't be true."

Chloe sat up, gently dislodging the kittens. Rejuvenated from their nap, they leapt across the sofa arm, claws digging into the upholstery, then bounded toward the kitchen. Chloe didn't notice. "All Ethan cares about is his iPhone."

Tess suppressed a sad smile. Chloe could seem take-charge with Dilly, but now she sounded like a kid herself.

"It's the first thing he looks at every morning," Chloe said. "The last thing he sees every night before bed. I don't think he hears a thing I say. He's too busy checking with this or that supplier, his and Grady's job sites..."

"Hmm." Tess was reminded of Merry's boyfriend and his remote control but with Ethan the distraction was work. On one hand, she understood. Running The Go-To Girl could easily take all her time. If she dared to expand, as Merry kept urging her to do, it would take even more effort. "So, you feel Ethan is neglecting you?"

"The only time he's home except to sleep is to eat. Even at the dinner table he works that phone—if not his iPad."

"You make it sound like a drug." Tess was hyper-aware of addiction in any form.

"He's attached to those devices like an intravenous line. We watch TV, take Dilly to the park, go to church, and the whole time his thumbs are flying over those little keys." She cast a look toward the upstairs, as if to make sure Dilly couldn't overhear. "I didn't know how else to wake him up except by leaving." Her lower lip quivered. "The night before I left, he took that thing to bed with us! Right under his pillow. Said he was expecting an important message about a contract." Chloe blinked hard. "Aren't *I* important to him?" Her cheeks flushed. "Can't he forget work long enough to...even make love? Tell me what to do, Tess. I worry Dilly will suffer."

Chloe looked miserable. And Tess could empathize. She'd spent enough nights and weekends and holidays alone while Grady indulged his passion not for her but for some game of poker. The worst week she'd spent in her marriage was in Las Vegas. During their supposed vacation—Tess's last since then —she hadn't seen Grady for days.

"I think I know how you feel, though in a different way. That doesn't mean Ethan doesn't love you." Still, no one knew better than Tess that sometimes love wasn't enough.

"I love him," Chloe said on a quiet sob. "But either we're a couple, a family, or we're not." She looked up, her eyes red-rimmed, which seemed to be a chronic condition. Another big shirt, another pair of baggy pants, hid her figure. Tess itched, as she did with Merry, to give her a makeover. "We had a tough time for a while, but just when things seemed to be going right—we bought our house and he went to work for Grady—Ethan stopped caring about us."

"Chloe," Tess said, "he adores you and Dilly."

She picked at a hangnail. "Then why did he barge in here the other night as if he wanted to understand then stalk out again when I wouldn't see things his way? You know what?" she said. "He was thumbing that darn iPhone when he went down the front walk! Maybe I should stay away for good."

Tess tried to block out the familiar sounds of scrabbling from the kitchen. If she didn't miss her guess, one or both of the cats was scaling the lower cabinets onto the counter. Had she forgotten to put away the leftover chicken?

Frowning, she sensed she was hearing only part of Chloe's story, but obviously she wasn't ready to voice the rest or to tell Tess what was missing from her life. For now, Ethan was taking the full blame.

Tess framed her next words with care. "I hope you didn't come to me with some notion that I'd tell you how happy I am on my own. I'm lonely sometimes without Grady," she admitted. "Our situation wasn't the same, sweetie. Ethan brings home his paycheck, he pays the bills. If anything, he's *too* responsible." She smiled a little. "I think he was born that way. The last thing in the world I'd suggest would be ending your marriage to Ethan."

Chloe stared at her hands. Her normally husky voice wobbled. "But will you talk to him?"

Her stomach sank though she wasn't The Go-To Girl for nothing. How could she let Chloe down?

"Yes, I'll talk to him."

. . .

E than met his mother at Don Diego's, his favorite Mexican restaurant. She was already talking as she approached the table. Although she'd been the one to call him, she didn't have much time. He knew she and Merry seldom managed more than a burger and fries from a fast food location but, as Tess hastily explained, Merry had offered to spend today's lunch hour in the china department at the Kenwood Towne Centre picking out crystal for one of next weekend's brides so Tess could grab lunch with Ethan.

He still wondered why his mother had asked him to meet her today.

He was ticked at Chloe, worried out of his mind that she and Dilly would never come home. Was that why Tess was here? "You look frazzled, Mom."

"Such flattery. Thanks." She leaned close to kiss his cheek then slid into her chair at their corner table in the rustic restaurant. Ethan was halfway through a bowl of tortilla chips with salsa.

"Busy day?" he asked.

"We're swamped." Then she continued to babble, as she often did under stress. "It's not bad enough that every bride in Hamilton and Warren Counties needs our services *now*, the Henderson and Pickett weddings are next weekend." She paused with a rueful smile. "I'm not complaining, mind you. Three or four years ago I would have given an arm to feel this rushed."

Three or four years. Right after she'd left his dad.

"Why don't you hire another person?"

She studied the menu. "Now it's a consensus," she said. "Everyone suggests that, but I'm not ready to expand. You look tired, sweetie. Have you been sleeping?" Neatly, she'd changed the subject. "I see dark circles under your eyes, white lines at the corners of your mouth." Chloe's fault?

His mother reached out to touch his face, and her expression softened. In her mind he was still a boy. Her boy. "Ethan, except for the shadows you look so much like your father."

"You should do something about that," he said. "I mean about Dad."

He and Grady had their plan but now wasn't the time to mention them. Ethan glanced at the table where his now-vibrating phone sat right by his water glass. He didn't want some discussion of his parents and their failed relationship, not when he was worried Chloe would leave him, too. For good. He checked the incoming call on his screen then frowned. "I need to handle this. Sorry."

The conversation didn't go well. Ethan could feel his mouth grow taut, his eyes darken. He pointed at the menu so his mom could order for them, mouthed the words "lemon soda," then hung up and placed another call.

"Dad, that guy from Larson Lumber hacks me off. Yeah, I know. They were supposed to deliver yesterday. Now he has some song and dance about next week." Pause. "Sure, I told him. With pleasure." He hesitated again. "Yeah, how'd you know? She's right here."

When he looked her way, his mother shook her head. Talking to Grady, he knew, always rattled her equilibrium. She showed him her watch. In her defense her time was as short as Ethan's. "She's on the run," he reported to Grady.

"How's his foot?" she asked anyway.

"How's your foot?" Ethan repeated, tempted to grin at her. Did she really not understand that she still cared about his father? A second later he ended the call. "He says it's still there." The waiter set down their plates and Ethan studied her, remembering Grady's words not long ago. "This is like old times, Mom—me playing go-between for you two." He paused. "You feel for him, huh? That's a sign."

She shrugged. "Don't read anything into it. You're talking to a woman who rescued two cats from certain death along the road. I have a soft spot in my heart for all creatures great and small."

Ethan's mouth tightened again. "Which one is he?"

"You know what I mean."

"No, Mom. I don't." He dug into his combination plate, scooping up black beans with more salsa and guacamole. No wonder he didn't sleep. Tonight he'd have heartburn for sure. Twenty-five, and his insides were turning to pure acid. "I know you weren't happy when I signed on with Dad. Can't you see that he's changed?"

"I can see."

But Ethan couldn't let the subject go. "I know all about Grandpa and how you grew up, but I also know Dad. He even goes to Gam-Anon meetings now. Doesn't that tell you something?"

"He went before, Ethan," she murmured. "And quit—more than once."

"Because you pushed him then! This time he's doing it himself." He drew a harsh breath. "Why not give him some credit?"

That seemed a bad choice of words even to Ethan. His dad had been forced to apply for one of those low-limit credit cards to even get his business restarted.

"I'm trying. Really, I am and I'm sorry about your father's foot." She was offering him an olive branch.

"Dad says those cats of yours need some kind of exorcism."

His mother half smiled. "He only says that because he got clawed. A cat, I'm told, can tell when someone doesn't like

him. Which apparently made the kitten all the more determined to 'make friends.'"

"You call that making friends?" He paused. "And who are
you kidding? You're such a fraud. You may be divorced, but
you still take care of people. Grandpa, for one," he said, "and
whether or not you'll admit it, you take care of Dad."

She attacked her chicken-filled taquitos. "Can you blame
me for worrying? A little?" As if in spite of her best effort, her
tone quavered. "Your grandfather isn't getting any younger.
And I do...care for your father on some level, yes. I even feel
proud that he seems to have turned his life around, but that
doesn't mean I trust him. Let me remind you, he's the one
who broke that trust."

Ethan pushed his plate aside. He'd always gotten caught
between her and his father, between the proverbial rock and a
hard place, even when he tried to avoid it. He was their
hostage because he loved them both.

"Whatever you say. But *I* do trust him. And *I'm* shooting
for a partnership in O'Neill Construction by Christmas.
Before we get into a fight, why don't you give me your
message from Chloe—" To his further frustration, his voice
cracked on her name like a twelve-year-old. "That's why we're
here, right?"

Tess gave up on her lunch, too. "Yes, sweetheart, but the
message is from me. I don't claim to understand why you two
are having problems. Chloe said she feels neglected, but
there's more to it than that, I suspect."

"I *miss* her," he said. "I miss Dilly too until I ache."

"Chloe thinks you're married to your iPhone."

Ethan glanced at it. "I never knew running a business
would take so much time. But we're going to make a success
of this company, you'll see. Chloe will too. Who does she
think I'm doing this for?" He shoved back his chair. "I've got
a mortgage now, a child to raise, and one of these days, all too

soon, I'll have Dilly's college to pay for then her wedding. If Chloe thinks that will happen with her tripping down the stairs every five minutes, she's dead wrong."

"Ethan!"

"Don't you understand? I need to protect her. I need to keep her safe—from herself." He tossed money on the table, grabbed his phone, and headed for the door, already regretting his words. He'd said too much.

Outside he climbed into his pickup truck, seething. He and his dad had a plan all right: Work their butts off. Show Chloe and his mom just how good they were. How much they loved them. How else could they prove it? He had just cranked up the engine when his phone pinged—and he saw a text message from his mother.

Thanks for lunch. But this isn't over.

U pset about Ethan, Tess didn't feel her mood improve until Meredith led her through the crowded china department at Macy's. Unlike Chloe, thank goodness, Merry wasn't accident-prone. The teetering pyramids of sherbet glasses, the delicate displays of crystal everywhere would have caused Chloe to stumble for sure. Bless her heart.

Merry was a terrific assistant, even in her lime green Capri pants and tight orange sweater, and Tess wouldn't trade her for the world.

Lately, though, Merry's concentration had been spotty at best. Their previous talk about Frank, like Tess's lunch with Ethan, hadn't done much good. Merry hadn't been able to decide here at Kenwood either on a crystal pattern for her next bride and needed Tess's input.

Merry stopped at a wall of sparkling Waterford pieces. The variety of wine glasses alone might confuse anyone, but it only made Tess's heart beat faster. Shelf blur was never a problem for her. Here, if not with her father, Chloe or Grady, she was in her element.

For these few moments her misstep at lunch with Ethan could be set aside with Chloe's insecurities, their inability to talk, the effect of their separation on Dilly.

"I sort of like this pattern," Merry said, reaching for a deeply carved, footed glass in the Heirloom line. She turned it in different directions to catch the light. "But it might be *too* traditional, even for Ashley Henderson." Merry set it on the shelf and took down another, more airy-looking pattern. "How about this?"

Tess studied the quality crystal. "Maybe." She smiled. "Maybe not." She plucked another glass from a shelf. "How about this Reidel instead? Clean, pretty, yet basic. Ashley could do anything with this design. It should complement her china beautifully."

"You don't like the Waterford?"

At first Tess didn't hear the tears in Merry's voice. She'd become almost immune to crying with Chloe in her house. And Merry never cried.

"Possibly. Twelve glasses each. Wines, whites and reds, water goblets..."

"Lucky Ashley." Merry released a small sob. "I'm never getting married."

Surprised by the outburst, Tess took the Waterford from Merry's grasp before the expensive object wound up on the floor. "How thoughtless of me." She set down that glass and the Reidel she'd been holding then gathered Merry close. Good thing they were the only two people in the department As Merry began to howl, Tess was reminded of her cats.

"I tried to talk to him, like you said. Frank doesn't love me."

"Did he say that?" Tess asked, horrified by his insensitivity.

"No, but..."

"Shh, don't cry."

She smoothed Merry's hair like a mother comforting a child, as she'd done with Chloe, and been tempted to do with Ethan at lunch. "I shouldn't expect you to handle this bridal shopping when you have troubles with Frank."

Tess abandoned making a decision about the crystal. She pulled Merry through the store and out into the hall. She urged her down onto a seat by a pool filled with coins from well-wishers to benefit charity—which gave Tess an idea.

"What's your fondest wish?"

Merry didn't hesitate. "A diamond ring like Sybil Shallowford's on my hot little hand. Permanently." She gave a watery laugh. "Not from Emery. From Frank."

Tess squeezed Merry's hand.

"True, the Shallowford diamond is already taken," she teased, "but if you have your hopes set on Frank—" Tess wouldn't have him on one of the gold-trimmed Noritake plates from Macy's china department "—let's make sure his heart is set on *you*." Tess was on a roll now. Lose some, win some. Nothing restored her like a good shopping trip and finding the answer to someone's wish list. She put her hands on Merry's shoulders. "I think three carats—the gold standard these days—would be perfect. Don't you?"

"Frank doesn't have any money."

"His wallet, we'll deal with later. He can finance."

"He won't propose, Tess. I know he won't. He'd have to shut off the television long enough to ask, 'Will you marry me?' That won't happen, even after this year's World Series is over." Merry heaved a sigh. "Then there'll be Monday night football. Hockey season, which goes on forever. This isn't a World Cup soccer year, is it?"

She looked into Merry's eyes.

"You and Chloe," she said. "I'm surprised you don't

believe in yourselves. If you really want Frank, you'll get Frank." *And I hope you won't be sorry.*

Fifteen minutes later she and Merry sat across from Tess's travel agent friend in a Hyde Park office. The last of a dying breed since many people now booked their trips online. Tess told her what they wanted, and in another half hour they walked out with a romantic weeklong package for Merry and Frank at a country bed-and-breakfast. She'd known Merry wanted a vacation. Why hadn't Tess suggested this before? Merry had had to front the money, of course, but...

"No TV," Tess crowed, wheeling out of the parking lot. "It's perfect. You're within driving distance—only a few hours —and Kentucky should be beautiful. The trees and flowers will be blooming slightly ahead of Cincy. All meals included, except you may want Frank to take you out at least once for a candlelight dinner, somewhere utterly romantic."

"What if the timing of this trip's not right for Frank?" Merry fretted.

"He's out of work," Tess said. "Time is not an issue."

Practically drooling, Merry studied the brochure again. "They have Porthault sheets! Down duvets. Cashmere blankets. The breakfast room is vintage antebellum." She jabbed the folder in Tess's face. "Look at those plantation shutters."

Tess pushed away the brochure, which had blocked her vision through the front windshield. "I can't. I'm driving. No cell calls for me either, no texting, no putting on makeup in the rearview mirror." She paused. "Did you know some people actually watch movies while they drive?" But Merry was single-minded.

"There's a terrace with our room, a garden below...a fireplace, Tess!"

"And nothing to do but focus on each other." Tess wagged her eyebrows. "Even Frank should be able to handle that— assuming he's really a man, not a La-Z-Boy on two legs."

Merry snickered. "Sometimes I wonder."

"You'll just have to keep him away from the Louisville Slugger Museum. Stay on the highway until you get to Bardstown."

Merry was silent for a moment. "You think this will really do the trick?"

"Well, maybe not the ring part. He won't be prepared to give that—unless I nudge him beforehand to do some shopping...No, I don't want to jinx this. Nothing to alert him to our real purpose." With a grin Tess added, "After we're through, he'll propose all right. He'll beg." She turned onto the ramp leading to I-71 north and their Fields Ertel Road office. "They don't call us the best personal shoppers in town for nothing."

"They do?"

"They will," Tess amended.

Merry studied her from the passenger seat. "How can I thank you?"

She waved away the need. "Nonsense. This is our job. If you know where to go, who to talk to, you can solve any request in a heartbeat."

But Merry still had second thoughts. "What if this *doesn't* work? And what about the crystal for Ashley Henderson? Her mother will be a basket case if we don't deliver those glasses on time. Her father will have a fit. That's only part of their wedding gift but—"

"Two weeks in Aruba. Can you imagine? And that fiancé of hers...tall, dark and handsome doesn't begin to cover it."

Merry folded her arms. "I'll settle for Kentucky. And Frank."

Tess hoped *settle* wasn't the operative word. They were almost at the office before Merry spoke again.

"Tess, what about you? We have those two weddings this weekend, and next week is jammed. There isn't enough time to get everything done for a dozen different people with me gone. You can't be everywhere at once."

Tess groaned. "That reminds me. Nell Whitman called this morning. She wants us to preview her mother-of-the-bride outfit then find accessories. High-end stuff. The commission will be great, but she's *impossible*."

"I can't go to Kentucky," Merry decided. "It wouldn't be fair."

"Who said life was fair? I'll give up sleep," Tess said with a smile. "Thinking about you with Frank will lend me all the energy I need."

Merry touched her shoulder. "This is a really bad time for me to take off."

"It's not vacation. It's therapy. Like shopping. And don't worry, I'll find Ashley's crystal on time."

"You'll still need help, Tess."

"I'll think of something. I always do."

🏵 6 🏵

EVERY TIME GRADY rang Tess's doorbell, he felt instantly tongue-tied. He didn't expect a warm welcome from her. Or her cats. But tonight, he felt especially bad. His brain wasn't working as it should, and his foot throbbed. In fact, his whole leg ached—which he didn't intend to tell Tess. Still, he'd promised Ethan he would give it the old college try, not that Grady had gone farther than high school graduation.

When Tess answered, he took a painful step back, surprised not to have the kittens attack him or Dilly fling herself at her "Poppy."

Grady stepped into the foyer, then closed the door behind them. And heard silence. He slipped off his shoes. "Where's Chloe?"

"At the mall." Tess made the sign of the cross. "Shopping for me."

He arched an eyebrow. "You think that's wise?"

She winced. "No, I think I've lost my mind. But this is kind of a test for her," she said, leading the way to her kitchen.

With a stifled groan he sank down on a chair at the table,

grateful for the relief of pressure on his foot and for these few moments alone with Tess.

"Okay. What's the matter?" she asked.

"You think the only reason I come by is when there's something wrong?" Which likely reminded her of Larry. He glanced around the homey room, surreptitiously looking for the cats but nope. The kittens weren't perched on top of the refrigerator, glaring at him from a counter top or about to fly at his sore ankle. Maybe they'd gone to the mall with Chloe. He forced himself to relax. "This place isn't half bad, Tess. But Ethan and I could kick it up a notch for you—*bam*," he said like that chef Emeril on the cooking show she used to watch. "Raise the ceiling, put in can lights overhead, maybe some under-cabinet ones too. You need more wattage in here."

"This isn't my house," Tess said, her teeth gritted.

Grady's jaw tightened too. "Ah. The dreaded reminder that you're no longer a homeowner." His fault, of course.

For different reasons—Tess because she tried to avoid him whenever possible, but he kept showing up; Grady because he wanted her back but couldn't have her—this seemed to be the effect they'd had on each other since the divorce. Sooner or later, they'd both break a molar.

"My landlord would never approve any upgrades," she said.

"Maybe you need a new landlord."

"Maybe I need you to—" She stopped. "No, I'm way too tired to argue."

Any second now she'd tell him to leave before he said what he'd come to say. "I'll take a cup of that coffee," he said, tilting his head toward the half-filled carafe on the counter. The stuff looked like tar.

"It's old. From this morning. Burnt, actually. The coffee

maker doesn't turn off automatically as it once did, and Chloe forgot to hit the switch."

"I'll take some anyway." Maybe the jolt of caffeine would kill the wicked throb in his foot. Open his veins, or something, and let his blood flow faster, bottom to top. His brain always needed a boost.

"What do you want, Grady?"

"Loaded question." He couldn't help the small grin. With a resigned sigh she took out a mug, splashed in dark brown sludge like mud at a wetlands site, then pushed the cup at him. The coffee sloshed over its rim. He took a sip. It felt cold but tasted familiar. She'd remembered he wanted no sugar.

"Thanks." He took what he could get from Tess these days—at least for now. He didn't dare ask her to heat the coffee for him. He was lucky to still be sitting here. He propped his bad foot on the rung of the chair next to him. "So. How's Chloe doing?"

Tess gave up. She took the chair across from him, scooting it back from the table so their legs couldn't touch underneath. "Better. She hasn't burst into tears since I hired her to help at The Go-To Girl while Merry's out of town."

Grady raised both eyebrows. "Taking a chance there. Wow. Pretty soon you'll begin to reconsider our divorce."

As if she realized she'd surrendered to his presence, she said, "Don't get too comfortable. I was just about to go to bed."

He grinned again. "TMI, Theresa. I might feel tempted to join you."

"Grady. Don't get cute." She turned her head to pick up a scrambling sound he could hear from another room, and a corner of her mouth kicked up. "One wrong move, and this time I will sic those cats on you."

His gaze sharpened. "Where are they?"

"Locked in the downstairs bathroom. I couldn't take any more tonight. There's not much they can do in there—except, of course, to shred the wallpaper."

"Sounds like they need some serious training."

"That isn't their opinion," Tess said, unable to suppress the rest of her smile. "They're training me. Didn't you know? Cats are bent upon world domination, and in this case I'm their first conquest."

He laughed. "No, that would be me." He could still feel the one she'd called Big Boy hooking lethal claws into his foot. In perfect timing, it pulsed like a Taiko drumbeat.

Tess shook her head, looking puzzled. "I don't know why, but Chloe and Dilly have no trouble with them. Surprising, isn't it? Chloe has trouble with most everything."

"Including Ethan," he said. "That's why I'm here, actually. He sent me."

Tess stiffened. "Ethan and I had words today, yes, but we'll work that out. Without your help."

That was news to Grady. Ethan hadn't said anything about Tess. "Wrong, he thinks maybe I can reach Chloe when he couldn't. And it seems you haven't tried very hard."

She frowned. "I have tried, believe me." She told him about her talk with Chloe. "I still think there's something more going on with her," she finished. "Something beyond Ethan and what she sees as his neglect of her and Dilly for his job. Something that—" she waved a hand in apparent frustration "—I don't know, makes her clumsier than usual, causes Chloe to stumble and drop things...sabotage herself by trying too hard."

"Like what?" Grady had always assumed Chloe was just Chloe. But in his experience women looked for a hidden meaning.

"Something deeper, emotional." Tess paused. "I hope I'm doing the right thing. Maybe while she helps me with The

Go-To Girl, I'll be able to discover her problem." Tess rolled her eyes. "Merry's going to take a week off to repair her relationship with Frank."

"That loser?"

"She says she loves him. What do I know?"

Grady enjoyed their banter, the way Tess's cheeks grew rosy at his teasing, but even more their shared concerns for their family. He was getting that edgy feeling of anticipation, the familiar itch to play his cards and rake in the pot.

"You know a lot. Take us, for instance. You and I were damn good together, Tess. Don't let my problem—*former* problem—ruin that. Remember your bathroom that night?" He nodded toward the very place where Tess's cats seemed to be scaling the door inside now. She ignored them. Tried to ignore him, too. Grady leaned closer and raised the stakes. Taking risks had been so much a part of his life until a few years ago, and he still liked feeling the rush wherever he could find it. "If I'd kissed you then," he said, voice low and soft, "you would have kissed me back, Tess Trueheart. Don't bother to deny it."

She turned a deeper pink. "I have no idea what you're talking about."

He laughed again. "You're the biggest chicken. You know that?"

Tess reared back. "Maybe, but that's what keeps me safe."

Grady made a quick tactical retreat before he went too far. "How safe can you be? You just hired Chloe. I love that girl like a daughter, but in one week she could destroy The Go-To Girl."

Tess had to agree. "Please. Don't remind me."

At that moment the still-confined cats set up a howl. Loud enough to make Grady's foot pulse even harder. He was about to say *don't let them out* when Tess shot from her chair to open the bathroom door.

"Have mercy," she said to them.

Déjà vu. Grady moved faster than he thought himself capable of in pain. He was halfway to the front door in his sock feet before the kittens skidded around the corner into the hall.

Tess ran right behind them. She scooped up both cats, taking a chance Grady wouldn't have thought *her* capable of then held them against her chest. His favorite chest. Their blue eyes glinted silver, reflecting oddly in the light like zombies.

Intent upon escape he limped another step but couldn't hold back a grunt of agony.

"Your foot," Tess said, alarm in her voice. "Let me see."

Grady felt torn. Should he allow her to fuss over him and maybe earn some points? Or chance getting his skin flayed from his body again by her evil pets?

"Not with Igor and Frankenstein around," he decided. It was probably the first time in his life he hadn't taken a risk and said to hell with whatever happened next.

"Don't be silly." She gently dropped the kittens in the living room and closed the French doors onto the hall. "Show me."

He briefly shut his eyes, his tone husky. "I'll show you mine if you'll show me yours."

"Grady."

"Yeah, okay. Sure." He bent to pull up his jeans leg, rolled down his sock, and bit his lip against the pain that streaked from his ankle to his thigh. "It's nothing. Only a big scratch."

Like a man's favorite fantasy at the worst time for Grady, Tess dropped to her knees in front of him.

She shook her head. "This is no scratch. These are holes. They're deep—and look infected."

"Sore, that's all," he insisted.

"They're red and swollen. There's a pustule." She gazed up

94

at him, her eyes strangely bright. "Grady, you're an *idiot*. You could get blood poisoning. Do you want to lose your foot?" Her voice wobbled. "Or your *life*? You have to see a doctor. I'll drive you," she said.

"Tess—"

"You need an antibiotic. Now."

This time he didn't argue. Grady's heart beat faster and so did the throb in his foot. Tess really cared. She was already grabbing her purse from the entry hall table, jingling her keys, and to be honest, he did feel alternately hot then cold all over. It occurred to him that he hadn't come running to Tess simply on Ethan's behalf. Still, he couldn't resist.

"Hey, Tess. Does this mean you don't hate me after all?"

Chloe had an inordinate need to be liked. She accepted that. It was one reason, she supposed, why she and Ethan had married so soon. Well, that and her love for him, and then too Dilly had already been on the way. Chloe had yet to live down that miscalculation, at least in her father's view.

For once, today she was determined to do well.

"Am I doing this right, Tess?" she asked, juggling a huge box wrapped in white wedding paper with a big puffy bow. She picked her way across the vast green lawn at the Henderson house, which was a mansion, really, praying she wouldn't drop all that crystal. This much glass—with some fancy German name—must have cost the whole planet.

"You're doing fine." Beside her, wearing a trim navy suit, Tess wrenched an ankle in the lush grass. She pulled her four-inch Prada heel out of the divot then grinned. Her box of glassware hadn't shifted an inch. "Look at me. Staggering in these insanely pricey shoes. I got them on sale at Saks. Tell me again why I started this business. We've been running non-stop since seven a.m."

Clearly, she was in her element. In contrast, Chloe wore a dress borrowed from Tess that showed too much cleavage for her comfort. She liked its vibrant color, though. Maybe she should dress a little better more often. Maybe then Ethan would notice her.

A big white tent reared up behind the enormous house. Chloe heard the band warming up for the reception, and the tinkle of glassware and china as the white-gloved wait staff checked place settings and champagne flutes. Someone was putting ivory tapers on every table.

Chloe and Ethan had gotten married in their college chapel. No guests, no flowers. Their wedding had been just shy of an elopement. She doubted Tess had forgiven her missing the chance to create the perfect wedding day for her son.

Chloe felt her eyes widen. She'd never seen so many limousines. The sedans and sports cars weren't bad either. Beemers, Lexuses, even a Bentley or two, crammed the edges of the driveway and spilled over into a nearby field. Half a dozen guys in tuxedos, no less, were directing traffic to the grassy spots. Talk about valet parking. Not that she cared about money. She and Ethan lived simply. But...

"This place looks like a fairyland."

"It should," Tess said. "This is what a few hundred thousand dollars can buy for one day."

"Really? Good grief. That much?"

"And more. Tomorrow's the Pickett bash. You won't believe your eyes. Sometimes," Tess said, "I think there's a competition here in Indian Hill to see who can spend the most money on a single event. But the Picketts aren't having their reception at home. They reserved the Country Club five years ago."

"Good thing Dilly stayed home," she murmured. "I wouldn't want her getting ideas. Although with Ethan working day and night, he might be able to pay that much for her wedding someday."

"I hope that's light years away," Tess said with a suddenly worried frown. "I hope she's all right now being with Larry. If he tries to teach her to play craps..." Tess appeared to shake the thought away. "I wish we could have left her with Grady, but he had a problem at his construction site where Dilly wouldn't be safe." She made a face. "Medicine or not, can you believe he's working with his bad foot?"

"I'm glad you took him to the clinic." Chloe felt inadequate. "But I wish I could be more help here. If I could do half as good a job as Meredith would..."

"You can. You are," Tess assured her but in a weak tone.

As if that were a cue for Chloe to bungle this event, her borrowed pumps plunged into another hole in the lawn. She didn't avoid it as successfully as Tess had. The big box in Chloe's arms wobbled, and the ominous, if muffled, sound of delicate glass chimed like wedding bells through beautiful embossed white wrapping paper. And several rolls of bubble wrap.

She cried out and heard in her mind, *Chloe, pick up your feet. Watch where you're going.*

Somehow Tess managed to hold onto her own box and steady Chloe at the same time. Practice, Chloe imagined. Or better coordination?

Tess saved her with a too-cheerful announcement. "Here we are."

They had reached the rear patio of the Tudor mansion where what appeared to be a million gifts were artfully piled on long white-clothed tables.

"Let's slip these two right in the center."

Wedding guests were now flooding from the house onto

the rear lawn. The band began to play. A waiter carrying a silver tray of filled glasses offered one to Chloe then Tess. All stressed out from her near-fall, Chloe was reaching for the champagne flute when Tess stopped her.

"No, thank you. We can't stay."

"We're working," Chloe added. Too late.

The waiter sent them a thin smile then floated into the crowd.

Chloe flushed. "Sorry, I didn't think." The champagne had looked to her like a life saver. She was so nervous she could barely walk. Her knees kept knocking together, and her arms quivered from having held the box. Tess appeared cool and collected.

"I'll just tell Mrs. H that we've delivered the glasses—better late than never. We're lucky they came in at all. When she chose the Schott Zwiesel for her daughter from our suggestions, I didn't realize their Fortissimo design in this quantity would be a problem. Thank heaven for FedEx Overnight."

Tess left Chloe at the gift table while she searched for Mrs. Henderson. After a moment, Tess approached a woman with big beige hair and the most garish orange suit Chloe had ever seen. Costly, no doubt, but there was no accounting for taste. Or the lack of it. At least she knew that much about fashion.

Chloe turned around—not checking the area first—and bumped into a youthful-looking, middle-aged woman in a much prettier pale blue dress, her blond hair styled in a chic feathered cut that suited her kind face.

"I'm sorry. I didn't see you there," Chloe began. "I'm clumsy."

"Nonsense, my dear. I wasn't watching where I was going," the woman said, repeating Chloe's mantra. "I can be a bit fluttery, and I was focused on this table full of glittery gifts." She flashed her own enormous diamond solitaire. "Aren't you a pretty thing? Sister of the bride? A college roommate?"

"No. I'm...working." She couldn't keep the note of pride from her voice this time. Chloe didn't care that she wasn't part of the festivities here. She had a *job* with Tess, at least until Meredith came back. "We're The Go-To Girls. We can find anything for anyone from crystal—" she put a light hand on the two boxes on the table then focused on the woman's huge, and showy, ring "—to diamonds. If you like sparkle, you've come to the right people."

Eager to help, she fished in her pockets for a business card. Tess had given her a bunch to carry because "you never know when we might meet a potential client." And Chloe wanted to be prepared.

The cards were well-designed on heavy stock. They bore Tess's logo, the name of her business, and below that *Your Personal Shopper* above all her contact information. The cards coordinated with her stationery, her invoices, even her web site. Of course they did, knowing Tess.

Handing the card to her new acquaintance, Chloe saw that her gaze had wandered across the lawn. To Tess herself.

Chloe waved a hand toward her, but Tess had her back to them and was talking to a tall man with a booming voice. Chloe saw him bend close to Tess and whisper something in her ear. His hand lingered on her shoulder, and when he laughed the sound was low and husky, like Ethan's bedroom voice. She missed that tone with every fiber of her being. Missed him.

"She's my boss," Chloe said. "Tess O'Neill." *My mother-in-law. My hero.*

"We've met. And he's *my* husband," the woman murmured, her tone a shade cooler than before. Her blue eyes had taken on a hundred-yard stare. "Excuse me," she said abruptly then left Chloe standing alone. The woman marched right over to Tess and grabbed the man's arm. A few blistering words snapped through the air like an exposed live wire, but Chloe couldn't quite hear them. Tess, who had turned slightly, just stood there, a frozen smile on her face, as if she'd dropped the crystal glassware, like Chloe almost had, and ruined the reception.

When Tess finally spotted Chloe, her face looked white. She came over to Chloe, and they both watched the man and woman stalk toward the parking area, the wedding forgotten. The woman did all the talking.

"That was Sybil Shallowford," Tess said. "Her husband's a client of mine. I should have known they'd be here. They're practically neighbors."

"Did you see that diamond?"

"Merry and I picked it out. And by the way, mum's the word, Chloe." She groaned. "Sometimes I don't think it pays to get out of bed in the morning...and I don't mean Emery Shallowford's. Sybil must think we're having an affair. He claimed she was the jealous sort."

"Oh, boy. As soon as she saw you with him, she set off across the yard like a Hummer in full off-road mode."

What had Chloe done wrong?

"Let's go," Tess said with a sigh. "Too bad Indian Hill is such a small world. We'll just hope they don't show up at the Pickett event tomorrow."

I*f wishes were horses...* Whatever that meant.

All Tess knew, and thank heaven for small favors, was that Emery Shallowford hadn't turned up at the Pickett reception the next day, but on Monday when he did meet up with her at Saks Fifth Avenue, he wasn't happy.

"I spent a very bad night on Saturday," he told Tess, *sotto voce*, from behind a clothes rack in the bridal department. The store was bustling, and somewhere out there, according to Emery, Sybil Shallowford was circling through Designer Dresses like a shark in the water.

Tess made another fervent wish. She should have sent Chloe instead—God help her—to preview Nell Whitman's mother-of-the-bride ensemble. The Go-To-Girl had been charged with finding the jewelry to go with it.

Instead, to her surprise Emery had cornered Tess as soon as she walked into this room full of filmy white wedding gowns. She noticed the sales associate had made herself scarce and there were no other shoppers in the area, as if he'd paid for a private showing—starring Tess.

"How did you find me?" she asked, as if she were evading one of Larry's gambling pals from Dayton.

"Your assistant."

"Chloe?" At first, she'd thought he meant Merry. She would have to speak to her daughter-in-law again. Tess didn't like being tracked down by a disgruntled client when she was on other business.

"I don't remember her name. Sybil has banished me to the living room sofa," Emery reported, looking miserable. He peered at her above the billowing silk taffeta skirts of a creamy gown, and Tess struggled not to smile. Emery looked like a bride in drag. "You have to help me, Terry."

"I'm sorry, but if your wife chooses to think the wrong thing about us, there's not much I can do."

"I didn't pay fifty-thousand bucks for that ring—to end up divorced."

"Emery, you're putting me in a very bad position." Tess stepped away from the dress rack and from Emery's health club-tanned face, but he stopped her.

"You'd better find a way to get me out of this. If rumor gets around that I've been cheating on Sybil, I'll be a walking scandal at the hospital. If she leaves me, I'll be crippled financially..." He trailed off, a look of utter despair in his eyes.

Tess felt sorry for him, but she also pitied herself. Just for a moment. She had enough to contend with. The cats, Chloe and Dilly, Ethan and Larry. Grady. If only Meredith was back from Kentucky, she would have been here instead. At worst, Tess would have faced Emery in her office on home ground.

She squared her shoulders, determined not to let him intimidate her.

"You know, my daughter-in-law had a point. She was with Mrs. Shallowford when they spotted you and me together. Frankly, Emery, your attitude can sometimes seem too familiar, even flirtatious. Ask yourself why your wife gets that wrong impression of me or the nurses at the hospital." He'd mentioned them at lunch. "If Sybil had seen us, for instance, together at that restaurant, there might have been a worse night for you than on the living room couch."

He had the grace to look ashamed but only for a second. He glanced toward the designer dress area across the aisle—and blanched. Emery ducked down. "Help me hide. Sybil just walked by."

Tess shooed him toward another rack where several dozen gowns in various shades of white hung like a convenient curtain. Emery blended into the voluminous skirts, his tasseled loafers poking out underneath the pleated satins and flowing chiffons. His tone was haunted. "I've been a physician in Porkopolis for twenty-five years. How long have you been shopping for a living, Terry?"

She began to sweat. The question was rhetorical.

"I'm not one to make threats," he continued, then proceeded to do just that. "But if you don't think of something to clear me with Sybil, you won't have a business to worry about!"

Wow. He really was angry. "Dr. Shallowford..." Then, on the verge of total desperation, Tess had a sudden epiphany.

Emery Shallowford had the ego of a surgeon, all right. His reputation in Cincinnati was stellar and well-deserved. Rumors of an affair wouldn't ruin him in the end, but if anyone took the fall, it would be Tess.

He was right. If word circulated about them, her phone might never ring again. As if Tess needed another reminder, she thought of the Henderson reception. Half of Indian Hill had attended, and that was only the start of the season. As a society matron from old money, Sybil, if humiliated, would talk. And Tess would soon have to file for bankruptcy.

This was her fight, too, after all. Again, as at their luncheon, she couldn't jeopardize The Go-To Girl, her means of survival. The means of buying a home again, of at last getting over Grady.

She shot Emery a look—and in spite of the jam she was in, almost burst out laughing. The eminent physician crouched among all that bridal finery looked like some peeping Tom. His shrewd gaze darted here and there, his eyebrows popping up every few seconds above the bunch of strapless necklines to gauge the shoppers in Designer Dresses, scoping the area for Sybil.

"If she finds me here now," he began, "with you...in this department..."

"Wait," Tess said. "I think I know what to do. There's a dinner soon for Angela Fortini to celebrate her engagement. I worked with her mother to find gifts for her daughter and her fiancé. My son went to school with Angela. They were very close for a while, and he and I are invited to the party." She took a deep breath. "So are you and Sybil, I understand."

His brows rose again. "The joys of living in a city with a small-town feel."

"At the party I'll try to get Sybil aside and talk to her.

Assure her after she relaxes with a glass of wine or two—which will be your job to provide—that she didn't see what she thought she saw. Let's hope that puts an end to it."

"You don't know Sybil." He huffed out a breath to show he wasn't happy, but Tess didn't know what else to offer. He bobbed up like a jack-in-the-box long enough to give her a look before he glanced across the way. "God, there she is. Quick! Don't let her see me." He dived back into the mass of wedding skirts, his voice muffled by the fabrics.

"No, that won't do." Tess tore a gown off a hanger. She grabbed Emery's hand, threw the dress over his head like a lampshade, then dragged him into a nearby dressing room—and, to her horror, ran smack into a half-naked girl wearing a luscious Vera Wang creation around her hips and nothing else but a lace demi-bra.

"Ms. O'Neill," the sales associate called, rushing from behind Tess toward the room. She stopped dead at the door, her voice shocked. "Dr. Shallowford."

"Sorry," Tess said. "I'm terribly sorry."

A moment later she and Emery had been evicted from the bridal department. Tess would have some explaining to do, later. Now she hurried Emery toward the stairway. "Go down to the main floor then come back up on the elevator. Walk right into Designer Dresses and find Sybil. She won't know you were here. Tell her you went to Starbucks."

But Emery called her back.

"Terry," he said, poking his head out of the stairwell, his face the color of a pomegranate.

"Yes?" she said.

"About the Fortini dinner. Bring a man."

. . .

"So, will you do it?"

Fingers crossed, Tess perched on the corner of Grady's cluttered desk in a trailer at his latest construction site. From outside she heard men's voices shouting, a jackhammer drilling concrete, a backhoe—or some other enormous machine—grinding its gears. Dust was everywhere. Tess could barely breathe.

"Emery Shallowford? Are you kidding me?" Grady studied her from the doorway, one broad shoulder against the frame, his arms folded, his biceps bulging in a black T-shirt smudged with dirt. The masculine sight made Tess's senses hum. "Why would I try to bail him out of trouble? Why would I want to attend a party for some woman I've never met?"

"Free food? Open bar?" Tess tried a smile. "You do know Angela Fortini. She went to the senior prom with Ethan."

"I can't drink." Grady glanced down at his foot. He wore some kind of low-cut sneaker that wouldn't rub his ankle. "The antibiotic I'm on says 'no alcohol.'"

"You're feeling better, though, right?"

"Not as sore." He didn't elaborate except to say, "Thanks for asking."

Tess swallowed her pride. Emery Shallowford's "suggestion" had been clear. She was to show up at the Fortini function with an escort. Or else.

"You won't have to do a thing. Just look pretty."

"Now we're getting somewhere." Grady glanced at the low ceiling of the trailer where Tess saw cobwebs he didn't seem to notice. "Am I being manipulated here for some reason?"

"No, um, not really."

"Come on, Tess. What's going on?" One problem with having an ex-husband was that he could almost read her mind. He peeled away from the doorway to sink down in his battered chair behind the desk. Tess assumed his foot still hurt.

She angled to face him. "You won't have to walk around, mingle, or anything. It's a sit-down dinner. You like P.F. Chang's, right? If I remember, their coconut shrimp is your favorite."

"I'm watching my cholesterol."

He was making her squirm. But then, so had Emery, who held her career in his capable surgeon's hands.

"This won't be a real date." Tess didn't realize her mistake until she said the words. "You don't have to kiss me goodnight."

"Lost me there," he said, a smile tugging at his too-appealing mouth. His dark gaze slid over her. "I don't see an incentive, then, to play Man of the Evening."

That was exactly what she needed, and he knew it. She wasn't being fair to him, though, and he knew that, too.

"You'd make a very sexy Man of the Evening."

Grady grinned. In the next second, he was out from behind his desk, ambling toward Tess with hardly a limp. He leaned over her, too close, caging her with his well-muscled forearms, and her heart began to race. This time they weren't in the bathroom of her rented house. The backhoe or whatever ground to a halt nearby, engine humming.

"Persuade me," Grady murmured, his mouth mere inches from hers.

His eyes were both hot and amused.

Tess couldn't move. Her mind scrambled for some other enticement he wouldn't be able to resist. She couldn't find one—except *her*, and she was definitely off limits—but before she could say so, the trailer door swung open and Ethan poked his head in.

"Hey, Dad, we're done. Want us to—"

He broke off with a knowing look at Grady, then Tess. She

saw hope, not a lingering anger from their lunch at Don Diego's, in his eyes.

Tess mentally groaned. Did a child, even a grown child, ever give up praying that his parents would reconcile?

"Never mind," Ethan said, tongue in cheek. "We'll find something to do till quitting time. You two have fun."

The door shut behind him. Tess heard Ethan chuckling to himself outside. Like her, Grady hadn't moved. He was still leaning over Tess, closing her in, tempting her. She swallowed. "Grady, please. Come to dinner."

"You don't know any other men?" Now he also sounded hopeful.

"Not at the moment." She swallowed again. "On short notice you were the only one I could think of." No, that didn't come out right.

"Gee. Thanks. I feel much better."

"I didn't mean it that way." Tess dared to put a hand on his bare forearm. His brawny forearm. Grady was in far better shape than he'd been four years ago when she finally left him.

Every time she saw him these days, he looked good. Healthier. Happier. More comfortable in his own skin. Enthused about his new business. He even dressed better, took more care with his appearance. Yet at the moment, even wearing tattered jeans that had seen better days, he could still have modeled for *GQ*. His five o'clock shadow was a nice touch too.

"How did you mean it?" Grady straightened, walked over to the door, and peered out the modest pane of glass.

Good question. At first inviting him to the Fortini engagement party had been an act of desperation. It was true she didn't have time to foster a new relationship, as both Merry and Emery advised, nor was she inclined to start one anyway. Still, it amazed—and frightened—her how fast she'd thought of Grady.

Tess stared down at her wedding band still welded to her finger.

"I *want* you to go with me," she said and meant it.

Grady turned his head. "Finally, the right words." His gaze checked out her sincerity. "Okay. Then I'll go. You can repay the debt later."

Tess surged to her feet. "Thank you. You don't know what this means to me, Grady. I'll meet you—"

He shook his head. "No, I'll pick you up." Tess had already lost her advantage. They were playing by his rules now. "What time?"

"Sevenish?"

"I'll be there. With Tinkerbells on. Good enough for you?"

"Yes." More than good for Emery Shallowford, perhaps, if not for Tess.

"One thing," Grady said.

"What?"

"It's a date, Theresa."

7

Tess loped through the neighborhood behind the new pet stroller she'd bought. The two cats hunkered inside the mesh-windowed carrier on wheels, looking unhappy.

Tess had recently begun her long-delayed exercise program. This morning, after the Fortini dinner last night, the bathroom scale had confirmed her hope that she'd already lost a few pounds, and now she jogged along the sidewalk faster than usual. Her jeans were starting to feel looser. When she shed the rest of the weight she'd gained after she left Grady, she'd be able to take off her too-tight ring. Maybe that would inspire her to date again, as Merry and Emery had urged. As soon as she forgot Grady.

Which seemed to be getting harder.

Last night he had charmed Sybil Shallowford—which was great—but he'd also charmed Tess, which was definitely bad.

To make matters worse, in spite of her vow she'd given in after all to a goodnight kiss and then another.

"Jesus, Tess," Grady had muttered, his mouth finally leaving hers. "That was worth every bad joke Emery Shallowford told at our table." He paused. "Come home with me tonight."

"Chloe will wonder where I've gone. How would I explain to Dilly?"

"No explanation necessary." He'd run a hand through his hair. "It's not like we haven't done it before. A million times."

"Who's counting?" she asked weakly.

But in the end Tess had sent him home. This morning she was still feeling the heat, but after the night-before-that-hadn't-happened, she saw no sense in giving false hope to him, to Ethan or to Chloe for that matter. Even Dilly had been known to ask: "Why don't you and Poppy live together anymore?"

A four-year-old child didn't need to hear the answer to that.

As it was, thanks to Grady, Tess had narrowly squeaked out of the sticky situation with Sybil. She really was a nice woman—when she didn't assume her husband was interested in someone else, meaning Tess—and in parting, as a Realtor she'd suggested Tess meet her today at a nearby Open House.

Crisis averted. Emery's jealous wife seemed convinced that there was nothing going on between him and Tess. For that, she owed Grady anything except a night in his bed. But oh, the idea...

The touch of his mouth, his hands...She was only human and so was he. What did a few kisses mean? No use beating herself up after the fact. It wasn't as if she'd actually shown him her less-than-perfect body.

"Isn't this fun, guys?" she asked the kittens, picking up her pace.

They didn't seem to agree. Big Boy glowered at her like the tough little macho kitty he was. To her frustration, lately he'd become even more aggressive, at least around Tess. Always the shy one, Little Girl curled into a ball, and mewed pitifully, as if they were both about to be given away on a street corner. Did cats have long-term memory? Tess crossed the intersection, using the sidewalk ramp not to jar the kittens over the curb.

"I need exercise. You need fresh air. If I were cooped up all day and night, I'd act just like you. I can't blame either of you," she said, rolling along the path through the park, feeling just a little winded.

And hoping the brisk walk would help her forget Grady's kisses.

"Honestly," she muttered. "You'd think I was fifteen, not forty-four. Of course, it's only physical attraction. A woman's never too old for that, huh?" A shiver ran down her spine. "Doesn't mean a thing."

Except that, after four years, even when she knew better, she still missed being in Grady's arms, missed their night-time conversations after making love, missed sleeping spooned together until morning. Better to remember all those nights when he hadn't come home at all; when he'd shown up late, like Larry, smelling of beer and desperation; when he'd lost again at cards. Lost his car and their month's mortgage payment.

On the other side of the small park, Tess drew up in front of the house that was being shown. To her surprise, this was a home she'd often admired in the neighborhood but knew she couldn't afford. For a moment she felt the urge to turn around, not to waste Sybil Shallowford's time just when they'd made a truce. She could call her cell to cancel their appointment. Then she wouldn't be tempted to want something else she couldn't have. But did she dare risk angering Sybil again? At last night's dinner she had gone out of her way to tell Tess about the house, which had just come on the market.

Keep your mind on business, Tess. Not on Grady. Or some

daydream of last night that might turn into another one of her If Onlys.

"There you are." To her dismay Emery, not his wife, was standing on the front porch. A beautiful wraparound porch with a pair of inviting white rockers and a pretty table between them like an invitation to sit down, stay a while, and drink a glass of lemonade. "Come in," he said.

Tess almost hadn't recognized Emery who wore a pair of well-pressed khakis and a golf shirt with a high-end logo discreetly displayed on his chest. He looked casual, approachable—and content.

"Where's Sybil?" she asked.

He swept a hand toward the open front door. "I'm your host this morning. Sybil had another unexpected showing. She'll be here afterward but I offered to fill in for her until then."

Tess felt rooted to the steps. Had she misread him after all? Maybe Sybil's fears had a sound basis. Last night she'd caught Emery staring at her more than once. Even Grady had noticed. "What's his problem?" he'd asked.

The two men were hardly friends. Emery had a long memory, and he hadn't forgotten the unfinished patio at the Shallowford house. Emery wouldn't hire Grady now to walk his dog.

Tess looked toward the street but didn't see any cars at the curb. No one else had come yet to view the house. She glanced at her watch, then read the sign out front: Open House. 12-5.

"I'm early," she said. It was only eleven. She guessed she'd been offered a private showing. "I'll come back when Sybil's here."

"You're here now. Let me show you the house, Terry. You can be the first. No telling how many offers Sybil might get today. Why lose this opportunity?"

Tess hesitated.

She didn't want to appear silly, or overly suspicious. Last night had changed the dynamic with the Shallowfords, and Sybil's soft sell about the house had seemed to Tess like an apology. So, Emery liked to look. That didn't mean he intended to touch.

He reached out to take her hand, but Tess avoided contact. "If you like the place, Sybil could do the paperwork with you this afternoon. I think this is just what you're looking for."

"You make a good salesman."

He grinned. "I owe you one. I can't say I was thrilled to see you walk in to the Fortini dinner with Grady, but it worked. If he was playing a part, from the way he looked at you, he's a better actor than he is a contractor. Seeing you with someone else—even him—put Sybil's jealousy to rest."

She paused. "You didn't spend the night on the couch again?"

His grin widened but he didn't answer. "Come on. You know you want to walk through these rooms, imagine your own furniture here."

"I can tell you live with a Realtor."

Chiding herself for her renewed suspicions, which appeared to be unfounded, Tess left the cats in their stroller on the shady porch then slipped past Emery into the foyer.

And held her breath.

This house had everything on her wish list. Keeping her distance from Emery—just in case—Tess let herself be charmed by the big living room fireplace with marble mantel, the updated kitchen with stainless steel appliances and a sunny breakfast area, the three large bedrooms upstairs all with en suite baths. The huge attic was another plus, and so was the roomy garage. On the finished basement level the current owners had a family room with cozy seating and lined with gleaming cherry bookshelves that flanked an entertainment center and occupied an entire wall. By the time she'd toured the house twice, she'd almost forgotten Emery was here.

"See?" he said, startling Tess from her contemplation once more of the dining room wallpaper. The taupe with gold French pattern was obviously expensive but not her taste. If she bought the house, she would change it. "You didn't need to go for the pepper spray after all," Emery said, sounding amused.

Tess turned. "I wasn't worried."

He smiled. "Yes, you were."

Chloe was determined to succeed in her job and not to worry about Ethan or anything else. In the past few days she'd dropped only three items, broken just one valuable piece of pottery and a crystal candy dish. She'd learned to properly answer the phone for Tess, and for the first time in four years child care wasn't an issue.

Today was Dilly's first day of nursery school. There'd been an unexpected opening in the facility between Ethan and Chloe's home and Tess's house, and Dilly was beside herself with excitement at being officially a "big girl." Tess had bought her a new pink outfit for the occasion.

With Dilly there half days now, Chloe could focus on herself.

Sooner or later, she'd find her special niche in life.

She already missed Dilly, though. Terribly.

Chloe blinked as she reached for the phone that wouldn't seem to stop ringing. Tess said this was a good thing.

But three phone calls later, which she'd managed perfectly, Chloe was still worried about Ethan too.

Last night he'd called to talk to Dilly, and Chloe had overheard her daughter's side of the conversation.

"You're going to Mex'co? Where's that, Daddy? Far away?"

Chloe's heart had stalled. She had an instant image of white sand beaches, the teal-blue ocean stretching as far as the eye could see, nubile young women in scanty bikinis everywhere. Why was Ethan taking a trip? Without her?

But, of course, why not? She'd left him.

"I wish I could go with you." Dilly's tone sounded wistful. At which point Chloe eased the receiver from her grasp.

"Let me say hi to Daddy, hon." She hadn't talked to him since their quarrel in Tess's living room. "Then you can tell him goodnight."

Dilly hopped off the kitchen stool and dashed off to play with the cats. She'd be back soon, though.

Trying to keep her voice light, Chloe spoke fast. "What's this about Mexico? Sounds exotic."

"So now you're talking to me?" He paused. "There's a big builders' conference in Cabo San Lucas. Dad decided I should attend."

"When?" Chloe asked, her heart sinking.

"End of the week. Four or five days in the sun. Tough duty, huh?"

She heard the edge in his voice. If they'd been together, maybe she could have gone too. She and Dilly. If she said she wanted to go, he'd only remind her that it had been her choice to leave home. And Chloe would have to crawl back, having accomplished nothing.

Besides, she couldn't walk out on Tess.

"Well, have a good time," she'd said instead.

After she hung up, Chloe had renewed her commitment to help Tess because Meredith was still in Kentucky. Everything was running smoothly, Tess insisted, with Chloe to fill in.

LEIGH RIKER

Yet Chloe knew how precarious her position was. At any moment she might tangle The Go-To Girl into knots, but at the sound of another incoming call, she dutifully snatched up the receiver.

From the other end of the line she heard a cultured voice. "This is Sybil Shallowford. Is Tess in?"

"Not at the moment." Chloe rushed on, "She's with a client in Lebanon who's planning a surprise party for her husband's fortieth birthday at the Golden Lamb, which used to be a coaching inn and is on the national historic register." Was that too much information? She tended to get carried away in her enthusiasm for this new job.

"So it is," Sybil agreed.

Stupid, Chloe thought. Of course, she would know about the inn. The woman was probably on some auxiliary committee dedicated to its preservation. "May I have Tess call you?"

"Please."

But Chloe, being Chloe, couldn't leave it at that. "Oh, Mrs. Shallowford! You probably don't remember, but we talked at the Henderson reception."

"I remember well. How are you, my dear?"

Momentarily, Chloe forgot she'd been the one to point out Dr. Shallowford and Tess together. "You're the lady," she remembered, "who got the diamond ring for your anniversary. Tess picked out exactly the right one. I didn't get a very good look at it the other day, but it's gorgeous—"

"*Tess?*" Too late, her tone registered with Chloe. "Tess bought my ring for Emery?"

Chloe tried to retreat. "Uh...I wouldn't really know. I just started to work here. I'll be sure to have Tess call you. Does she have your number?"

"Yes," Sybil said coldly. "And I have hers."

Suddenly Chloe was holding a dead phone.

She'd only been trying to help.

Oh, God. Now what have I done?

"Chloe! How could you?"

Tess paced the office from one end to the other. Just when she'd hoped things might work out until Merry got back, and Tess had been trying to shore up her daughter-in-law's confidence, Chloe had made a terrible error. Emery, who shouldn't have lied to his wife in the first place, was sure to throw a fit. Just when it seemed Tess had gotten off the hook with Sybil too.

"I left you in charge for no more than a couple of hours. I come back and this is what I find?"

"I'm sorry. I shouldn't have told you."

"Shouldn't *tell* me?" Tess's voice rose. "And then what? I get blindsided? Emery comes barging in here later today, takes my head off—rightly so—and my business goes down the tubes? I cannot afford to lose this place, Chloe. Do you understand?"

Chloe nodded and Tess felt like a tyrant. Every vein in her neck seemed to be standing out. She was surprised she didn't have a stroke. But she remembered Chloe was fragile, so Tess deliberately lowered her tone.

"I'm sorry, but this is important. Vital. All I needed you to do was answer the telephone and take messages. Apparently, you decided to expand your duties again." She hadn't been pleased when, with Chloe's help, Emery found her at Saks. "But with *Sybil Shallowford?*"

Chloe's voice was barely audible. "She's a nice lady."

"Yes, but she's terribly jealous. You knew that. No sooner did I get her ridiculous assumption about me with Emery corrected when this happened. There was no truth to the other, but he asked me—told me—never to let his wife know he'd hired a personal shopper to buy her such a personal gift." And, *mum's the word*, Tess had warned Chloe after all as she had Meredith but not strongly enough. "If she were anyone else, maybe it wouldn't matter so much. Lots of the corporate wives here would probably expect nothing else." Tess picked up the phone then set it down again. "I can't call her yet. I have no idea what to say this time."

Her dreams since the open house had gone up in smoke. She'd told Sybil she might be able to go over her budget, see if she could manage the mortgage, and would be in touch soon. But...it wasn't bad enough that the numbers were dismal. Now Sybil wouldn't work with her.

Chloe's shoulders slumped. "Do you want me to go home?"

Tess didn't know if she meant to her house or to Chloe's home with Ethan.

With a sigh she slipped an arm around Chloe, felt her trembling, and all her anger dissipated. Tess hadn't quite yelled, but obviously she had hurt her feelings.

In Tess's embrace, Chloe shrugged. "I shouldn't have talked to Mrs. Shallowford. I said too much."

"Yes, you did. But it's done. We'll get through this." Somehow.

Chloe glanced up, hope in her eyes. "You're not mad?"

"My business is essential to me, but you did nothing intentionally wrong. It was an accident."

"*I'm* an accident," Chloe said miserably. "I always mess up. I've been messing up since I was *born*."

Tess frowned. Who had given Chloe this dreadful image of herself? For one awful moment Tess feared that Ethan had shattered her self-esteem, but that wasn't like him. And Grady adored her, too. Tess had never said a cross word to her before, not through ruined holiday meals or burnt stew or shriveled cashmere sweaters. They all chalked up her mishaps to Chloe's tender heart, her eagerness to please.

Tess had thought there was something more to her problem with Ethan than his obsession with his phone. Now she decided to go fishing. If Ethan wasn't fully responsible, Chloe's troubles must go farther back. Tess took her hand. "You don't talk much about your family," she said, "but I've met your parents." Once, when Tess and Grady had hosted a post-wedding dinner, and again when Dilly was born. "I'm sure they're good people," although, to Tess, Chloe's father seemed like a cold fish. "Is there anything you'd like to tell me?"

For a long moment Chloe stared down at her hand, nestled in Tess's grasp. Then she murmured, "No."

"Are you sure? Just between you and me. Whatever you say won't go any farther than right here."

Chloe shrugged again. "Nobody should trust me to do anything right. Even Ethan—who's the kindest person I know, except for you, well, and Grady too—even he just smiles when I drop something or say the wrong thing."

"We all love you. We don't think you could do anything *really* wrong." Tess patted her hand. "Dropping things is just your way, Chloe." No, that didn't sound very kind, did it?

"Like yours is to do everything right?"

Shocked, she said, "If I did, I wouldn't be in trouble with Sybil again."

Chloe drew away. "That was my fault."

"Partly, and I could have elaborated on my warning, but frankly Emery should be the one in trouble. He lied to Sybil. As a professional I'll do my best to smooth things over, but he'll have to deal with her and their marriage."

"What if he doesn't hire you again?"

"Then I'll cope with that." Tess mentally crossed her

fingers. At the moment her business seemed less important than Chloe's wounded feelings.

Chloe buried her face in her hands. And at last, along with the tears, the words spilled out. "He always said 'Chloe, pick up your feet. What did you break now? Don't be so clumsy. Make something of yourself...'"

"Who?" Tess said carefully.

"My *father*. He doesn't like me."

"You're his daughter, Chloe. He may not be able to show it, but I'm sure he does love you. He doesn't understand you, that's all."

"Ethan doesn't either." Tess could only imagine how long Chloe had been holding in these feelings. "He's going to Mexico," she said, as if that were the ultimate betrayal, "without me. He's probably afraid I'd embarrass him."

Grady had mentioned the trip to Tess last night. He thought it would be a good opportunity for Ethan to promote their fledgling firm. A reward for all his hard work. "It's business," she said.

And if Chloe continued to alienate her customers, Tess's business would soon be in jeopardy. Her dream of buying a home—never mind the one Emery had shown her—might never happen. Yet she couldn't shatter Chloe's shaky self-esteem by firing her. Tess wasn't the Go-To Girl for nothing. *Find the solution...*

She put a finger under Chloe's chin and looked into her still brimming eyes. At any business conference there were always social events too. Suddenly, she knew what might just work.

"How would you like to have a second honeymoon?"

Chloe blinked. "We never had a first."

"Ethan was probably afraid to invite you to Mexico, sweetie." She smiled. "Try to forget that little voice inside that keeps telling you you're a bad person."

"We can't afford the trip. Grady's company will pay for Ethan but not for me."

That didn't stop Tess. If she robbed Peter to pay Paul, or rather, Larry, she could afford one coach plane ticket for Chloe. Ethan would already have reserved a hotel room. She'd call Grady whose firm could darn well pick up the food costs for one more person.

"Call this an early anniversary gift," she said, remembering Sybil Shallowford's diamond with a wince. "From me."

"Tess, I can't accept that."

"Merry's spending her break in Kentucky with Frank. You can join Ethan. It'll be like a marriage encounter. Maybe you'll both come home with smiles on your faces. At the very least you'll be forced to talk to each other." Like Merry and Frank, she hoped.

It was all she could do. If only she and Grady could have done something similar...before their marriage fell completely apart.

Chloe looked tempted but still unsure. "What about Dilly?"

"I'll work when she's in school. Between me and Grady, she'll be fine." Now all she needed from him were the dates and Ethan's hotel information. "Let this be a surprise for Ethan. All you have to do is pack your bikini—then take that phone away from him."

8

INTENT UPON GETTING through security unscathed, which almost never happened to her in any situation, Chloe inched her way in the TSA line at Cincinnati-Northern Kentucky International Airport. The crowd snaked along a circuitous route hemmed in by stanchions toward the scanners, and Chloe's heart beat faster.

Was she claustrophobic? She'd never thought so, but the notion that she couldn't escape from her spot—wedged between a large family behind who were all speaking Spanish and a self-absorbed woman in front with a huge wheeled suitcase that kept rolling over Chloe's toes every time the line moved, was making her crazy.

And she was already late. Usually, Ethan was the one who arrived at the last minute. Tess's idea for Chloe to surprise him in Mexico had all the earmarks of another disaster.

She'd never flown out of the country before, except with her father. Those family trips had been a lot of fun—*not*—and she wasn't sure she wanted to repeat the experience. A good thing her documents were in order, her boarding pass and—

Chloe scrabbled through her carry-on. Where *was* her passport?

The duffle bag was dark, serviceable, and borrowed from Tess, like the rest of her luggage. Crammed full of makeup, an extra pair of shoes, birth control in case Ethan didn't send her home, and a small album containing recent pictures of Dilly, the carry-on didn't seem to hold the now-missing passport.

She began to sweat, hair drooping in damp wisps around her face. *Hurry.* She didn't have time to go home to search for it there.

And it was then that she saw him.

Ethan stood in line too, maybe ten people ahead of her.

All at once they all seemed to be moving at the speed of sound. For a second Ethan vanished into the scanner then emerged on the other side. Chloe saw him scoop up his pocket change, his wallet, and the hated iPhone from a plastic tray. If he glanced back and saw her, the surprise would be ruined.

In no time at all, the woman in front of her turned a bit and was hauling her wheeled bag over Chloe's foot once more, then disappearing through the same portal as Ethan had.

Panicked, Chloe rummaged through her borrowed bag again. Ah, there! How could she forget that she'd tucked the passport away behind the hidden zipper under the flap for safekeeping?

Blowing out a gust of relief, she tried to breathe easier.

She set her carry-on on the moving belt then managed a smile for the TSA agent who held out his hand for her passport and boarding pass. Feeling better, she walked into the scanner then out again without setting off an alarm.

Much better. She wouldn't be wanded or searched.

Her relief was short-lived. Her carry-on didn't glide along

the belt back to her and, waiting, Chloe saw the woman behind the monitor stop its motion. "This your bag?"

"Yes."

"Please step aside."

Another agent hustled the carry-on to a nearby table. With her agreement, he began to search her bag, taking out every item, piling it on the table, frowning. "What's wrong?" Chloe asked.

He didn't answer.

Her pulse kicked up again.

He held up a tiny pair of manicure scissors, and when Chloe nodded that they too were hers, he confiscated them. Then, "Powder," she heard him mutter as if he'd found gold. He carried the bag to yet another table to conduct some test. Chloe couldn't catch her breath now. She would never travel again. Not even for Ethan.

Finally, the agent returned to show her the thin film of milky dust in the bottom of the duffle that had caused all the trouble. Then he dumped her belongings back inside.

"Am I free to go?" Chloe said in a small voice, as if she'd been arrested.

"The residue in the bag...what is it?"

Chloe's stomach sank until she remembered taking the kittens to the vet in that same duffle bag for want of a proper carrier... "Flea powder."

He started to smile. Couldn't seem to help himself.

Which was the effect Chloe had on everyone when she didn't even try.

Her father would have already embarked on a stern lecture. *Flea powder? Chloe, don't you ever think? To the TSA it must have appeared to be an explosive.*

Blinking, she gathered her stuff then, still rattled by the experience, took two steps away from Security—and spied Ethan. Waiting for her.

"Let me guess," he said. "Cincinnati via Dallas to San Jose del Cabo?"

"Um, yes."

"Me, too. Quite a coincidence, huh?"

To her dismay he wasn't smiling.

"Is this Mom's doing?" he asked.

"No," Chloe lied. "I—I decided we need a few days in some relaxing place with nothing to do but look at each other."

"Chloe, I'm headed for a conference."

"Yes, I know, but Tess said there'll be time too for social—"

"See? I knew it. Mom put you up to this." He didn't sound angry, though. He sounded disappointed, as if he'd really hoped Chloe had planned the trip all by herself.

"I packed my bikini," she informed him. "Now all you have to do is give up your—"

He was already thumbing the hated phone. Probably calling Tess.

"Ethan, please. Tess may have paid for my ticket but it's a good idea."

"I'm not saying it isn't. The timing sucks but if you want to lie by the pool or at the beach all day while I'm in meetings that's okay with me."

"Then you don't mind?"

"I don't mind," he finally said, studying his phone. "But guess what? While you were detained in Security, we missed our flight. I'm trying to get another."

"Oh, no!" she cried. "I'm sorry, Ethan. When's the next one?"

"Looks like tomorrow. There's not a lot of choice."

She mentally wrung her hands. "Now you'll miss some of your meetings."

Ethan must have heard the despair in her voice. He

slipped the phone in his pocket. Then he put his arm around her shoulders, and Chloe couldn't help herself. She buried her cheek against his broad shoulder. Felt him kiss the top of her head.

"Baby, nothing you do disappoints me." He walked her a little way down the concourse. "It'll be all right. We'll rebook at the sky club—then go home for tonight."

Chloe stiffened. Normally, his suggestion would have appealed to her. Heaven knew, she missed him. So did Dilly. But Ethan clearly expected her to follow his lead, to forget— or overlook—their differences. It was only a matter of time before he pulled out that smartphone again and started reaching out to someone else.

"What was the hold-up in Security anyway?" he asked.

Chloe told him.

Ethan laughed, a rich, deep sound she usually loved. "*Flea powder?*" He ruffled her hair. "What a great story. Dad will love it."

"Ethan, it's not that funny," she heard herself say. Was she the family joke?

"Sure, it is. I've heard all about those cats from Dad."

"They didn't mean to hurt him." Chloe pulled back so they were no longer touching. Suddenly it seemed important to her—no, vital—to take a stand. "Being everyone's constant source of amusement is no more appealing to me than one of my father's harsh sermons about all my faults and failures." In either case she felt demeaned. Belittled. No one took her seriously.

For an instant Ethan looked startled.

"Come on, Chloe. There's no need to get huffy." He started walking again. "We'll grab a bite to eat, have a glass of wine in the club, and talk. Our trip will be one day short...no big deal. We'll try for the same flight tomorrow, clean the flea powder out of the bag. Better still," he said, "I'll buy you a new one."

She pulled a big word out of the air. "Don't patronize me, Ethan." She took a breath. "What if I don't want to fly to Mexico with a man who thinks I'm nothing but an airhead?"

"I never said—"

"No, but that's how you treat me. Everyone does."

"Chloe, you're overreacting." He sighed. "If this is about your dad—"

"It's not about him! It's not about your parents either—and how you fall all over yourself trying to make up for their divorce."

He blinked. "How did they get into this?"

"You've never been able to face the fact that maybe Tess left Grady because she had to. Sometimes that's a woman's only choice."

"Meaning you? What the hell—?"

"And maybe that's what Grady needed in order to save himself!"

Chloe was breathing fast. But strangely enough, she felt a little thrill of power. Of *being*. It was a heady feeling, and for once in her life she didn't hear her father's voice inside, chiding her.

Ethan had drawn her to one side of the busy concourse. All around them people hurried past, a few sending them curious glances. The smells of popcorn and onions from nearby restaurants mingled in the air. Chloe couldn't seem to catch her breath, yet a strange peace had welled up inside her too.

"I am not going to argue about this," Ethan said, the very model of exaggerated patience.

"Why not?" For the first time in her life, she wanted a fight.

"Because it's crazy. Come home, Chloe. You sound just like my mother."

"And you're like Grady." She didn't know where the thought had come from. But there it was. Maybe she did sound like Tess. To Chloe that was a really good thing. It certainly felt right. "At least the way he used to be," she said. "No wonder Tess left him. He might have been a gambler, but you're addicted too to that...that iPhone! Well, you can sleep with it instead of me for all I care!"

She turned on her heel and marched off.

"Chloe! Dammit!"

Shoulders squared, she buzzed through the terminal without looking back.

W ith a contented sigh Tess settled into her favorite easy chair. For once, the house was quiet. Dilly had been invited to a new friend's home after nursery school. By now Chloe was on her way to Mexico. Even the kittens were taking a nap somewhere, and Tess meant to enjoy the rare peace when it seemed half the world was beating a path to her door these days.

Her mind wandered to a far more personal interlude on the night of the Fortini engagement party. And to Grady, who wasn't the safe memory she might wish for. Still, their after-glow celebration in the parking lot outside P.F. Chang's had been, indeed, memorable.

Holding hands, their bodies touching now and then, Grady had walked Tess to her car. They stood talking in the dark near Joseph Beth Booksellers at the Rookwood Commons, alone except for a few stragglers from the party who waved then drove off like Ethan, who sent them a quick toot-toot on his horn when he whizzed past. Smiling to himself, Tess remembered.

If only his wish for her to reconcile with Grady wasn't strictly that—a wish. Unfortunately, it was also the precursor to another of Tess's fantasies now in which things had gone even farther than they actually did...

G rady edged her up against his car. He held her caged between his arms, his face just above hers, as he'd done in his trailer/office, his lips half parted. His intent gaze made her feel as if this night was preordained, their nearness meant to be, and it would be useless for Tess to refuse him.

"Makes you feel like being twenty again, doesn't it?" he asked, though Tess felt his question was rhetorical. "Must be the Fortini bash tonight, all those gifts for the bride and how she and what's-his-name kept looking at each other." His gaze lowered to her mouth. "And kissing," he added, the word running across her senses like a velvet caress. "Remember, Tess? How we never could get enough of each other?"

Already breathless she said, "I remember."

He tilted her chin. "Remember too that this is supposed to be our date?"

"Then you can drive me home now."

"In a minute. Don't rush me."

He angled his head and kissed Tess softly, then with firmness, his tongue slipping easily between her lips to explore her mouth. Tess's murmur of acceptance turned into a moan, and without stopping to consider what this meant, she pulled his head down again and went back for more.

Within seconds Grady had her right where he obviously wanted her. Up against that car, his body pressed to hers, his stance wide enough to frame Tess's legs, his obvious erection nestled in the cradle of her hips exactly where it would do the most good.

Tess groaned. "Oh, God. Grady."

"Yeah," he whispered, his hand inside the V-neck of her dress. He palmed one breast, teased its nipple into a tight, hard bud, then

focused on the other. By the time he drew back a little, she was pant-
ing. Ready to beg. When his fingers skimmed down to her waist, then
her thigh, she almost did.

"Jesus, Tess." He rested his forehead against hers. "Come home
with me."

Another instant and she would be begging him not only to take
her with him, but to take her in his bed until she didn't know where,
or who, she was and didn't care. She made a weak protest. "Chloe will
wonder where I've gone—"

W ith that the desperate fantasy shattered and Tess
straightened in her chair. But, wait. Those moments
outside P.F. Chang's in the dark hadn't been a total fantasy.
Not just one of her If Onlys after all.

Tess touched her lips. Nothing had happened, really,
except some harmless groping and more than a few less-than-
harmless kisses. Yet now she wished she'd gone home with
him, and she and Grady had made love. Tess scolded herself
for wool-gathering, whatever that meant. She should spend a
few hours on her home computer or the phone for business ,
but Sybil Shallowford had so far refused her calls and Tess
didn't want to try again.

Instead, she put her feet up on the hassock and opened
her new book. *Living with Cats* wouldn't normally be her first
choice for leisure time reading. She preferred Jim Grippan-
do's thrillers. Still, it was high time she learned something
about the two small creatures that had taken up residence
with her. Chloe wouldn't stay with Tess forever. Without her
to run interference, Tess would again be on her own with the
kittens. And Big Boy was becoming a definite problem for
Tess.

She flipped through the chapter headings. *So You've*
Decided to Adopt.

That page-turner was followed by *Litter Box Habits to Love*. Tess finally chose *The Indoor Cat's Rules for Happiness*.

She should start at the beginning of the book, but she couldn't seem to focus. She'd dip a toe in the water here first. She'd just begun to delve into the subheading of *Toys and Safety Tips* when the front door banged open.

Tess sat up with a start. If Larry had used his key when he could plainly see her car sitting in the drive and know she was home, she'd throttle him for not knocking first. He'd already used up his father quotient for today with an early morning call about—what else?—more money. As she'd expected, Tess had been right that her twelve hundred dollars were only a down payment for "the guy in Dayton." The word "extortion" came to mind.

She was on her feet, eyes blazing, when instead Chloe stomped in.

"We had a fight," she informed Tess. "Ethan is impossible! I don't know what I ever saw in him—Oops," she added. "I'm sorry, Tess. I know he's your son and you love him—"

"Chloe, you love him, too." Until recently she'd never seen a pair of lovebirds like those two, not even herself and Grady in their early days. Or in her continuing fantasies, um, memory. Chloe and Ethan belonged together. "How could you have a quarrel? You left for the airport three hours ago. You wouldn't see Ethan until late afternoon..."

"We were on the same flight," she said. "We missed it. The only flight left today. So much for my surprise."

"Oh, Chloe. I was hoping you'd—"

"Yeah. I know." She flopped onto the sofa. "But maybe this will give him something to think about. Ethan isn't nasty but he does put me down without knowing he's doing it."

Tess felt lost.

Chloe explained about her troubles in Security. She and

LEIGH RIKER

Tess laughed about the flea powder, but Chloe hadn't finished.

"Then Ethan blew it off, like 'so what, Chloe always gets in some jam, but we love her anyway. Poor thing.' How do you think that made me feel? Like an imbecile," she answered herself. "It doesn't matter whether my father is telling me I don't have a brain or my husband is kissing the top of my head as if that will make a problem go away." She took a sharp breath. "It's still a problem...and I needed to leave for a while until I know where I'm going in *my* life."

Tess could empathize, but she saw her dreams of a quiet, solitary late afternoon vanish like David Copperfield, the magician, during one of his illusions onstage. Still, she had an obligation—called love—to help Chloe.

Then Tess noticed something strange. Through her entire tirade Chloe had been filled with newfound passion. Now her face glowed and a smile blossomed on her pretty face. She looked better, happier, than she had in some time.

"I think you've discovered the real issue here," Tess said.

As quickly as it had come, Chloe's smile slipped. "I feel awful about Ethan, but you're right. This is about me. Now all I need to do is figure out what floats my boat. Except for Dilly, of course." She glanced around. "Where is she?"

"At a friend's house." Tess smiled. "She's quite the social butterfly since she started nursery school. It's good for her to have playmates. And this gives you some free time. Maybe now you can finish college?"

"Maybe. I'm not sure." Chloe brightened again. "I don't need to be sure. Not yet." Then she asked, looking puzzled, "But what about Mexico?"

"You could leave tomorrow."

"That's what he said. He was going to change our tickets but I left before that happened." Chloe shook her head. "No,

132

Ethan needs time to realize how he treats me, as if I need to be protected from myself."

Tess remembered he'd said just that at lunch. She opened her mouth to argue that in a more neutral setting Chloe and Ethan would have time to work out their problems, but she could see that Chloe was adamant about staying home.

"If I went after all," she said, "I'd feel I was giving in. Nothing would change. Let Ethan miss me a little while he's gone. In the meantime, I still need to think about what it is *I* want." She paused with a worried frown. "Does that mean I'm being selfish, Tess?"

Tess had gone through a similar struggle before she started The Go-To Girl. Maybe she still was, or she'd be ready to expand the business as Merry urged her to do. "No, I think it means you're exploring new territory. Take your time."

Tess could have meant herself too, but Chloe grinned. "Thanks."

"You're very welcome."

"Your support means a lot to me, Tess." Chloe dug in her carry-on and came up with a boarding pass. "But I have an idea right now. You've been working way too hard. This is the flight number you'll want. You go to Cabo instead. I know your dad drives you wild, and then there's the Shallowford mess. My fault." For an instant she looked guilty again. "I'd really like you to have a vacation."

"This is one of my busiest seasons at work—"

"Isn't Merry coming back?"

"She took a few extra days but—"

"Then I promise. I won't mess up again at work. And I'll watch the cats," she said. "Now you have no reason not to go."

"I don't have a hotel room reservation," Tess pointed out. "Buying a new ticket at this late date would cost—"

Chloe's eyes sparkled. "Airline points!"

"I don't have any," Tess said because she rarely flew.

"My father does. He belongs to a bunch of frequent flier plans. He has about a gazillion miles. I figure he owes me a few thousand. I sure put up with a lot from him when I was a kid. And I know he feels a little guilty that he didn't help me and Ethan like you and Grady did when we got married." She searched the duffle for her phone. "I'll call him."

"But, Chloe—" Tess was astonished. Even yesterday Chloe would never have considered approaching her father for what amounted to a handout.

"You don't need to thank me. You're going." In the doorway she looked back at Tess. "If it makes you feel better, just remember I have an ulterior motive. While you're gone, maybe you can talk sense into Ethan."

Ethan rapped on the edge of Grady's desk. His dad was deep in concentration over some blueprints. "Hey, I'm back."

With my ego smashed to pieces. Chloe had gone nuts at the airport, but at least now he knew what her problem was—if not how to deal with it.

His father looked up with a frown. "You should be on your way to Cabo by now."

"Missed my flight." Ethan sank onto a chair and felt all the air go out of him like the dust that rose from the seat. "You won't believe this."

"What about Chloe?"

Ethan narrowed his eyes. "You *knew* she was going?"

"Uh, well, yeah." His dad rubbed the back of his neck. "Busted," he admitted. "Tess decided Chloe needed a vacation—with you. I, uh, provided some info so she could make her plans."

"Then thanks for sending me into a female ambush."

Exhausted, he told his father about the scene with Chloe. "Women are loony," he finished. "So, hell. Let her stay home. She can wear her bikini in Mom's backyard. I could care less."

"Oh, you care," Grady said. "You ought to see your face. That expression is a dead ringer for Dilly's when she wants ice cream before dinner and Chloe says no. That kid could pout for a living."

"Or act on the stage." Ethan hauled out his phone, checked its display. Just in case Chloe had texted him an apology. Nothing. "I don't know what to do with her. It seems the harder I try to understand, the less I do."

"Been there, done that," his dad said with a little shrug, as if he didn't care that he and Mom were still on the outs when Ethan knew better. "So, you'll leave tomorrow instead."

He shook his head. "I don't have the—" he started to say *heart*, but that didn't sound manly "—stomach for this trip now."

"Ethan, we paid the conference fee and booked the hotel."

"I know, I know." He looked down at the phone again, as if to find answers on the screen. "I just can't leave, that's all." Ethan glanced up. "Hey. I know. You go instead."

"I can't use your reservation. Pay another full air fare? No way."

"You can dock my pay. I'll work for free next week."

"And pay your mortgage how? Look, it's not that I can't come up with the money. I don't have one foot in bankruptcy court these days, but you're the one who signed up to do that workshop about cost-cutting without sacrificing quality in construction."

"I'll give you my notes. You can take my laptop. It's all there. All you have to do is show up at the workshop, use my Power Point presentation. It's a no-brainer."

Grady winced. "Thanks."

Ethan backpedaled. Grady's smarts, or what his father perceived as their lack, were always an issue. "Dad, please. Consider this a favor, okay? I am not leaving town with Chloe having such a hissy fit. I'll let her cool off for a day or two then we're going to talk turkey. Or else."

"You can try."

"You should too. With Mom." He slipped the iPhone into his inside jacket pocket. "I told Chloe she's acting just like her, taking off when something bugs her." He left out Chloe's accusation about Ethan's behavior compared to Grady. "You and I know how to hang in there and get the job done. Whatever it takes. Isn't that what we agreed?"

"Ethan..."

"When you get back, go see her."

His dad looked away. "Who are you? You sound like someone out of a Disney film. We're all too old for *The Parent Trap*." But Ethan could tell the notion appealed to him.

He leaned forward to catch Grady's gaze. "I thought we had a deal. Whether or not you did it directly, you made the Mexican connection possible for me and Chloe." He half smiled. "Now you're stuck, Dad. And you're right. Why waste company money on a no-show for this conference? You might as well do it. Could be really important for us."

"I don't speak Spanish," his father tried but his objection failed.

"You don't have to. Just enjoy yourself. After the workshop's over, you can spend the rest of your time while you're there writing a speech to give Mom."

Ethan's mood lifted. With any kind of luck, he and his father were looking at a win-win situation. Chloe would be home with him, and Mom with Grady again, before the two women knew what happened.

9

GRADY COULDN'T BELIEVE his eyes.

Midway through the process of shoving his carry-on bag into an overhead bin, he froze, arms in the air. And did a double take. Was that really Tess sitting on the aisle midway back in Coach? Couldn't be. Yet it was. For sure.

He hadn't seen her since the Fortini dinner and their necking session in the parking lot. Grady's sore foot almost stopped hurting. He pulled his bag from the cramped, over-crowded space then strolled toward her seat. Feeling suddenly, unbelievably, lucky.

"Surprise, Theresa."

Tess lifted her gaze—in shock.

"What are you doing here?"

"I might ask you the same thing." And here, a moment ago he'd been grousing to himself because his foot still ached. Things were looking up. "Guess you're headed south of the border too, huh?"

"Chloe was supposed to join Ethan but—"

"—They had a big flap and—"

"—she came home," Tess finished.

Grady explained his side of things then said, "Long story short, I'm Ethan's substitute."

This news only made Tess, who was obviously standing in for Chloe, appear more stunned.

He could practically see her mind spin before she said, "It didn't sound too crazy for me to spend a week with our son, but if you think for one minute I'll fly there with you—"

Grady couldn't help it. He started to grin. When Tess stood, he gently pushed her back into her seat. "Relax. Any way you look at it, this will be a vacation. Bet you haven't taken one since you walked out on me."

"And long before that." Her gaze narrowed. "Did you and Ethan cook this up?"

He spread his hands, all innocence. Grady had been a gambler for much of his adult life. In fact, he was gambling now on his newly reorganized business. Sometimes a guy still had to take a chance. And when Tess fell right into his lap, so to speak, what could he do but seize the opportunity? He might be dumb, but he wasn't crazy.

Upfront the flight attendant asked if anyone was willing to change seats. Apparently, a pregnant passenger tended to get airsick when sitting in the rear of the plane. Intent upon staying near Tess, Grady started to offer his seat closer to the front of the cabin, but the expectant mother and her husband needed two of them. Fortunately, another pair not traveling together, agreed to make the switch. The expectant mother and father ended up sitting across the aisle from Tess.

A second later the flight attendant announced, "If Cabo is not your destination, this would be a good time to deplane."

The door was about to close, and Grady smiled to himself. As if anyone in his right mind, except Tess, would pass up an unexpected trip to paradise.

She made one last attempt to leave. Using his greater size, Grady blocked her, then dropped onto the surprisingly vacant middle seat beside her. The woman sitting by the window sent him a look of displeasure as if to say she'd reserved the cramped space for her laptop and briefcase.

"Lover's quarrel," he explained, tilting his head toward Tess. And with a faint frown the woman returned her attention to her book. "You've already paid for your ticket," he said to Tess in his most reasonable tone of voice. "Sit back. Enjoy." He leaned closer, keeping his voice low. "Is this your first trip to Mexico, gorgeous?"

Tess struggled not to smile. His teasing had hit home, making her realize she wasn't going anywhere but to Mexico, and as the cabin door closed with a definite thud, she ran a shaky hand through her glossy hair. "I'd planned to room with Ethan, assuming he booked two beds instead of a king, but I imagine you're taking that. As soon as we get to the resort, I'll ask the desk for another room."

"Tess, Tess," Grady murmured. "You don't know what you're missing."

"That's the trouble," she said. "I do know."

The flight to Dallas went smoothly, and Tess was glad she'd been able to get a morning one, but once they were airborne again on the connecting flight to Cabo, it was bumpy and the choppy ride over the mountains south of Texas wasn't doing much for Tess's uneasy stomach. It was either the power of suggestion—that airsick pregnant woman across the aisle—or because she'd skipped breakfast. Or, could it be due to Grady's nearness?

His broad shoulder kept rubbing against hers, and Tess shifted in her seat. His arm felt hot. They hadn't been this close, physically, since their divorce—except for that night in her bathroom. And in the construction site trailer. Not to mention the aftermath of the Fortini party. Such incidents were adding up. She had to fight herself now not to touch him again. Every cell of her body cried, *He's still mine*.

On a more rational level Tess didn't want to agree. She shouldn't forget their history. The good parts especially, which tempted her, even the ones she'd imagined. If she wasn't careful, she'd experience another of her If Onlys right here. Another hour of proximity and she'd be climbing all over him.

"You okay?" Grady asked for the tenth time. He looked a little pale himself.

"Fine," she said.

"Sure?"

"Yes. Double sure." She wouldn't let him know that he still got to her. Maybe it was the wine. Tess stared at the empty split bottle she'd tucked into the seat pocket in front of her. Grady had insisted on buying her a drink to go with the minuscule packet of peanuts the airline doled out. She should have paid for a cheese platter instead. On an otherwise empty stomach the alcohol had surged through her bloodstream in a heartbeat.

She unfolded the pashmina she'd brought in case it was chilly. "I'm just...tired," she admitted. "I didn't have time to eat this morning. Dilly needed to hear 'just one more story' before I left. A few more hugs. And Chloe had a million questions about the house." She shuddered. "I think she has some idea to organize my closets while I'm gone. And then there's the office."

"Chloe may be accident-prone but she's smart. She'll get it."

"I know she's smart. That's not her problem." Tess almost told him about Chloe's father, the apparent cause of her low self-esteem, but there was no sense getting into a family discussion, which might lead to a quarrel. Instead, she decided to take Grady's advice. After all, this was supposed to be a holiday for her.

In fact, because most people aboard were also on vacation, a party atmosphere prevailed on the plane—until a groan sounded from nearby.

The cry had come from across the aisle in the same row. The pregnant woman, who'd changed seats earlier and looked to be roughly Chloe and Ethan's age, clutched her swollen abdomen. His expression stricken, her husband met Tess's gaze.

Tess hit the call button for the flight attendant.

"This is our first baby," the man said, patting his wife's hand. "She's not due yet. Our doctor certified she could take this trip. How can she be in labor?"

Tess tried a reassuring smile. "Babies don't always arrive on schedule."

Grady leaned across her. "Ours came early too."

His reminder surprised Tess. Grady was right. In her haste to blame him for not showing up at the hospital in time, she always forgot that Ethan hadn't waited for her due date.

The flight attendant hurried up the aisle.

Tess said, "Would you please page a doctor?" She turned to Grady. "What are the chances with several hundred passengers that one of them practices medicine?"

He lifted an eyebrow. "You're asking me for odds?"

But the flight attendant soon hustled back to them empty-handed. Her announcement hadn't yielded a physician.

"What about diverting the plane to the closest airport?" Grady asked.

Having a limited view from her seat on the aisle, Tess glanced over, but they were still over the rugged mountains, their barren peaks just visible. The woman sitting by the window in their row abandoned her book and said, following

Tess's gaze, "There's nothing down there but rocks, not even roads."

"We're only forty minutes from Cabo," the flight attendant added. "The captain says he'll push it as much as he can."

The woman in labor writhed in her seat, as if trying to find a comfortable spot, but the pain seemed to overwhelm her.

"Breathe, honey," her husband kept saying. Tess recalled that stage with perfect clarity. If you didn't breathe and stay on top of the contractions, the pain controlled you. It was easy to break the rhythm and panic.

"Lay her down across the seats," Grady suggested as the third person in the couple's row got out of the way then headed for an empty seat in the back. "Can we get extra blankets to keep her warm?" The air conditioning system was working overtime, and the cabin did feel cold.

"We no longer carry blankets in Coach," the flight attendant informed him. "I'll try to find one in First."

"No, I've got it." Her queasy stomach forgotten, Tess went down on her knees in the aisle beside the laboring woman with her own pashmina then covered her. "What's your name, sweetie?" she asked as if talking to Chloe.

"Mar...Marnie. Are you a doctor?"

"No, but I'm a mother." Which sounded lame. "And I was there when my granddaughter was born." Not exactly the best credentials, but that was all Tess had—except her experience as the Go-To Girl. Which would have to do. "You'll be fine, don't worry." She didn't dare point out that the baby would be premature. Or that something could indeed go wrong.

"We've taken classes," her husband said.

"You're doing a great job as her coach."

"I'm Ned." He held out a clammy, trembling hand.

"Tess O'Neill."

Grady reached around her to introduce himself as "Tess's husband."

The bizarre scene grew even more strange. A cluster of passengers had gathered in the aisle and some were peeping over the seat backs. Everyone seemed to offer some advice.

"Raise her head."

"No, her feet."

"Give her water."

"Heck, give her some Scotch. Makes a great anesthetic."

"Give her twenty bucks," someone said, "to not have the baby here," and everyone laughed, clearly nervous.

"Please, people," the flight attendant said, "return to your seats."

Tess glanced at Grady. She'd noticed before that his color seemed off, but now he looked even worse. He didn't have experience with imminent childbirth. Grady had been out gambling the night Ethan was born. He'd arrived at the hospital minutes after the premature birth, shame-faced but too late to be part of the action.

Of course, once Grady did arrive, he'd been the very picture of a proud and emotional new father. Tess had the photos to prove it. Maybe she hadn't been quite fair to him all these years.

"You'd better sit down, Grady," she said now.

But to his credit, as Marnie's contractions grew closer together, he moved to support her shoulders. Ned gripped her hand.

The jet, out of the mountains, skimmed over the Sea of Cortez headed for the Cabo airport. It wouldn't be long now, the flight attendant reported, hovering close. Could Marnie hang on until they landed? "Maybe if she crossed her legs..."

"Oh, that'll work," Tess murmured. "She's already in transition."

The primitive urge to push soon followed.

"Showtime," Grady said, his face an interesting shade that Tess could only call puce. Or should that be puke?

Looking equally alarmed by the process, Ned counted breaths and pushes, offering moral support in a quavering voice. Tess stationed herself at the business end. She could see the baby's head now and a sense of excitement rushed through her. She forgot the other passengers, most of whom had taken the flight attendant's advice to return to their seats. From all around she heard concerned murmurs but no more helpful suggestions. The world narrowed for Tess to the expectant parents. "Come on, sweetie...one more."

And all at once, a slippery little human being shot into her waiting hands.

"You did it! Yes!" Tears welled up then streamed down Tess's cheeks. Marnie was crying too. When Tess looked at Grady, his eyes also seemed suspiciously bright. "Marnie, she's beautiful," Tess said. The new father's eyes were brimming as well. "You have a little girl, Ned. Congratulations, you two." She wrapped the baby in the pashmina she'd lent the new mother. Remembering Dilly's birth, Tess met the tiny girl's unfocused blue gaze. "And how are you today, princess? Happy birthday."

The baby was tiny but, to Tess's relief, a healthy pink and breathing on her own. As she began to cry, the news traveled throughout the cabin like a flurry of instant messages on the internet. The flight attendant announced the birth over the PA system, a round of cheers went up, and then, "If we weren't on our initial descent, drinks would be on the house!"

"Virtual champagne," someone called out.

Their pilot had radioed ahead. When the big plane glided down onto the runway between the other mountains near the sea, an ambulance was already waiting on the tarmac. Grady and Tess lingered before following the other passengers being herded toward the terminal by uniformed police.

Tess and Grady waited until Marnie had been loaded onto a gurney, and Ned and their daughter were with her in the van. Tess still felt choked up. At the bottom of the portable steps with the blazing sun high in the sky, and heat shimmering off the pavement, Grady pulled Tess into his arms, holding her tight for a moment before he drew back to gaze into her eyes.

"Good work, babe."

"You too, Doc. It was nothing." No, it was really something.

He grinned, still obviously overcome by the event they'd shared. Maybe the first thing they'd truly shared, except for Dilly's birth, in years. Well, that and often in Tess's fantasies, which Grady didn't know about.

"Wasn't that just the most amazing start to a vacation?" he asked.

"It'll be hard to top," Tess agreed.

A half hour later she felt tempted to change her mind. As she emerged from the terminal, having gotten through Immigration and collected her luggage, Tess was enchanted. The week's weather forecast for Cabo San Lucas was for partly cloudy, but to Tess, who endured the long gray winters in Cincinnati, that seemed relative. The blue sky with only a few high puffs of white looked perfectly clear to her.

The natural environment—a primal joining of mountains, desert, and ocean, two of them in fact, Grady read from a travel guide as they rocketed along the new road from the airport in a cab—was awesome to behold. In its own primitive way, the very scenery at Land's End, the southernmost point of North America, was grand. And oddly sensual.

Once she got over her fear of imminent death on the winding two-lane highway, she began to enjoy herself, as Grady had advised. Never mind that everyone drove like maniacs, and many didn't bother to obey traffic rules.

"Not much out here but cactus and dry wash," Grady murmured. "I like it."

As the car approached the end of the road then merged onto another, Tess caught her breath at her first sight of the blue ocean. Along what was known as the Hotel Corridor between the two towns of Cabo San Lucas and San Jose del Cabo, on either side of this road many resorts were at least partially hidden from view, strewn along the hillsides that sloped down to the sea, but The One and Only Palmilla particularly drew Tess's attention. The tropical landscaping at the five-star vacation spot contained lots of bougainvillea in brilliant hues, which must have taken thousands of gallons of water to maintain in the arid climate where it rained only a few days each year.

As soon as they walked in to the open-air lobby of their own resort, Tess saw a vast expanse of travertine floor amid bold colors, rosy pink and sharp yellow framing a panoramic view of deep blue ocean to the horizon. A staff member handed her a Margarita from a tray as if to say even she had to relax in such a place.

At the front desk Tess did her best to get a second room. But Grady's conference took up the entire venue and the hotel was fully booked. Every few seconds another van or taxi drew up at the broad stone steps leading to the lobby and disgorged another party with mountains of luggage.

"Two beds, then," Tess tried again.

"The *reservacion*, Senora O'Neill, was for one King," the clerk said, eyeing her then Grady. Both had the same surname.

Grady grabbed the folder that held his room key and hers. "One King it is."

"How dare you," she said on the way to the elevators, but she couldn't help but smile at his brashness. Tess wasn't a prude. After all, she and Grady had been married for over twenty years before their divorce. They would have celebrated their silver anniversary soon, something Grady never let her forget.

Now, she hoped, there might be a sofa bed he could sleep on.

A few moments later Tess stood on the threshold of their spacious room. As in the hotel lobby, the sturdy, rough-hewn Mexican furniture lent an authentic air, echoed the audacious yet restful colors of the lobby, and boasted the same gleaming floors that invited her to go barefoot. All that space, the fluffy white duvet and piles of pillows on the huge bed, seemed to beckon Tess. Entranced by the ocean front view, she felt drawn to the balcony like a barnacle to a coral reef. But the low-slung, two-cushioned love seat in the room would be too short for Grady, even for Tess, to sleep on comfortably.

If only they were still together...still happy.

Tess gazed longingly at the king-sized bed. What a waste.

But as she'd unpacked, even the thought of baring her forty-something body to any man was enough to give Tess anxiety. Still, was this the same man she'd once married? Or rather, divorced?

She was no longer sure.

First, Grady had helped her deliver a baby. Now, after an evening welcome reception for his conference, they were strolling through the grounds of the resort, stopping here and there so he could greet people he knew, and it was obvious to Tess that those people respected him.

She heard someone say, "Great to have you back, Grady. Man with your talent shouldn't let that go to waste."

"Good to see you," said an attractive woman in a fetching floor-length print dress. She and Grady exchanged business cards. "Looking forward to your presentation."

As she walked away Grady tucked the card in his pocket, then twined his fingers with Tess's before she could think to stop him. "Ready for dinner?"

Her head was buzzing, but the sensation was pleasant. Earlier she'd downed that Margarita in the lobby and, before that, wine on the plane then more at the cocktail party. Tess needed to put some real food in her stomach. "Feed me before I get the overwhelming urge to sleep." She was a bit jet-lagged from the time change.

He smiled. "You won't be sleeping alone, babe."

"The sofa is all yours," she reminded him though she knew better.

"That over-sized chair with the wooden frame? Not gonna happen."

Tess needed her wits re-sharpened. And yet there was always that temptation, not only to relax here, but to generally give in, to see where she and Grady might go again.

The restaurant at the top of the hilly resort overlooked the dark nighttime sea, and on the horizon Tess could see the glimmer of lights from a ship.

"One of the cruise lines leaving," Grady said, "headed for the mainland of Mexico. We should go sometime."

Tess studied her menu. If she didn't get a grip on herself, she would end up in Grady's bed, in his arms. Disaster. Even though his changes were easier to see here, to believe in, she still couldn't trust him. Old habits died hard.

She focused on a choice of entrées. Normally she would pick the least pricey item on the menu, one of her economy moves since the divorce, but with the Sea of Cortez on the east side of the Cape and the Pacific Ocean on the west, seafood seemed the wisest option. The ocean's bounty was no more apparent, or abundant, than here.

Grady chose Kobe beef from Japan. Exotic and expensive. In her mind, as a gambler he had always been the bigger spender.

As if lulled by the ocean breeze, their conversation drifted from travel to The Go-To Girl and, finally, to Grady's conference.

"I'm sorry we missed the first day—but that panel Ethan was scheduled to be on should be good for us. Show the flag," he said. "I can do some networking. Make more contacts..."

She remembered the people they'd already met, but tensed, unable to stop the small frisson of alarm that shivered down her spine. "Ethan says he's shooting for a partnership."

"By the end of the year, I hope." He sent her a look. "It's possible, Tess."

"I never said it wasn't. You did great years ago before—"

"The cards got the best of me. Ethan knows that, too. Which doesn't seem to frighten *him*."

"It's not his job to keep you on the straight and narrow," she said.

He paused, his fork full of salad. "What's the matter? Can't trust me to do *my* job?"

His edgy tone put Tess on alert again. She didn't want to quarrel. Yet she couldn't seem to stop herself. Maybe as self-protection?

"Grady, I can see that you've changed." She couldn't meet his eyes as she voiced a long-time fear. "But is the change permanent? Maybe some night you'll be at another conference like this but one where there's a casino, and you'll feel the urge to play poker again."

He studied her for a long moment, a hint of temper in his

dark eyes. "So, in your view, I've changed but it won't last. Should I be grateful for an even temporary reprieve?"

"I can't help it, Grady. That's how I feel."

"Well, consider another possibility—there are two sides to any issue." He set his salad aside. "For instance, mine. What about your obsession with shopping?"

"That's not the same. It's my business."

"Now," he agreed. "A few years ago, I would have said you didn't know when to stop. For yourself then, not for someone else. Even when the money wasn't there, and it was *our* money, not yours, to lose. Just like me with poker. What's the difference, Tess?"

The pleasant evening threatened to disintegrate into a full-blown argument. What could she say?

Grady's mouth tightened. "Maybe I gambled sometimes hoping to make up for your spending."

"That is no excuse, Grady."

"No, but it's true. Things got pretty desperate on both our parts." He hesitated. "What if you ran up the credit cards again and couldn't pay them off?"

"I pushed those credit cards to their limits—when you weren't doing the same—because that was the only way I could pay the mortgage after *you* gambled away your pay!"

"Partly," he said, his tone relentless. "But that was then. This is now. What if you couldn't resist 'just one more' trip to Saks? Or Victoria's Secret? For yourself."

"But I can resist," she said, her tone weaker than she intended.

"Don't be too sure. Once an addict, always an addict."

Stung, Tess opted to withdraw. She'd never considered her shopping to be an addiction, like his, but she didn't want to ruin the trip either. For almost a week they'd be sharing a hotel room, if not a bed. "Our food is here. Let's eat, okay?"

After that, Grady's silence was deafening. Deliberately she scrambled to find another topic. Naturally, she chose family.

"Tell me. Did you and Dilly have fun at the zoo last weekend?"

He smiled, although his eyes didn't warm. "Ethan went with us, and between us we managed to get her on the elephant ride."

Tess dug into her sea bass. "I'm impressed. She's always been afraid."

"Dilly's not afraid of anything," he said, as if to contrast their granddaughter with Tess. "At least not anymore. We created a monster. She stood in line three times. After the first Ethan claimed he had vertigo and could ride with her only once."

"How was it?" Tess asked, guessing Grady had gone with Dilly.

"Rocky. But the kid never noticed." His reluctant smile grew. "Wait till you see the pictures. I don't think I've had that much fun—until I walked onto the plane today and saw you sitting there." He was trying to make peace, letting her know he was no longer angry.

"Grady."

"See, Tess? We can get along, if we try."

"If we stick to *safe* subjects," she said. "Like Dilly."

Grady didn't comment. He focused on his steak and polished off the bottle of wine they'd ordered. It didn't seem to affect him as it did Tess.

"Ethan and Chloe can manage too," he said at last with a frown. "I hope they're having that deep-hearted talk he promised."

Tess had the same hope, but it didn't seem wise to contribute her opinion. Too close to the other minefield of their own broken marriage, and Tess clung to their tentative truce.

For dessert two cups of rich, dark coffee arrived with a tiramisu to share. As if he wanted to apologize for his harsh words about Tess and shopping, Grady offered the first fork full to her mouth. When she felt the lush blend of coffee, chocolate and thick whipped cream touch her tongue, even the added alcohol couldn't make her refuse the treat. She finished her half with a sigh of pleasure.

Grady's eyes darkened.

"That's my girl. Ready?" The question held more this time than a simple need to know if she was done with their meal, which made Tess remember her resolve not to get naked with him.

"Yes." The bill lay on the table and, hoping he wouldn't see the flush in her cheeks, Tess reached for it. She often picked up the tab for clients, for Merry, for Chloe. With Larry she didn't even have to think before she paid.

"No," Grady said, "let me."

She held the leather restaurant folder aloft so he couldn't grab it. "That's okay. I've got it."

His gaze deepened another shade. She could see fresh anger though his tone stayed deceptively mild.

"You think I can't pay?"

Tess rolled her eyes. "Don't get macho. You refused to let me pay half for the room so why shouldn't I pick up a few meals?"

"You think I *can't* pay." This time it wasn't a question.

"Grady, don't make a big deal of this." She took out her credit card, opened the folder then stared at the check. The sum looked huge. Then she realized the total was in pesos. "With the exchange rate—this would be $120 not $1200?"

"Something like that. Give it to me, Tess."

She shook her head. It seemed important to let him know that she would remain independent, in and out of bed, even for this one week. "My treat. I insist."

"*Dammit*, I said hand it over." Without warning, he snatched the folder. He slapped her credit card on the table between them then whipped out his instead with a gleam of triumph in his eyes. "My AmEx trumps your Visa."

Tess grabbed her card then rose from her chair. A couple was staring at them from a nearby table.

"You're drawing attention. I should have known this wouldn't work."

She didn't wait for Grady. Driven by her own need to escape from a confusing mix of feelings, she stalked from the restaurant out into the balmy night. Grady soon caught up with her.

"What are you doing? You left your credit card," she said. There hadn't been enough time for the waiter to return it.

"I signed dinner to the room instead. Right now—"

"Don't," Tess warned him. Feeling miserable, she increased her pace, but he was taller, faster, and before she knew it, he had lightly grasped her arm.

In the middle of the lush gardens that wound through the resort, with the scent of the ocean and the sound of its waves in the distance, and no one else around, he gently nudged her up against a stone retaining wall. Tess felt its lingering warmth from the daytime sun through her light summer dress. And Grady felt so good, so warm. How could they quarrel in such a beautiful place?

"You're being unreasonable, Tess. No surprise there. Why else would you turn a pleasant meal into a power struggle? Impugn my ability to take you out to *dinner*? As if I live on handouts. Make me feel like a...damn *loser*?"

Tess remembered his lifelong sense of inadequacy. In Grady's mind his two brothers, the whiz kids, never failed. She shouldn't add to that, but he was standing way too close... Her voice shook.

"I think that's your problem, not mine."

His grip loosened. He stared down at the path between them. "Hell, maybe it is."

Startled, Tess made her own concession. In the restaurant she'd felt small and petty. Ethan kept telling her how hard Grady was trying to redeem himself, and as Grady had said, she wasn't exactly blameless either.

"Maybe I did have a little problem myself," she admitted, "buying some item I didn't really need. With money I—we—didn't have. I was like a bird pecking at a shiny thing. Loving the way it looked." She hesitated then said, "The way it made me feel."

"Like you could afford it. Like me with poker," he murmured.

She nearly whispered the truth. "We both made mistakes, Grady."

"Ah, Tess." He rested his forehead against hers, his eyes briefly closed. "How did we go so wrong? Why didn't we love each other enough? We could have conquered our problems together."

"Maybe not...then," she added. A light shiver ran down her spine. The warmth of the stone wall couldn't prevent the cold that touched her deep inside. Made her say the words she'd hidden, even from herself, for too long. "I didn't *want* to leave you, Grady."

She heard him swallow. "I didn't want you to go."

Somewhere in the distance the shush of the surf was overlaid with the haunting strains of a poignant song being played on a guitar. A man sang in Spanish, probably at the patio restaurant on the next level down of the hillside resort.

"He's serenading us," she murmured, her throat tight.

"Wonder what he's saying."

Tess raised a hand to his warm cheek, felt the faint scratchiness of his five o'clock shadow. She loved that rugged look, loved the growing darkness in his eyes.

"You know what he's saying." She felt reckless. "So do I. It's universal. A love song."

With a murmur of assent, he turned his head to plant a soft kiss in her palm. Then Grady drew her hand down to mesh with his warm fingers and pulled her closer. He looked at her, hopeful but clearly hesitant to risk the next step, which wasn't typical of Grady.

"Remember how I kissed you after the Fortini party? How hard it was to stop when you wouldn't come home with me?"

"Yes," she said. "I...didn't want to stop either, Grady."

"Then trust me now, Tess." He held her face in his hands and kissed her.

Tess felt the thrill of desire from the roots of her hair to the tips of her toes. She'd been feeling it all day and possibly for some time. Would she never forget? Maybe...just maybe she didn't need to. In another second, she had her arms wound around his neck, wanting, clinging, kissing. At this moment she couldn't seem to remember their bad times. Within seconds the touch of his tongue, the warmth of his mouth, turned her soft and weak with need. Like one of her If Onlys becoming real.

The heat of his body.

But did she dare surrender? Tess pulled back. Gray seemed to radiate heat.

"You're much too warm," she said, playing for time.

He shook his head. "Hot." He meant for Tess.

She touched his face, tested as she might have with Dilly or, years ago, with Ethan. "You were pale on the plane, but now you're flushed."

"I got some sun this afternoon." He nibbled his way along the arch of her throat to the indentation at her collarbone.

Tess resisted the shiver of awareness. "Have you taken your medicine?"

"I'm fine." He added, "Done."

She did a quick mental calculation. He should have more doses left. "You took *all* of the antibiotic?"

"Finished." He avoided her gaze.

Her tone turned suspicious. "You had wine tonight. And on the plane." He'd told her he couldn't drink alcohol with the drug. "You stopped the pills."

"Side effects," he mumbled, working the top button on Tess's dress. "Didn't seem smart to add them to the change of food and water here. Or we wouldn't be having this conversation. I don't need Montezuma's Revenge."

"Grady, what if the infection isn't gone? Just because you feel better—"

"Stop fussing, Tess. You sound like a..." He smiled. "... wife. I'm not getting sick in this place." End of discussion. "You're deliberately ruining the mood. And don't think I can't figure out why you started that fight in the restaurant. It was a perfect way to avoid climbing into bed with me. Could we concentrate, please, on just making each other feel good?"

She planted a soft kiss on the top of his head. He was right about the quarrel. "Yes, but—"

"Look. If I need more medicine, there's always the *pharmacia*. You can get anything here over the counter. Antibiotics, cholesterol busters, Viagra..."

Tess wasn't satisfied, so to speak, but she let it go.

"As if you need that," she said, knowing she'd run out of excuses not to go upstairs with him. He was right about that big bed—which had been her thought too—and Grady was too hot, but in several ways. Maybe she did need to stay close tonight. Later, she would find a thermometer, take his temperature.

And who are you fooling, Tess O'Neill?

"That bed's still waiting in our room," he said against her lips. "Be a real shame to squander the opportunity."

"You've got me there." She leaned into him, taking more. And then more.

By the time they pulled apart at last, alerted by the approach of another couple in the garden, they were both breathing hard.

Lightly, Grady brushed away tears she hadn't known were on her cheeks. "It'll be all right, Tess. I promise. I won't hurt you again."

He meant his gambling. The loss of her trust. What could she do but give him that, if only for tonight?

"What happens in Cabo, stays in Cabo," he whispered, his mouth pressed to the tender skin beneath her ear.

With a shaky laugh she laid her head on his shoulder. He felt solid, and, oh, yes, warm, and, above all, here.

"I guess so. Yes," she said.

"Then what do you say? Sex with your ex?"

There was no other answer. Maybe there never had been.

"*Yes*, Grady."

10

I T's true what people say. Sex is like riding a bicycle.

Tess hadn't forgotten how, and neither had Grady.

Which was part of the problem. Grady was worn out. The next morning, while he slept late, Tess went shopping. In times of turmoil a good retail therapy session helped to ease her mind. Not that she intended to overspend. She'd buy a few souvenirs, a locally made toy for Dilly....

Tess stood at the jewelry counter on the resort's mezza-nine level of hotel shops, staring at a display of glittering fire opals, and silently fretted. Last night she and Grady had barely made it up the stairs from the gardens to the bank of elevators. When the doors slid open at their floor they'd scarcely managed to walk to their room, kissing all the way. Certainly, they hadn't made it to the bed.

By then his heat was all around her, fire in his eyes like the gems now on display in the shop window.

In the hotel roomTess had tried once more to stall for time.

"I don't look...I'm not the same," she said. Standing against a wall in the darkened garden with her clothes on was different from undressing for Grady, letting him see her changes. "Cellulite," she muttered.

"You think I care?" He drew back to study her then gestured at himself. "No more six-pack abs, babe. Marshmallows."

"That's not true." Grady still had a beautiful body. She could see that his work kept him fit, and hard. He leaned into her, showing her just how much.

"I love..." *You*, she feared he'd say but he didn't. "...your shoulders, your breasts, always a personal favorite—"

"My not-quite-narrow waist?"

"—that little flare of your hips. The way they twitch when you walk. Drives me crazy, Tess."

"What about the rest of these stubborn extra pounds I can't seem to lose?"

"Don't. You sound like Chloe. Any difference I can see," he went on, "just makes you more of a woman. Any changes are from having Ethan, the son you gave me."

Tess blinked at his sweet words of acceptance. If he didn't care that her body had changed, and not for the better, then maybe she shouldn't either.

Still...

When he undid her last button and was spreading the front of her dress wide, her nipple hardened into a wet pearl and she couldn't help asking, "Do you have protection?"

"I'm a real Boy Scout," he murmured. "Ever hopeful where you're concerned," not that he'd been expecting her to join him in Cabo. Tess wondered how long he'd been carrying a condom around.

But then, lost, she'd stopped wondering. And finding excuses.

Even now, the next morning, the very familiarity of their remembered lovemaking was enough to turn her face bright red. Thank goodness the sales clerk was in the rear of the store and couldn't see her. Tess's whole body tingled from the memory of Grady's touch.

"Come on," he had whispered in her ear. "Just you and me," his erection pressed, hard, against the juncture of her thighs. And Tess turned soft, pliant, like Dilly's Play-Doh in his hands.

"Oh, Grady."

His voice grew husky, pleading. "Don't make me stop this time."

Her first orgasm had come—so to speak—almost before they landed on the marble floor of the room. With the mere brush of his fingers her second followed almost without a pause. By the time Grady stripped off the rest of his clothes then covered her, entered her, Tess was already peaking again, quivering.

This morning it didn't seem quite as easy to tell herself that Grady was the wrong man for her. It wouldn't be difficult to convince herself that their divorce had never happened, that she and Grady loved and laughed and still lived together in their little Cape-style house.

She had trouble reminding herself that she couldn't trust him for more than one night. Despite their divorce, as Merry had insisted, Tess cared for him. Still, for her own good she had to try again to keep her distance.

With a frustrated sigh she turned away from the opals, dozens of them sparkling a clear, bright orange-apricot in the morning light. If she had her mind on something other than Grady, lying warm—too warm?—and asleep upstairs in bed, she wouldn't be able to resist buying just one gem. That little pendant set in gold, for instance. Or the beautiful pair of earrings that glittered in the corner of the display case. But for once, she felt no desire to buy—even, this time, for herself.

Better to remember that she and Grady were quits. Sex—

last night, all night—had been only a physical act. Not to be repeated. No need to feel guilty. They were both consenting adults. Never mind the remembered feel of Grady's fingers on her breast, his lips on hers, the low, endless groan he'd uttered.

Weren't more than twenty years of an often-difficult marriage enough?

Like her mother's?

A sudden flash of a different memory took Tess by surprise.

Larry. Stumbling into the darkened house at night, tripping over Tess's toys on the floor. Cursing. Waking up Tess and her mother. Shouting. Telling them they would have to move again, that he'd lost his job. Blaming everyone but himself. No wonder a man needed to drink a few beers, play a few hands of poker or Blackjack. He'd lost, of course.

Tess remembered hiding on the stairs, hearing her mother, weeping. Trying her best to calm him, to reassure him that they would, somehow, manage. Larry would find another job. He'd had a hundred of them over the years— until his latest employer would decide he was unreliable, undependable, and certainly expendable. Then let him go.

Tess blinked. The past was a good teacher. Whatever had possessed her to fall into bed again last night with her ex-husband? Taking a final look at the shimmering opals in the case, she left the store and wandered back to the room.

On her way she intended to buy a thermometer but forgot as she rehearsed her lines for Grady. It would be better for her to find another hotel, to let him complete his conference without her. The extra money she would need to spend on a room would hurt her house fund, which had a habit of shrinking rather than growing, or maybe she should go home early, but in either case it wasn't fair of Tess to let Grady keep believing they could have another chance.

To make sure she got the same message, Tess stopped in the hallway outside their door and stared at her third finger, left hand. Thanks to hours of jogging around the neighborhood with the cats, she was actually five, maybe six pounds lighter. Her clothes did fit a bit better, and her stomach was getting flatter. Even her fingers looked slimmer. The sight of her naked forty-something body hadn't turned Grady off last night. This morning she felt womanly, sensual again. But still, it was time. Taking a determined breath, she twisted the gold wedding band on her hand, tugging at it until finally, after far too many years of wearing this reminder of Grady's love, she removed it.

A sudden wave of sorrow pulled at her heart.

Tess pressed her lips tight. Her pulse thudded in her ears. Well, it was done. She slipped the ring into her pocket, unlocked the door, then entered the room.

At first, she didn't see Grady. To her surprise he wasn't in bed where she'd left him, and she didn't hear the shower running. Still, when she poked her head into the bathroom, the air felt warm and humid. She turned back into the bedroom—and saw Grady wearing nothing but a towel and a big smile.

He shut the closet door, a shirt and pants in his hands.

"Hey, babe. Where'd you go?"

"Out." She couldn't say *shopping*. She hadn't even bought the thermometer. "You were still sleeping..." She meant to say *sleeping off last night*, but the words didn't come out. Tess stared at his broad, bare chest, the dark silky line of hair that trailed from his pectoral muscles down his front to the white towel slung low on his hips.

Her mouth went dry. Fingers twitching, she felt for the gold band in her pocket, then hastily pulled out her hand, and Grady's eyes tracked both motions. As if to chide her about the ring, which he couldn't see, his smile turned into a cheeky, very sexy grin.

Tess couldn't speak. What had happened to her plan to straighten him out on their relationship? The darkening expression in his eyes reminded her of the night before, every moment of a night to remember. And promised more.

He ran a sun-browned hand over his jaw. While she was gone, he'd shaved and showered, and he smelled like Aramis, her favorite men's cologne. Because Grady wore it?

He strolled toward her.

The tingling all through her body hadn't lessened. To her discomfort it only grew stronger with his every step.

Inches away from Tess, Grady stopped. The white towel edged even lower on his lean hips and Tess couldn't help it. Her pulse sped into higher gear, like the crazy traffic along the Corridor highway, and before she knew what had happened Grady had drawn the ring from her pocket.

Obviously, he'd noticed her bare finger. Recalled that she'd been wearing the band the night before.

"What's this?" he said softly, holding it up. "Morning-after regrets?"

She cleared her throat. "Something like that. Grady—"

His grin slipped a little, then firmed again and grew lazy, sure of itself. Of him.

"Waste of time, Tess," he murmured, all sheer male confidence.

He drew her close, put his arms around her. His skin was still damp from his shower, and warm. Too warm, she thought again with a slight frown.

"Grady, this isn't smart. I can't deny last night was...nice—" a huge understatement— "but we have separate lives now."

He frowned. "You seeing someone else? Since the Fortini dinner?"

"Well, no..." She couldn't lie.

"Me either. So, what's the problem?"

Taking his time, he turned to set the ring on the stone dresser top, the band's burnished gold gleaming in the morning sun through the windows. Like another reminder of all the years they'd shared.

"You think you can wipe away what we had—all we did here last night—by taking this off? Why now, four years later? I have my theory about that, Tess Trueheart." He paused. "I also have a no-return policy."

And with a flick of his tanned fingers, the towel fell away. Along with Tess's resolve. She couldn't help but realize the truth of what he'd said.

What happens in Cabo stays in Cabo.

A t six o'clock, after his last meeting of the day, Grady walked back into his room to find Tess seated at her computer in a cotton sundress the color of the sea outside the windows.

She was the brightest spot in his already stellar day. He had come to the conference determined to make contacts, though he didn't have high hopes of doing business in Mexico. The conference was well worth the money to attend, but this country seemed to operate, as it traditionally had, on whom you knew and how you were connected. Grady was just glad to have made contacts that might bear fruit in the U.S.

And he had learned plenty. His presentation in Ethan's place had gone so well that Grady was then asked to take part in the panel discussion as well. His knowledge of the best mix of sand and cement to make concrete was well received by both the locals and people from the States. For once he didn't feel dim-witted, or "slow on the uptake," as his brothers might say.

And for Grady the pleasure factor in this room worked equally fine.

His only regret was that, because Tess wasn't registered at the conference, she hadn't been able to hear him speak.

At the end of the day he was limping a little. His foot ached, and he felt slightly dizzy, which was new. He also had a nagging pain centered not far from his groin. Too much sex? This morning, after he'd dropped his towel, he and Tess had skipped a late breakfast. They'd almost skipped the entire day, his conference, and stayed in bed to make love again— except that Tess had wanted to sightsee until his meetings were scheduled. He'd wondered if it was another attempt for her at self-protection.

After telling himself to be patient, they'd taken a cab twenty-some miles from the resort into Cabo San Lucas where he saw bars on every street corner and more than a few in between. Grady had long since outgrown his party years, so places like The Giggling Marlin and The Nowhere Bar didn't appeal to him, but at the famed Cabo Wabo Cantina, he and Tess each bought a blue bottle of the house tequila. They'd then toured the many silver shops nearby where to his surprise Tess didn't buy anything. Shopping or The Go-To Girl didn't seem to be on her mind.

His fault? He hoped.

Maybe their lovemaking that morning had indeed sapped his energy. Not to mention the long walk in the sun around the Cabo marina to ogle the expensive yachts, their leisurely lunch beside the water, and the taxi boat ride by *panga* out to the Arch, the rocks carved by water into that shape at land's end. By then Grady felt like one of the lazy sea lions they'd seen lounging on the rocks. He and Tess had even taken a stroll there on Lovers Beach, which absolutely required a few kisses. No wonder he felt tired now, even a little washed out. His foot hurt worse than it had earlier. He wouldn't tell Tess that, though. She would fuss over him again like the caring woman she was.

Instead, now in their hotel room he stepped closer to the computer, bent low to nuzzle her neck and saw she was checking her e-mail. She reached back to touch his hair.

"Hi. I'll only be a minute," she said. "Look at this."

He saw a picture of a red-faced baby. "Ned and Marnie's?"

"Amy Theresa." He heard the note of pride in Tess's voice, the threat of tears. "I would have told her I'm not really Theresa, but wasn't that sweet? I have a namesake. Marnie says they're doing fine. Ned, too. I'm so glad we exchanged contact information before the ambulance left the airport."

As if to evade her feelings, she exited the post then opened a message from Chloe. Grady smiled. He felt better already. They were actually talking, enjoying each other's company in and out of bed. "What's going on at home?"

She arched her neck to give him better access to her throat. His hands roamed over her breasts, lightly kneading them through her silky cotton dress.

Tess moaned. "She and Ethan are 'negotiating.' That sounds positive."

"Um," he agreed, all too willing at the moment to let Ethan and Chloe settle their own differences. "I made us a seven-thirty reservation in San Jose. Restaurant's right on the beach. Thought you might like to see the opposite end of the Cape before we leave. The town is quiet, historic. Sound good?"

"Hmm," Tess agreed, sounding more relaxed than she had in years.

"Tell me. Just how far are you from Cincinnati?"

"Right now, I could be on another planet."

Grady kissed his favorite spot beneath her ear. The fact that she didn't resist, or pull away, made him happy—even if she was no longer wearing his ring. That could change. His hands eased away from her breasts. "Pretty dress. You look ready." He didn't have to say for what else beyond dinner.

"I spent an hour in the sun during your talk. I think I got some tan."

"You always glow," he murmured.

"Flattery will get you anywhere." She closed Chloe's post then paused at the next message in her inbox. "How did your presentation go?"

"Great." Grady glanced at the screen. He didn't recognize the e-mail address but obviously Tess did. The subject line read: *Tempted Now?* That caught his attention and his pulse jerked. He reminded himself that she'd told him she wasn't seeing anyone. "Go ahead. Open it, Tess. Don't mind me."

But he couldn't look away. He had a bad feeling.

The brief message seemed cryptic: *About the house you like. Let's talk.*

The one-word signature line rocked Grady back on his heels. He knew only one person with that name.

"Emery *Shallowford?*"

Her body tensed. "I've done some work for him."

"Me too," Grady muttered, remembering the Fortini dinner and the way Emery had looked at Tess. "Didn't know you and he were pen pals. He's a married man," he reminded her. "What's this about a house?" He knew Tess's dream was to buy a home again. Just for herself. Or did she want company now, and it wasn't his?

"Emery's wife is a Realtor. They've helped me find a property." She clicked on the attachment. "See? It's only a couple of blocks from my rental. Problem was I couldn't afford it. But Emery says the sellers have just lowered the price."

"Sure sounds like *he* has an offer."

She turned her head to look at him. "Are you jealous? Of Emery Shallowford? You can't be serious."

"He's the biggest player in Cincinnati."

"He appears to be," she corrected him.

"I've seen him with women, Theresa."

"I have too," she said.

"I saw him with you at P.F. Chang's."

"I can take care of myself, Grady. And I've told him his style can only hurt Sybil. Besides, it's not as if you and I aren't divorced."

Grady ground his teeth. "It's not as if you and I didn't spend part of the past twenty-four hours in bed together."

She practically crowed. "You are jealous!"

He sighed. "Tess, Shallowford and I go way back. You know that. Be careful. Bet you dollars to doughnuts—"

"Whatever that means."

"—he's just using you. To tick me off."

"*Using* me? Thanks so much—as if I couldn't possibly be attractive in any way to another man. Grady, your problems with Emery are between you and him. I had—have—nothing to do with that."

"Think so? I bet he'd love to throw a monkey wrench in my life again. He's never forgotten how I screwed him on that patio business. He does conveniently forget, however, that I made good on it."

"I didn't know that," she said.

"Yeah, I did, but he still used his position in Cincy as the great neurosurgeon to spread the word all over town that I couldn't be trusted. Sound familiar?" he asked her. "I lost so much business that year, it's no wonder I went under."

"You went under because you were gambling!"

His jaw tightened. "Like Larry, I suppose."

"Exactly. If I hadn't started the Go-To Girl I don't know what I would have done. I had no other way to pay our debts —the ones assigned to me in the divorce settlement—but that wasn't Emery's fault."

"He sure didn't help." Grady stepped back and walked to

the window. He stared out at the sea. The sky toward the horizon was a deep, cerulean blue and closer to the hotel a rich teal color like Tess's dress. There were no clouds overhead. As the sun started to sink, he could see a pale crescent of moon already rising. In a couple of hours, the stars would come out. Millions of them. A balmy breeze wafted up from the beach through the open window. A beautiful evening lay ahead—unless they continued to quarrel and ended up ruining the whole damn week. Yet he couldn't stop himself.

"I'm sure *Emery* would love to poke another sharp stick in my eye. And what better weapon than to use my wife?"

"Ex-wife. You think he's taking another opportunity for revenge with me? How? By being nice? That doesn't make sense, Grady."

Damn straight, but he was mad now. And, oddly enough, hurt. When he turned from the window, his foot pulsed harder with every heartbeat.

Tess punched a key and the computer screen went blank. "Thanks for letting me use your laptop. I'm ready for dinner now."

Grady blinked. His appetite had disappeared, but Tess was letting him off the hook again. When she took her pashmina off the bed, what else could he do? He draped it around her slim shoulders like an apology. Though he still wondered what Emery Shallowford was really up to.

At the beachfront restaurant, Grady asked for a corner table on the terrace away from the bar and at the opposite end from a noisy wedding reception that threatened to depress him. So much for the romantic evening he'd hoped for with Tess. Still, she didn't seem inclined to take their argument up again, for which he was grateful.

The Chilean pinot grigio Grady ordered slid easily down his dry throat. After a while his foot even stopped hurting. The soft cushions of the banquette where he sat close beside

Tess, and her nearness, almost made him forget Shallowford. The food restored his appetite.

"That was delicious," Tess said of her now-finished shrimp and pasta.

He smiled, his shoulder pressed to hers. Their contact felt even warmer and more thrilling than it had on the plane. "No argument tonight about who pays the bill?"

"I bow to your excellent credit."

Not that excellent yet, but he could handle the bill.

Leaving the terrace, they stepped down onto the beach for a walk on the sand, enjoying the warm night and the ever-growing display of stars overhead without feeling the need to talk. Then, in a taxi they drove through town, past the old square of the historic village, some souvenir shops, a rooftop sports bar, and even a French bakery.

Hoping he hadn't blown things between them, Grady held Tess's hand on the way home. In spite of the Shallowford incident, tonight seemed like many other nights back in the day when he and Tess had gone out together, leaving Ethan home with a sitter. Date nights, she'd called them then. Afterward they'd always made love, feeling like newlyweds.

At the hotel Grady guided Tess up to their room with a hand at the small of her mostly bare back. Her skin felt cool under his fingers. His head felt muzzy—from the wine and her?

They didn't speak. Words would have ruined the mood.

Inside the room Grady dropped the key card on a table, opened the draperies the turn-down maid had closed, and drew Tess out onto the balcony. The stars sparkled in the black sky. The breeze wafted across his hot face, drifted along his heated body. He sank down on the navy cushions of a teak deck chair with a sigh, tired, sated from food, and more than a little dizzy from Tess, he told himself.

He held out a hand to her.

To his delight she didn't hesitate. He pulled Tess down to straddle him, and she nestled against his body, her chest to his chest, her kiss welcoming.

"You are a wicked man."

"The best kind."

If he stayed lucky that ring would be on her finger again before their plane left Cabo. He wound his hands through her hair, and their kisses grew deeper, like the heat that rose from Grady's body. His hands strayed from her silken tresses to the halter tie of her blue sundress. He toyed with the knot, then, without untying it, moved on to slide his hands along her smooth shoulders.

He was floating on the high, as if they were on that honeymoon they'd never been able to afford. He wanted this moment never to change, or to end.

Then, like a dream come true, she wound her arms around his neck, set her mouth to his again and took him to paradise.

T ess woke much later in bed with tears in her eyes. She lay draped over Grady, feeling as boneless as he must with satisfaction, and the stars were out, but to her surprise he was fast asleep. For a moment she pressed her cheek to his chest, listening to the steady beat of his heart, listening to the sound of his soft snores.

Not exactly romantic, that part, but she could live on the memories of their lovemaking on the balcony for a long time...

G rady toyed again with the halter tie of her blue sundress. He untied it at last, no longer teasing, his fingers fumbling just enough to show Tess he felt as she did, a little hesitant to go on, a little afraid not to try. Then his index finger slipped inside the front of her *dress, his hand played with her breasts until she kissed him back again. With his other hand he pressed her closer until no space remained between their bodies, until Tess finally moaned into his mouth.*

Grady returned the favor. "Ah, this is what we do best."

He eased her legs apart, then farther still, and she pressed Grady deeper into the chair. His fingers trailed along the outside of her skirt, then up under its hem and the slim, sleek skin of her inner thighs to the heart of her. And found her bare. He stopped.

"Jesus, Tess. You went to dinner like this?"

"Commando. Just for you."

He groaned. "God, shoot me. I'll die a happy man."

"Don't die just yet," she said, her tone a silken purr in his ear.

Heaven.

Absolute heaven...

Tess sat up, jostling Grady but not enough to wake him. He slept on, oblivious of her tangled thoughts, the memories. After the Fortini party, she'd experienced a similar fantasy that had happened in part but not completely. She'd yearned then for the rest. This time she couldn't deny the closeness of his body, the beat of his heart. Tonight, making love with Grady had been real—not one of her If Onlys. And much better than any fantasy of what might have been.

The reality scared her.

If only she could risk taking another chance on happily ever after.

The next morning Grady was still asleep when Tess got up.

For a long moment she stood over him. He seemed to sleep a lot. Had she worn him out again? The dark shadow of beard along his well-defined jaw and across his lean cheeks softened her smile. His broad shoulders, bared and gleaming in the diffused light of the room with the draperies drawn, made her own heart beat faster. Was he sleeping too much?

She bent closer. Grady had a noon conference workshop to attend, but he hadn't stirred. Not a single well-toned muscle moved. Even his long legs, which sometimes jerked in his sleep, as if he were running, lay still. His breathing was so quiet Tess had to lean even nearer to detect the shallow rise and fall of his chest. Or thought she did. A flash of panic made her straighten.

"Grady?" she said softly.

He didn't react.

"Grady."

Still nothing.

She shook his shoulder. "*Grady, wake up.*"

Tess started to worry.

There was plenty to be said for *sex with an ex* but, like her, Grady wasn't in his twenties. Like a lot of men his age, he didn't always take good care of his physical health. Hadn't Tess forced him to visit the twenty-four-hour clinic in Ohio for that antibiotic prescription?

Pills he hadn't bothered to finish.

And who knew how strong his heart was at forty-six?

She grasped his shoulder, harder. Jiggled him again with no response.

Was he really breathing? She couldn't tell. What if he'd suffered a coronary after lovemaking? With her heart in her throat, she pressed her ear to his chest.

And heard...*nothing?*

Tess stiffened. Perspiration trickled down the valley of her breasts into her scoop-necked nightgown. What had she done to her ex-husband?

"My God. I've killed him!"

❧ 11 ❧

WITH A MOAN GRADY ROLLED OVER, drawn from uncon-
sciousness by the sound of Tess's voice calling his name.

He wasn't dead.

He just wasn't sure he was alive.

The world seemed to drift in and out, to come at him in
waves, like the pounding surf below the bedroom windows.
People—no, just Tess—spoke in sentences he didn't fully
understand.

"Grady!" Her voice hovered over him, full of concern.

He smiled a little or thought he did. "Hey." He tried to lift
a hand, beckoning her to come closer, to climb in bed beside
him. "Some night."

Grady might think he *had* died then and gone to heaven.
But for some reason he couldn't quite think at all. Good thing
he could still feel, though. On the darkened balcony last
night, in the deck chair with Tess's warm body touching his
from chest to knees, he'd definitely felt weak too, but hey, no
problem. That kind of kick had been missing from his life for
far too long.

Tess's mouth, that shallow indentation of her navel that

he'd always loved, the glide and flow of their bodies together later in bed—*together*, again—would be enough to kill any man. He couldn't seem to wake up to tell her he wanted more.

Grady cracked one eye.

"Thank God," she said, sounding about to cry. "You're alive!"

His eyelid felt heavy and dropped down again to shield the world from view. Not enough sleep, that was his problem. A few more hours and...

Wasn't he supposed to be somewhere? Across town to meet with a developer, or to grab a quick lunch with one of his suppliers?

The vague memory from his calendar refused to gel. Maybe he did need one of those smart phones instead of a basic model, as Ethan kept telling him.

Grady kicked off the covers. The white duvet weighed heavily on his legs, his chest, and he was sweating as if he'd climbed a ten-story scaffold in the hot summer sun. Underneath him, the sheets felt damp. But wait. He wasn't in his apartment in Cincinnati.

"Where...am I?" he managed to ask.

"Mexico," Tess answered, which only confused Grady more.

What was he doing in a foreign country? Were he and Tess really on their honeymoon?

A series of visions flashed through his foggy brain: Tess, wrapped around him like a warm blanket in the middle of the night. Tess, begging for release. Tess in the shower at three a.m., her smooth skin lightly tanned now, slick with soap as Grady spread the rich lather, smelling of lavender, all over her body. Tess, moaning against the marble wall. Tess...his bride?

But, no. Ethan was grown now, a family man himself and... Dilly, he suddenly remembered his granddaughter. Then,

Chloe. That reality jarred him too, but the memory of Tess and what they'd done together again, with perfect recall after so many years, refused to fade.

A cool hand touched his forehead. "I knew it," she said. "Last night you felt like a wood stove going full tilt. The night before that, too. I should have dragged you to a *pharmacia*. You have a fever, Grady."

"No way."

"You should have finished those pills from home."

"Rather...finish you," he said, eyes still closed, and probably a stupid grin on his mouth. He wanted to say *Get in here*, but nothing came out. A strange darkness kept rolling in around the edges of his vision. His joints ached. Hot one minute, he felt frozen the next.

She trailed a shaky hand along his stubbled cheek then disappeared. Grady heard receding footsteps. "I'm going to find a doctor."

"No," he called out, but she ignored him. Or had he even spoken aloud?

In any case Tess wasn't likely to join him under the duvet any time soon. Maybe last night and the night before hadn't really happened.

Maybe he'd only imagined...

The surf below the windows lashed against the sand, the sound lulling him into some other plane of existence where place and time and life itself didn't matter. The darkness sucked him back down as if he were caught in the riptide that all those black flags posted on the beach cautioned swimmers about, back into a world where he didn't know how, or even whether, to exist.

. . .

Tess spent a frantic few minutes on the phone. If she understood the person at the front desk, whose English wasn't perfect, the resort had a doctor on call who might make a house, or rather, a room call shortly.

Tess hung up then cast a still-anxious glance toward the bathroom where Grady was taking a shower. Some hot water and an aspirin would cure him in no time, he'd claimed after Tess finally prodded him awake again. But he wasn't singing some off-key rendition of an old pop classic ballad—his usual —and the silence, except for the rush of water, jangled her nerves.

"Grady?" She pressed her cheek against the bathroom door. "Maybe you should come out. Too much hot water could spike your temperature."

"Don't have one."

Tess gritted her teeth. He wasn't thinking straight. Despite her relief that he was, indeed, alive, no miraculous recovery seemed imminent. Despite the eighty-degree day outside, he'd been shivering when he stepped into the shower. His forehead had felt as hot as a griddle.

Stranded, she thought—even in a high-end resort—thousands of miles from home.

"Grady?" she called again. What if he passed out in the shower?

To her relief the water shut off. A minute later he stepped out of the now-steamy bathroom, holding a white towel, and whipped it around his hips as he had the first morning. Not before Tess had gotten a good view of his very appealing body in all its male glory. "You did that on purpose."

He gave her a weak grin, his eyes not quite focused.

"I've called a doctor," she said. "He should be here soon."

He frowned. "Tess, I'm fine. Hungover, maybe, but other than that—"

177

"You're lying." His cheeks had cherry-red patches, and from two feet away she could feel the heat radiating from him. When he took a step, he winced.

His grin tilted. "Worried about me?"

Her chin quivered. "Of course I am."

"After the last couple of nights, I guess that *is* reasonable." He stepped closer, and so did the heat. "We did more than okay, babe. If that's still between us, so is a lot of other stuff." He cupped her face. His hands burned her skin, and Tess blinked rapidly. They weren't talking about the same thing now.

What did she do with a sick man who would refuse the only help she could offer? She'd never felt so alone, helpless. For several years she'd relied solely on herself. Her business was to find solutions for other people's problems, if not medical ones, but how to help Grady now? What if the doctor never came? Or the front desk hadn't understood the urgency of the problem? What if Tess hadn't made herself clear?

Grady stared for a long moment into her eyes, his gaze with that faintly glazed expression she had come to know. Suddenly he tightened his hold on her, as if to keep himself upright.

He rested his forehead against hers, and Tess felt the blast-furnace heat rising from his skin. He started to shake, as weak as a proverbial kitten—except for the two cats Tess owned, which weren't weak at all.

"Know something?" His voice rasped in the stillness. "I don't feel so good."

Well, at least he'd made a major admission.

Tess held him tighter, comforting herself as well with the steady, if too rapid, thud of his heartbeat against her. And made her decision.

"I know," she said. "I know. I'll take you home."

. . .

Grady ended up at the hospital, where he belonged, near Tess's house. Getting him to Cincinnati hadn't proved to be easy, but Tess was nothing if not determined. *Just call me the Go-To Girl.*

Fighting the temptation to wring her hands, she crowded into the small curtained cubicle in the Emergency Room, intent on seeing to Grady's care.

She couldn't get the image of him on the trip home out of her mind. Getting their bags checked and passing through Security had been hard enough. By then Grady couldn't help, and Tess had feared he might collapse. He'd waited for their flight while slumped on a plastic chair in the terminal. On the plane he'd curled into the window seat, head lolling against the backrest, Tess's pashmina, the only blanket available, wrapped around his fevered body.

She fed him water and in-flight snacks, hoping to maintain his strength and to keep him hydrated. But at times on their connecting flight he fell into a too-deep sleep from which Tess feared she wouldn't be able to wake him.

Lucky for her, they'd gotten on the full flight in the first place. Not long ago, Tess had read of an ill young woman who'd been denied boarding, and although she doubted Grady's condition was contagious, she wasn't eager to have anyone except a doctor in the States examine him.

Grady had needed her in Cabo. He still needed her. Sure, he'd tried to pretend otherwise. Despite the obvious weakness he felt, at Baggage Claim in Cincinnati he'd even tried to send her away. Going through Immigration and Customs, he'd managed to stand on his own. He was a big boy, he'd said, who could take care of himself. Which only meant to Tess that Grady felt worse than he let on. He wanted to go home and lick his wounds in private.

Tess had refused to let that happen.

The physician who stood now by Grady's bed offered a snap diagnosis. Why did doctors, except for Emery, look so young to her these days?

"Possibly drugs," he said. "The tox screen will tell us what's on board."

She craned her neck, trying to see around the doctor. From her limited view she spied what looked to be a dozen vials filled with Grady's blood to be analyzed. Her stomach flipped over.

"Drugs? He has a fever." Tess knew the doctor was wrong. "Grady has had an infection. He doesn't do drugs," she said.

Looking irritated, the resident turned to her.

"Are you a relative?"

She hesitated. If she said no, she would surely be ejected from the cubicle. Privacy regulations. She'd already called Ethan, who might have permission to discuss Grady's case, but he wasn't here yet. If she said yes, what kind of statement would she be making about her relationship with Grady?

Tess chose a variant she hoped would work. "I'm his ex-wife." Which still didn't explain her presence. "We were, uh, in Mexico together when he got sick." She frowned, knowing how that would sound. But maybe this wasn't just the infection. "You don't think this could be something else like dengue fever? Malaria? West Nile? And I'm told there's hepatitis there."

"That's what lab work is for," he said in a condescending tone, then steered her toward the hall. "You can wait in the room over here, Mrs....O'Neill. I'll let you know when we know."

Oh, thank you very much. But no, thanks. What did this say for her problem-solving abilities? Tess had no authority here, and for an instant she felt tempted to call Emery who was an attending physician at this very hospital. She cast a glance at

Grady, lying still and pale under a white sheet, and had a flash vision: a drawer sliding out in the morgue to reveal a corpse. Grady's body. The infection wasn't that serious, was it? No, he couldn't die...but if she called Emery, his worst enemy, Grady might truly have a coronary. He wouldn't be happy to see the surgeon at his bedside.

"I really think I should stay in the room until our son gets here." As if she could keep tragedy at bay on her own.

With an aggrieved sigh, the doctor pointed at a chair then hurried off to give more orders.

Tess sat. Waited. And worried.

When Ethan finally arrived, she threw herself into his arms. And cried.

For the first time Tess wondered what she'd do without Grady in her life. After their time in Cabo, to say she would miss him didn't begin to cover it.

"Grammy! You're home! I missed you!"

The instant Tess set her luggage down by the front door, Dilly sped across the entry hall into her arms. Tess leaned down to rest her cheek against the top of Dilly's head and inhaled the herbal scent of freshly shampooed little-girl hair. For the first time in many hours, she felt her pulse slow into its regular rhythm.

"Hi, love." She kissed Dilly's hair. "Were you a good girl while I was gone?"

Dilly nodded with vigor, nearly knocking out Tess's lower teeth before she could lift her chin out of reach. "Real good." Dilly whirled in the center of the hall like a pajama-clad ballerina. "But I've been busy. I'm the best helper in my school, and me and Mommy cleaned your house. We organized *everything.*"

"Thank you," Tess said but with a sinking feeling. She

looked around the foyer but could see no obvious damage. "Did you wait up for me?" she asked Dilly. "It's way past your bedtime."

"I'm special," she said.

Chloe appeared from the kitchen, wiping her hands—and what appeared to be the remains of half a bottle of ketchup—on one of Tess's best Irish linen dish towels. She hugged Tess hard, which left her looking like the blood-spattered victim of some horrific crime. Chloe didn't seem to notice.

"I told Dilly this was a 'special time.' How's Grady?"

"Poppy's sick," Dilly intoned, her eyes like saucers.

"Yes. He is." Tess touched Dilly's hair again and tried to give Chloe a reassuring smile along with her explanation. She'd spent the evening at the hospital. As she expected, the tox screen showed no evidence of drugs, which took the wind out of that young resident's sails, but Grady's white blood cell count was high. Further tests were ordered, he'd been admitted, and he was now settled in a private room. Without a diagnosis yet, the staff had isolated him. "We should know more tomorrow," she said. "Ethan's there now."

This news didn't appear to trouble Chloe. Instead of the usual quick welling of tears in her eyes whenever he was mentioned, she seemed somehow...stronger. Maybe Tess's trip had forced her to come to terms with Ethan, with herself. Tess would find out later.

Still worried about Grady, she welcomed this heartfelt homecoming. The house seemed peaceful and Tess could use a little peace. Or was it too quiet?

"Where are the cats?" she asked.

Dilly tugged at her sleeve for attention. "They're having a time out, Grammy. Big Boy was being very bad."

Tess didn't dare ask. She felt too exhausted. Too grateful to be home.

But Chloe seemed to hear her unspoken question.

"There's a little problem with the kittens. We can talk about that later. You should rest." She took Tess's tote bag, watched Dilly race up ahead of them, then edged Tess toward the stairs. "We missed you. So did half the population of Cincinnati," she reported then seemed to think better of that news. "But all your messages can wait. I filled in for a few days but Merry—she's back now—finally told me she could handle it until you got here." Chloe took a breath. "Larry called. He can wait too, Tess. Oh, and Sybil Shallowford."

Tess held back a groan. *The office is probably in shambles.*

She felt the beginnings of a serious headache. The Go-To Girl had sustained her since the divorce, but after the idyllic —mostly idyllic—hiatus in Mexico with Grady, she wasn't quite ready to face work. As if she would have a choice.

"Did you talk with Ethan while I was away?" she asked, already heading for her home study to check those messages before bed after all.

Chloe lowered her voice so Dilly couldn't hear. "We tried. He spent the whole time looking tortured. I just know he wanted to check his iPhone. He also knew I'd brain him if he dared. I'm afraid we didn't accomplish much."

By the time Tess had skimmed her call list, she felt ready to fall into bed for another week. Maybe by then she could stop worrying about Grady, alone and sick in his hospital room with only the nurses to look after him.

THE MINUTE TESS walked into her office the next day Merry homed in on her missing wedding ring. "Ah-ha." She put her own bare hand over the telephone receiver she'd been holding when Tess came in. "Something interesting happen south of the border?"

Tess smiled like a sphinx. "What happens in Cabo stays in Cabo."

She braced herself, but for once Merry seemed to take her comment at face value and didn't probe for personal information about Grady. She did, however, ask about his health and Tess told her what little she knew.

"I'm headed for the hospital now. I dropped by the office first to see you—and begin the re-entry process. It's always hard to get back in the groove after being away. And now with Grady sick..."

"Must have been some week for you two," Merry began.

Here it comes after all. But before she could go on Tess said, "Quick. I need to go but tell me about Kentucky."

Merry ran a hand through her spiky red hair. "Frank lasted

one night at the inn. The next day we moved to a motel with high-definition TV."

"Meredith, I'm sorry."

"Not your fault." She changed the subject before Tess could ask what Merry intended to do now. She waggled the phone. "There's someone on the line from Visa. Before you go, you'd better take the call."

This turned out to be a prophetic statement. Tess already owed enough without adding more, but these few unauthorized charges stemmed from the time when she'd been with Grady in Cabo. For one second Tess's pulse jammed. Did he use her card after all, switched with his at dinner that first night like some game of three-card Monte on a street corner?

But he'd said he signed their tab that first night to the room, and the other restaurant meal wasn't one of the bogus charges. They were all local. And it seemed harder now, after their time together at the resort, to blame Grady for anything. She was being unfair again. At the moment he was lying flat on his back in the hospital, and surely he hadn't conned her. On the other hand...her heart sank.

Someone had charged a hefty amount at an internet web site called MegaPoker. Tess had an actual aversion to cards, and she became nauseated at the mere sight of a clean deck. Grady? But no, he'd been with her. The only times he had used his laptop were during his presentation at the conference or to check email with Tess in their room. Then suddenly, she knew. She should have known.

Larry! Her father had paid to gamble with Tess's credit card! But how?

He must have been more desperate than usual. This was a new modus operandi, even for him. Without naming her father as the culprit, Tess denied the unauthorized charges, which bought her some time. She hung up and hit speed dial.

She would deal with Larry, personally.

Larry didn't answer Tess's call. No surprise. He was in hiding, she supposed, but she could wait. Better to let her temper cool first. Unfortunately, Sybil Shallowford would not wait. She had left half a dozen messages at the office too for Tess, who hoped she wasn't still angry about the diamond ring.

But then why hadn't she responded to Tess's return calls last night?

And before she went to visit Grady, she needed to tell Emery's wife she still couldn't afford to buy the house. No price could be low enough. If she got stuck with Larry's charges that would wipe out much of her house fund. *What have you got for sale, say, in cardboard boxes? With a gorgeous view of a Dumpster?*

"I've been trying to reach you," Sybil said when Tess finally connected.

"Yes, I know. I was out of town." Tess decided on full disclosure. "Dr. Shallowford sent me an e-mail—"

That didn't seem to bother Sybil. "What do you think? The house is a steal now."

She hesitated. "First, Mrs. Shallowford, I want to apologize."

"Call me Sybil."

Tess blinked. Was it possible Sybil had forgotten Emery's lie? And Tess's part in buying the ring? "I know you were upset about the diamond and my firm's part in selecting the gift, but I assure you I was only trying to do my job."

"Then let me do mine," Sybil said, brushing aside her apology. "Let's meet to see the house again."

What was going on here? Sybil's silence until now, her more friendly approach today, threw Tess every bit as much off balance as the call from Visa about Larry. Had Sybil forgiven her in order to make a sale? Business was business, after all.

"I hate to waste your time, Sybil. You see, something has come up and I still don't think I can afford—"

"My dear, you won't be able to resist."

Still, like Larry, Sybil and the house would have to wait. At the hospital Tess found Grady sitting up in bed, his eyes bright and clear. She refused to look at all the tubes attached to his body, and the constant beep of monitors did nothing to soothe her nerves, but to her relief apparently his fever had come down.

"Better?" she asked, not daring to give him the kiss he obviously expected.

Grady's gaze shifted to his lap. "Better," he said, "and happy to see you."

Her face warmed. "Taking your Viagra?"

"Huh?" he said. He didn't remember their conversation in Cabo.

Her gaze sharpened. "What day is it, Grady?"

"Thursday. No, that's not right. Could be..." He paused as if trying to remember the days of the week. "Saturday?"

"It's Tuesday." Tess sat next to his bed. Had anyone else noticed that his brain wasn't functioning well? She took a closer look at his unconcerned expression. His eyes appeared normal, but he had a goofy look on his face that told her he wasn't quite present. "Tell me. How old are you?"

His grin widened, as if they were playing some entertaining game. Too bad for him it wasn't poker. Then, when he couldn't come up with the right number, his smile faded.

"Let's see. I was born in..." He named the proper year. "Subtract that from...if this is when I think it is that would make me...um, forty-one?"

Tess gaped at him. He'd supplied the wrong age by half a decade.

"No, you're forty-six." Amazing. He'd calculated his age by using arithmetic, not memory. He didn't automatically remember the answer but had to work it out. And still, he'd been wrong. She felt a fresh wave of alarm. "Maybe I should call a nurse. Do you know how long you've been in this hospital?"

He lay back against the raised head of his bed. His gaze wandered over her, lazy and hot. "I'm in a hospital?" He glanced around, taking note of all the tubes and monitors as if for the first time. "No way. I'm not sick!"

Grady flung back the sheet, revealing a hiked-up hospital gown and way too much skin.

Tess twitched the gown back down.

"Seen it all before, babe," he muttered.

"Grady, I'm worried. What have your tests shown?"

"What tests?"

This was useless. Tess pushed the call button. Five minutes later no one had answered. She jabbed it again, only to have Grady catch her arm and haul her down on the edge of the bed. His face, covered with beard stubble, hovered inches from hers, and Tess knew he meant to kiss her.

"Be careful! You'll pull out your IV lines."

One arm around her, he stared down at his other arm.

"What's this for?" he asked, sounding as offended as one could with a broad grin to rival that of a circus clown. Before Tess could prevent it, he yanked out the line. In the next second, he was out of bed, nearly dumping Tess on the floor.

A nurse spoke from the doorway. Finally. "What is going on in here?"

Tess scrambled upright. Grady was shuffling toward the hall.

"I'm outta here. Home," he said, trying to push past the nurse. "Work."

"Oh no, you're not." She'd stopped him. "Now see what you've done," she said as if to scold a naughty child. Blood had pooled on the floor. "Let's get you back in bed, Mr. O'Neill, and put your line in again before the doctor comes."

"I hope he has a diagnosis." Tess had never seen Grady like this, and in spite of the humorous comments he'd made, his condition frightened her. What if his mind was gone?

Quickly her own brain zoomed forward into the future, ready to fix things. Grady wouldn't be able to live alone. If he couldn't work again, if he couldn't remember, he'd be totally dependent upon someone else to care for him. And hadn't Tess always been his personal Go-To Girl?

Yes, they were divorced, but after Cabo how could she turn him away? At the moment Tess was his only advocate. She would have to rent a hospital bed. Move Grady into her spare room or turn over her home office on the first floor. Hire part-time help. Chloe would be willing to step in too, but Ethan would need to work even longer hours to manage O'Neill Construction on his own, which wouldn't be good for his already threatened marriage.

If Grady remained in his present state of semi-lucidity, they would all have their hands full. And Tess, her heart. Expanding her business wouldn't be an option then, or buying any house.

After an orderly had cleaned the floor, Tess heard a quick rap at the door and looked up. A white-coated physician, not the resident she'd met before, walked into the room. He wore a puzzled expression and a frown.

"Mr. O'Neill, are we being difficult again?"

"Stubborn," Grady answered with that silly grin. He seemed oblivious of the nurse's efforts to reinsert his IV line.

"Tess always says I am." He spoke like a happy four-year-old. Like Dilly.

The doctor turned to her. "You have permission to discuss his case?"

Tess felt her temper rise. "Let's assume I do." Privacy regulations be damned. "I'm the only one here. Obviously, my husband—ex-husband—isn't in his right mind."

The doctor turned his back on Grady then lowered his voice. "Frankly, I'm stumped." Not the words Tess had hoped to hear. He waved a sheaf of computer print-outs. "We've run a battery of tests. Nothing shows up. No systemic disease process at any rate, viral or bacterial, with which I'm familiar."

That was confidence-inspiring. "Maybe we need a specialist. *Doctor*."

His frown darkened. "I am a specialist—in infectious disease. I understand you were in Mexico when Mr. O'Neill became ill. But the tests for malaria, dengue fever, even West Nile were negative. Any other ideas, Mrs. O'Neill?"

Tess worried her lip. "Before we left the country, as I told another doctor, Grady did have an infection on his foot..."

He shook his head. "We looked at that. He's getting medication, but it doesn't appear to be serious." The doctor glanced back at Grady, whom Tess saw beaming at them with curious interest. She had seen the exact expression on Dilly's face when she eavesdropped on the adults. "His MRI showed no apparent brain injury—stroke or aneurysm. But I'm calling in a neurologist. Mr. O'Neill seems to have suffered a 'break with reality.' He may need to be moved up to that department for closer observation."

Tess was stunned. Grady had his problems, but he'd always been one of the more rational people she knew. Until now. "You mean to the mental ward?"

"I don't know what else we can do here."

Pass the buck, Tess assumed. Her irritation grew. "But he had a fever...What does that have to do with mental illness?"

The doctor offered no answer. He merely rapped the sheaf of papers against the palm of his hand then withdrew with a quick, "I'll see you later." He was out of the room before Tess could call him back.

"Oh, Grady. What are we going to do?"

Tess was on the verge of tears, and feeling overwhelmed, when someone spoke from the doorway.

"Need help here?"

She glanced around, startled to see Larry, nattily dressed as always but sporting a worried frown. Oh, he should be worried. About that call from Visa. How could he have duped her like that?

"Yes, I need help," she admitted, perhaps for the first time with him since she was a child, "but I doubt that's possible."

Grady was staring at her father as if he'd never seen him before.

"New boyfriend?"

"For heaven's sake. He's my—"

"Oops. Larry," Grady said, as if the dawn had broken.

Tess supposed that was a good sign, but all she needed right now was for her father to ask for more money. He'd be lucky to leave this room alive.

"You rest, Grady," she said. "I'll be right back. Come with me, Dad."

She steered Larry out into the hall. She didn't want anyone else to hear what she had to say to him, but Tess had had enough.

Her father had the audacity to act as if nothing had happened. He'd come to see Grady not her. He probably didn't expect to find Tess in the room, but that didn't faze him either.

"What's wrong with Grady?" he asked.

She tried to keep the sharpness from her tone, and even worse, the fear, but failed. "Who knows? Certainly not anyone with a medical degree."

Tess had felt utterly alone in Cabo, trying to bring Grady home, and she felt even more vulnerable now. She always did, around Larry.

Yet his latest betrayal wouldn't go unanswered.

He and Tess stood by the windows at the end of the long hall, neither of them speaking for a moment. *He's such a user*, Merry had said, and she was right. As long as Tess let Larry lean on her, he would.

"Dad, I can't give you any more money. I sure didn't give you permission to use my credit card to pay MegaPoker!" At his shocked expression she said, "How could you?" She heaved in a breath. "How did you? I never lent you that card." Tess guarded her credit these days with an iron fist. Or thought she had.

Larry hung his head. "I—uh—saw your card on the kitchen table the night I stayed for dinner. It was right there, sugar-pie. I had that debt in Dayton, then I lost playing poker online—"

"With the computer I bought you for Christmas? I can't tell you how angry—how disappointed—I am. You know how hard I've worked to pay off debt from my marriage to Grady —" She stopped then started again. "You knew, but you took advantage of me anyway."

"Tess, I'll pay you back."

Her throat tightened. "*How?* I've reported your charges as fraudulent. Visa will investigate. And that trail, sooner or later, will lead straight to you. *You* need to do something about your gambling, Dad."

"I've tried," he said.

"Not lately—and not hard enough."

Larry didn't respond.

"You've been an addict ever since I can remember." Tess felt tears well in her eyes. "Do you know what that did to Mom—and to me? After she died, I felt obligated to help you, to try over and over again, because you have no one else. But you *never* change. Why?" Tess asked, barely able to speak past the lump in her throat.

"You helped Grady all those years. Why not me now?"

Tess didn't care to address the part about her ex-husband. "I can't. Not again. I'm sorry." She paused, almost blinded by tears. "No, I'm not sorry. This is for your own good. Call it tough love—"

"Trouble?" said a familiar deep voice.

Tess whirled away from the window to find Grady in the middle of the hallway, scowling at them, his IV stand trailing behind him like a comet's tail. For a brief moment he looked all there, like his normal self. Ready to protect Tess and have her see him as her knight in shining armor.

"It's okay, Grady." She took his arm to lead him back to his room. She didn't look at Larry again. "My father can take care of the trouble himself."

"Doesn't anyone seem to care? Why can't someone give us a diagnosis?" Tess heard Chloe ask later that afternoon. She leaned over Grady's bed, appearing to inspect his tubes and monitors as if to find some clue there to his ailment.

"I have no idea," Tess told her. "I've been asking the same question."

Chloe had opened her mouth to respond when Ethan strolled into the room—and stopped. He and Chloe exchanged pointed looks, part cool distance, part poignant longing. "Hey. Didn't expect to find you here," he said.

"I thought you were watching Dilly," Chloe responded.

"She went shopping with Meredith who agreed to babysit." He glanced at Tess. "Seems she inherited her grandmother's love of retail. God help me."

"Dilly is a sensible child," Tess said with a smile, hoping to reduce the tension in the room. "She also had a total of three dollars and fifty-four cents in her piggy bank. I'm teaching her the value of saving. If she spends every penny, it won't go far."

"Let us pray." Ethan walked to the other side of Grady's bed. Chloe was still bent over the equipment, her gaze now evading Ethan. "Hey, Dad. How it's going?"

"I'm ready to go home," Grady said, throwing back his covers again.

Ethan straightened them. "Whoa, not just yet. You get out of this bed too soon, you'll have every one of our suppliers knocking at the door. All the orders messed up. Wait a little bit. Rest. I almost have the Larson job finished."

"Larson?" Grady echoed, obviously clueless.

Ethan frowned. "I'll handle it. You concentrate on getting well."

"I'm not sick!"

"Just belligerent," Tess murmured.

"Get me out of here!"

Grady seemed to alternate between acting childlike and needing physical restraint. Ethan pushed his father back down with one hand. Chloe shoved at Grady's chest from the other side of his bed. Her eyes looked overly bright, and Tess knew she was as worried about Grady as Tess was. Her cooperative motions with Ethan might have been the first between him and Chloe in weeks.

He inclined his head toward the hallway. "Let's take a walk," he said, another good sign.

But Chloe hung back. "I'm trying to find out what's wrong with Grady."

"Chloe, you're not a doctor."

"Ethan," Tess began.

"Stay out of this, Mom." He rounded the bed to reach for Chloe's arm.

She stepped out of his way. "No one gives me credit, but I'm a pretty smart person," Chloe announced. "If I think about this, maybe I can come up with—"

"The answer to my father's illness?" Ethan murmured. "You flunked biology. Twice."

"Yes, because my dad was browbeating me to major in pre-med! He made me so nervous I couldn't study. You know that, Ethan."

"I apologize. But you're hardly qualified to practice now. What makes you think you can second-guess all the specialists assigned to Dad's case?"

"Why do I need a specialist?" Grady wondered aloud. As if he were watching the players at an NBA Finals game, his gaze darted back and forth between Chloe and Ethan.

If Tess hadn't been so worried about him too, she might have laughed.

Chloe punched a finger at Ethan's chest, forcing him to take a step back. "Didn't you hear anything I said at the airport? Or while your parents were in Mexico? Am I completely wasting my time on you here?"

Ethan's mouth dropped open.

"Now, Chloe," Tess tried again.

Ethan glared at her. "Mom, this is our fight. If Chloe wants to have it here, I'm fine with that. You can watch. But you can't say one word. Understand?"

What a day, Tess thought. "No, I don't understand."

Suddenly she was the odd man out.

"All my life you've been the one we all came to. Me, Dad, Grandpa, even Chloe...Well, this is between me and her. Nobody can settle this except us."

Tess had said a similar thing to Larry. And Chloe agreed.

"He's right, Tess. I know you want to help, but Ethan and I will figure out our problems—or we won't."

He eyed Chloe with new respect. "Now will you come out in the hall, away from prying eyes?"

Tess bristled. "Prying eyes?"

"Chloe may forget to watch where she walks sometimes, she might trip down the steps or drop your turkey platter, Mom, but—"

"You broke the turkey platter?" Tess asked, astonished.

Chloe's face turned ashen. "I didn't mean to. Or your Haviland dish."

Tess paled too.

"I'm sorry." Chloe's lip trembled. "Some day I'll be just like a normal person and then I'll buy you a new platter. Another piece of china. You'll see."

"I don't care about the dishes," Tess said weakly. "The turkey platter was a family piece, yours to keep. I care about *you*, Chloe. You and Ethan."

He patted her arm. "We'll be okay, Mom."

"I do just fine with the kittens," Chloe offered.

She and Ethan had reached the hall when Chloe suddenly whirled around. Her blue eyes went wide but not with the alarm Tess had so often seen there, or even remorse for the mishaps she'd caused.

"Wait a minute," Chloe said, not bothering to shake Ethan's hand off her shoulder. "The kittens. Grady, you had a sore on your foot, didn't you? From Tess's cat—maybe the only accident in the house that I *didn't* cause. Did you also have a, well, kind of bump...somewhere?"

Grady looked blank. "Bump?"

"You know...on your body." Chloe gestured toward the sheet that covered Grady's lap.

"In his groin, you mean?" Ethan asked.

She nodded. "His lymph nodes would try to stop the spread of infection from his foot, so it wouldn't reach his heart or lungs."

Grady stared down at himself. "A bump," he said. "Yeah."

Chloe's gaze touched Ethan, Tess then Grady in turn. She started to grin. "Never mind the doctors. I know what's wrong with Grady!"

WHAT A DIFFERENCE A WEEK MADE.

Grady was now out of the hospital. Chloe stood beside his bed—or, rather, by Tess's bed—holding a bottle of antibiotic pills. They weren't for Grady, not that he wasn't still sick.

That other day by Grady's hospital bedside, she had pronounced her diagnosis, "Cat Scratch Disease, sometimes known as Cat Scratch Fever," unable to suppress the quick flash of pride she'd felt at the discovery.

Once a further test had established her layman's diagnosis, Grady's prognosis was excellent. The disorder wasn't something his doctors saw every day, or even at all, and Grady became their new toy, a project to be written up in medical journals.

No big deal, really, on Chloe's part. She'd simply put two and two together and come up, for a change, with four.

All at once—for once in her life—she was the quasi-expert on a subject. And no one else knew, but Chloe's secret passion was veterinary medicine. In a small percentage of cases, she'd read later on the subject, the bacterial infection, which hadn't been picked up through standard blood work, could spread to the brain. Just Grady's luck.

As carriers of the disease, the kittens had showed no symptoms, but they were now being treated—or soon would be—as well.

Without the proper antibiotic, which this time should kill the germs, Grady might have died. Chloe short-circuited the thought. She loved Grady. He was the best father-in-law ever. Better than the dad she'd gotten stuck with because of a simple accident of genes. When Chloe was a girl, her only playmates were her pets. They hadn't judged or criticized. True, her father had more recently contributed his frequent flier miles for Tess's air fare to Cabo, one point in his favor, but Grady seemed to understand her when no one else did. She didn't want to lose him.

Now, at Tess's insistence, he was staying at her house where, to Chloe's satisfaction, he was making steady progress. Day by day, by some process that continued to fascinate Chloe, his mind cleared and healed. His mental function and his memory gradually returned.

"This arrangement is temporary," Tess kept telling him much to Chloe's frustration. Did she not hear how false her tone sounded? "Purely clinical," Tess went on now. "I could hardly let you go home to your apartment alone. I'd wonder every minute if you were all right."

Who did she think she was kidding? Talk about a heart-felt confession.

Grady grinned. "The lonely bachelor role has its perks after all."

Preparing to help with the cats' medicine, Tess fiddled with a pair of gloves intended to protect her skin from their claws. Chloe knew Tess cared about the cats, too. They had brought chaos into her house but also new life, even excitement.

The kittens, unaware they were about to get their pills, lay curled together on the carpet next to Grady's bed, appearing to be the very picture of innocent sleep. In reality they were quarantined in the same room with the very man they'd infected with illness. Chloe wouldn't risk letting Dilly rough-house with them and possibly contract the disease. It was more common in children.

But Tess remained in denial, not only about Grady. Obviously, she tried to ignore her attraction to him, and now she was spinning alibis for the kittens, despite all evidence to the contrary.

"These cats couldn't be responsible for your infection," she tried to reason. "I'm sure they're clean. They bathe often enough."

"That had nothing to do with it, as you know," Chloe said.

"We might have other issues, but I can't believe I've been harboring a couple of Typhoid Marys."

"One Mary, one Mark," Grady murmured.

Chloe couldn't help smiling. "You haven't been up close and personal with any other felines, Grady?"

"Only that one." He pointed at Big Boy. "I knew he hated me."

Again, Tess leaped to her cat's defense. "He knew you hated *him*. You said so the night he clawed you."

Grady leaned back against his pillows. "And here I am again." He patted Tess's mattress. "Maybe I should thank him."

Chloe stepped closer to the bed. "Tess, let's give these two their medicine." She grinned at Grady. "Your turn's coming, mister."

When Tess bent toward Little Girl, the cat jerked awake as if aware of some terrible fate then scampered off to chase an imaginary prey, her partner in crime in hot pursuit. Then as Chloe watched, they were stopped by the closed door. Big Boy backed up against it, his tail twitching in the air.

Tess kept one eye on Grady and the other on the cats. "What does his shaking mean?"

"Uh-oh. He's spraying," Chloe said. "How old did you say they were?"

"Couple of months I was told when I got them, but maybe they're older. Is that good, or bad?"

"Well, at the moment it's not good."

"How do you know so much, Chloe? I've barely started to plow through *Living with Cats*."

Chloe's grin reappeared. Tess and Grady looked to her for information, another first in her life. Big Boy's adolescent pheromones were on patrol, looking for a mate.

"We can talk about that later." She gave a pointed look to the gloves in Tess's hands. "Come on, put 'em on."

Tess turned pale. "Couldn't you give the cats their pills— I'll do Grady?"

He grinned. "Anytime, Theresa."

Tess couldn't ignore his remark. "I see you're really on the mend."

Chloe felt a twinge of envy. It had been way too long since Ethan had looked at her like that.

Having given Tess the spare bedroom, Chloe was spending her nights on Tess's living room couch next to Dilly on the carpet in her Dora the Explorer sleeping bag. Yearning for her own home, she ached even more for Ethan's stove-warm body snuggled against her in bed.

With a little sigh, Chloe popped the cap on the pill bottle. Though she'd avoided Ethan since their meeting at the hospital, he had convinced her then to at least have dinner with him soon. But she needn't think of that yet either.

Tess pulled on the gloves, looking none too eager to

repeat the twice-daily routine. Like a pilot ready for take-off, Chloe ran down their check list.

"Door shut to the hall?"

"Yes."

"Cats out from under the bed?"

"Yep."

"Then let's try Little Girl."

Tess hesitated. "This works better when we do Big Boy first. Otherwise he'll figure out what's coming."

"So did she a minute ago," Tess pointed out.

"But remember when he streaked out of here and we couldn't find him for hours?"

"Because the door was ajar then. This time we're covered. She's not as crafty," Tess added. "She's shy. She'll do whatever he does."

"You know them better than you think."

Both cats eyed Chloe with unblinking feline curiosity. She kept her voice low and soothing not to alarm them while Tess, having given in to Chloe's plan, dutifully scooped up Little Girl. Chloe had taken to calling her LG—like a brand-name appliance. "Tilt her head way back, put pressure on her jaws so she'll have to open them then I'll pop the medicine in her mouth. Just like before."

"She has sharp teeth, Chloe."

"If we do this quick no one will get hurt."

"Ha," Grady murmured. He liked to watch their routine with wary interest and, arms folded behind his head, he smiled at Chloe.

Her grasp impaired by the too-big gloves, Tess couldn't seem to keep a good grip on the kitten. "Hurry," she said, "or I'll drop her."

Chloe took command.

"No, you won't. Once she gets the best of us, this will only take longer."

From a safe distance Big Boy studied her as if to say *Yeah, right. You don't know by now that I'm smarter than you are?* Chloe experienced a brief loss of her newfound confidence. Unlike Tess, she found the cats childishly easy to deal with, but BB had developed his own self-esteem.

"Get her mouth open, Tess."

LG caterwauled in protest. Lightning-swift, Chloe took the opportunity to slip a pill inside her gaping mouth. She stroked LG's throat, forcing her to swallow. "Hold her for a second until we're sure she won't spit it out."

As soon as Tess released her, Little Girl flew from her arms onto Grady's bed, seeking refuge. To Chloe's surprise he caught her like a football.

"Hey, not bad, huh?"

"We're a team," Chloe said. "Go for it, Tess. We need the big guy now."

Tess shot a glance at Grady then seemed to realize that Chloe meant the other kitten, not him. BB, who'd been waiting for his chance, predictably bolted. Up on the bed he flew, across Grady's bare chest, and onto his head like a bird perched in a tree.

"Ow!" Grady tried to remove him, but he was holding Little Girl. Big Boy's claws sank into his hair and scalp, but the kitten had miscalculated. Caught between the headboard and the corner of two walls coming together, he had nowhere else to run. He gazed at Chloe with widened eyes.

Wincing, Grady said, "What's a little pain? I'm already on medicine and he's trapped. Get the pill."

Tess was closer so Chloe handed her the tablet. Among the three of them they managed to medicate the second cat. The instant Tess let go of his mouth he leaped over Grady like a pole vaulter. Little Girl jumped off Grady's lap to follow. Somehow, they both penetrated the perimeter of under-bed boxes Tess had lined up as a wall to corral them in the room then burrowed deep under the bed into the darkest corner.

Chloe bent down to see two pairs of blue eyes staring at her in obvious warning, but they didn't scare her. Let them settle down. They would come out when they felt secure. The pill-popping had been traumatic.

She straightened. "Are you okay, Grady?"

"Just a few more puncture wounds in my scalp. But hey, I've already got the disease. Know something? I'm beginning to like those two. You have to admire their spirit."

Chloe saw him looking at Tess with concern. "You all right?"

She held up her gloved hands. "Body armor. Works for me."

"Chloe?" he said.

She grinned, encouraged by her new skills. "I'm the cat expert here, remember?" Another flash of insanely strong pride whipped through her from head to toe. She glanced down at the shadowed, under-the-bed hiding place the cats had chosen. "Think I'll tackle surgery next."

She wasn't quite kidding. Who knew what she was really capable of?

A minute later Tess and Grady were alone except for the cats under the bed. Tess kept her distance from him. She was glad he felt better, but his presence in her house threatened her decision to avoid a repeat of Cabo. Their stay there had changed her view of Grady, but it had also made her more vulnerable to him.

"That was fun," he said, indicating the closed door to her room. Chloe had gone downstairs to phone the vet about something. "Now if we can only get rid of our chaperones..."

"Whatever you're thinking, forget it."

He grinned. "You know what I'm thinking. Take pity on a sick man."

Tess folded her arms. "In your dreams."

"I dream of you every night, babe. I picture you warm and cozy, naked under the covers..." His gaze darkened. "If I hadn't been out of my head in the hospital, I'd have pulled you into that high bed with all those fancy controls, tried a few new positions, and—I guarantee—taken you to the moon."

"Big talk. You hardly knew your own name." Yet she couldn't quell the fresh rush of desire that ran along her nerve ends. Grady was always appealing, damn him. Settled in her bed with the afternoon sun glinting on his dark hair, his bare chest exposed to her gaze, looking like her own fantasy in the flesh, he was even harder to resist.

"It's ridiculous that you can still make me blush," she murmured. "I'm a mature woman not the school girl I was when we met."

He raised his eyebrows. "All the more reason to tempt you now, Red Riding Hood. Notice I left out the 'Little.'"

Tess took an involuntary step toward him then stopped. "Chloe's downstairs."

But, no, Chloe wasn't downstairs. Tess could hear her climbing the steps. A second later she walked into the bedroom again, giving Grady and Tess a look of suspicion then delight.

"Hey, you guys. Want some privacy? I'm taking Dilly to the park to play. On our way back, I'll pick up Chinese take-out for dinner." She got down on her knees and somehow plucked both kittens out from under the bed.

To Tess's astonishment they nestled in Chloe's arms like babies.

"I'll just remove these last barriers to temptation. Enjoy," she said then was gone again, the door shut behind her, taking the cats with her to be imprisoned in the laundry room.

"Guess that does it." Grady held out a hand. "*Now* we're alone."

Tess cocked her head to hear doors closing, then the sound of Chloe's car backing out of the drive.

"I don't think this is a very good idea."

"It's not a good idea. It's great." His eyes had turned the color of dark chocolate, and Tess felt herself weaken then surrender.

She was in his bed—her bed—before she could form another objection.

"You want me," he whispered, his mouth at her throat, his hands busy with the button on her jeans. "God," he said seconds later, his gaze hot on Tess's now bare body. "On the plane coming home and in the hospital, I didn't know where I was at times, but you were there, Tess. Always. And I knew just who you were." He kissed her, his lips soft and warm. One hand strayed to her breast. "If I forgot everyone else in this world—Dilly, Chloe, Ethan—even for a minute, I'd remember you."

Tess was surprised, even stunned, to feel tears on her cheeks. All at once her fears during his illness burst from her. She tightened her hold on him. "I was so worried about you, Grady. I thought I'd never be able to talk to you again, make you laugh, make you angry. I'd never see that look in your eyes."

"What look?"

"This one," she said, lifting her head to that rich chocolate gaze, to the love she saw there. Grady didn't say another word. He knew. Tess's voice had been thick with need, with caring. She'd been wrong in Cabo. For both of them sex was just the start. For better or worse, although their wedding vows no longer applied, she still loved Grady. "You rat," she whispered. "You're way too good."

After that Tess let him have his way, and Grady's way was very fine, indeed. If anything, lovemaking in Cabo had only enhanced how their bodies came together, how they pleased each other.

The thought was both comforting yet frightened her.

She'd almost lost him.

Instead, would she lose herself all over again?

She didn't have long to wonder. Within the hour Tess knew she was in even deeper trouble than she'd been in Cabo.

"What do you think this means?" Grady asked after they'd made love.

She cleared her throat, trying to dislodge the swell of emotion she felt. "We were both scared before. You almost died, Grady. That's enough to make anyone re-examine his life," she added. "I guess this was a celebration."

He raised her chin, his gaze meeting hers and holding for a few long moments. Then he pressed his forehead to hers with a sigh. "We belong together, Tess. You know we do. Take a chance," he said.

To Tess that still meant trouble. Big-time. Even without her wedding band, which now resided in a dresser drawer, her awareness of Grady wouldn't quit, which should warn her. True, she hadn't had another If Only since Cabo, and maybe her late-night fantasies were no longer necessary. But now, she would have to make herself clear.

"Taking risks has always come too easy for you. For me, maybe someday," Tess told him, trying desperately for a lighter tone, "when I'm old and gray, and my house is paid for...if not the house in Emery's e-mail." She still had to tell Sybil no, but one day she would have a home. Then she'd know she could always survive on her own. Without Grady.

Without Larry. Without the fear that she could lose all she held dear again.

"You want a house," Grady said with an edge to his tone, "we'll buy one."

"Not we," she said. Her heart beating too fast, Tess slipped from bed. "I need a house that's mine. And no one else's."

Now, Grady was irritated with her. Hurt.

With his steady gaze on her, she dressed quickly, chiding herself for wanting so badly to give in, to trust for more than one night. For some reason that made her feel foolish and clumsy—not physically like Chloe, but emotionally. Still, she reminded herself, even Chloe seemed to be coming into her own. So where did that leave Tess?

Two days later Grady was out of bed and on his feet again, but she still couldn't look him in the eye. Tonight, although he didn't say much, he seemed to fill her dining room with his presence, snuffing all the air from Tess's lungs as if she were a candle and he was the flame.

To distract herself she worried about Larry. Tess hadn't heard from her father since she'd given him her ultimatum at the hospital. Was he okay? Or had someone in Dayton broken his knee caps?

Chloe stared down at her plate. Even Dilly picked up on the tension between Tess and Grady.

"You mad at Grammy, Poppy?"

"Nope."

She kicked one sparkly light-up sneaker against the rung of her chair. "You look mad."

Grady glanced at his watch for the tenth time since they'd sat down. "I have a little headache, Dill. Please pass me the peas."

Caught in her own stormy feelings, Tess had cooked his favorites for dinner, hoping that would soften the wounded look in Grady's eyes but not weaken her own resolve. *I didn't do anything wrong. I told the truth.*

The rest of the meal was silent except for Dilly's bright chatter about her day at nursery school where she'd gotten "*five* stars. I can write my name."

Tess squeezed her hand across the table. "That's wonderful, sweetie."

And Grady dutifully mumbled his praise.

By the time Tess served dessert, she almost welcomed the kittens' antics. They were halfway through their course of antibiotics and even more frisky than usual. As if to betray every warm thought she'd ever had about them, the two cats bounded into the dining room, startling everyone at the table.

Chloe jerked to attention. "How did they get out of the bedroom?"

"I must have left the door open," Grady admitted. "The latch doesn't always hold."

The two cats paid no attention to their humans. Focused on some goal of his own, Big Boy chased Little Girl out of the room then down the hall and through the living room before he circled back to tackle her at the base of the table. A second later he'd climbed like a monkey onto her back, and Little Girl gave the equivalent of a feline moan.

Everyone froze and Tess stifled a gasp. Even she, still stuck on Chapter 1 of *Living with Cats*, could guess what was happening. Big Boy had looked for love in the wrong place.

"What is he doing?" Dilly asked, leaning over the table to watch. She looked delighted. She hadn't seen the quarantined kittens in days.

Chloe clapped a hand over her daughter's eyes. "He's being naughty."

"Does he need a spanking?"

Chloe bolted from her chair to separate the cats. "He needs something, all right. That's partly what the tail-quivering meant, Tess. I've already talked to the vet." She looked back at her. "The last thing we need here is a new litter of—"

"Good grief," Tess muttered in horror. "He's her *brother*."

A fter dinner, to Tess's relief, Chloe prepared to take Big Boy and his sister to the clinic to be spayed and neutered, a necessary decision that seemed to alarm Grady.

He obviously identified with the male cat. "What if we did that to humans? It's hardly fair."

"So is a neighborhood full of homeless kittens," Tess insisted. "How else can these two practice any birth control?"

"Don't take this personally, Grady." Chloe hustled Big Boy into the new carrier Tess had bought. He tried to spread all four legs wide and arch his back like a Halloween cartoon cat, but Chloe deftly stuffed him inside anyway.

Dilly went with Chloe to "keep my kitties company." As soon as they left the house, Tess collapsed on the living room sofa. Alone with Grady. Again.

To her surprise he didn't sit down or go back upstairs to bed. He announced he felt stir crazy and would be going out for a while.

Tess tried to tamp down her instant concern. He did look healthier than he had before, and during his illness he'd lost a few pounds. He looked leaner, younger. His color was good. Maybe she shouldn't worry but, "Are you sure you feel well enough? You took your medicine?"

"Yeah. I'm going for a drive." Yet Ethan had dropped Grady at the airport before his flight to Cabo, and Grady hadn't been home since then. His car was still parked in the lot at his apartment complex. "Can I borrow your keys?"

Reluctantly Tess handed them over but worried anyway the minute he disappeared. Was he strong enough to drive? Or just unwilling to spend the evening with her?

If he could drive, he'd soon decide to go back to his apartment, and then she'd miss him. Maybe he was already on his way there...but even that wasn't what bothered her. She had a niggling feeling about his sudden need to escape.

She should be glad he was gone, relieving her tension as well as his. She didn't know how to deal with her need for Grady or what that meant for her future. But as she nursed a cup of coffee, she couldn't put him out of her mind.

She had no idea how long her thoughts spun in all directions.

Work seemed the safest topic. Tess had half a dozen items to buy for clients, gifts for retirement parties and christenings and more weddings. But he'd taken her car. Shopping wasn't an option, her usual means of finding peace, although that hadn't been working very well lately either.

When Chloe returned without the cats, having left them at the clinic for tomorrow's surgery, she put a sleepy Dilly to bed then went upstairs. Soon Tess heard the low murmur of her voice on the telephone. Was she talking to Ethan?

Tess spent the next few hours on the internet looking for a cheaper house to buy. Nothing compared to the one Emery had shown her. Finally, she watched two episodes of *House Hunters,* another of the international version in which a young engaged couple with the world at their feet found an apartment-to-die-for in central Paris. That fresh beginning reminded Tess of her early days with Grady.

These few days might be the last they'd ever share.

Intending to put her empty cup in the kitchen, she rose from the sofa, but the sound of her car in the driveway halted her in mid-step. Her legs went weak.

Grady was back. Home safe again.

When the front door opened, Tess was waiting there. But the sense of relief she expected to feel never came. As soon as he stepped inside, she knew.

The reason for her night-long disorientation hit her like a wrecking ball at one of his construction sites. All those other nights when Grady had gone missing then come home with a furtive look on his face flashed through her mind. The nights long before that when Larry had done the same, and her mother too had wept in despair.

Grady gave her a brief nod then continued past her to the stairs.

Tess stepped in front of him, feeling like the embodiment of her own mother with Larry. Now, with Grady, Tess's greatest fear had come true.

She couldn't control the quiver in her voice. "Where have you been?"

"I told you. Went for a drive."

"Grady, I know that look. You didn't only take a drive." She inhaled a shaken breath. "You borrowed my car to go *gamble*? You've been playing cards."

"Cards?" He reeled back. "But hey, sure, what else could it be? Every time Grady takes a walk, goes to the corner store, drives across town or, hell, anywhere else, he must be *gambling*?" He met her eyes. "That's a knee-jerk reaction if I ever heard one—and dead wrong, Tess. You want to know where I really was tonight? Huh?" He didn't wait for her answer. "I was with your *father*."

Tess stared at him. To her, that admission seemed even worse. If they'd spent the evening at one of the casinos or playing the horses...

But then, to her surprise Grady corrected her assumption. "Apparently you finally insisted he do something about his addiction. I have to applaud you for that." He paused.

"Tonight, Larry asked me to go with him to a Gam-Anon meeting."

Shocked, she put a hand to her chest. "He actually went? And stayed?"

She couldn't believe it. After all these years.

Grady nodded. "He admitted to a room full of people that he has a problem. You have any idea how important that decision was for him? How difficult a moment that can be?" He held her gaze. "Well, I do. The first time I went I had to leave twice. I threw up in the parking lot before I could go back and say a word to everyone there."

"You?"

"If it's any comfort, and Larry is as serious about this as I think he is, he can get better, too. If I were you, I'd pray." She heard the tremor in his voice. "As for me, I haven't picked up a deck of cards in four years. I've been attending Gam-Anon since the week you walked out on me. I've missed just one meeting—when I was in the hospital." He shook his head. "I know I screwed up during our marriage. I'd promise to change and go a few times then drop out again..."

As he trailed off Tess remembered something. Too late. She reached out but he avoided her touch. "Ethan told me you've gone back to the meetings."

"Yeah, but I have some pride. I keep a low profile even with him. Ethan would fuss over me if I let him." He half smiled. "He can be just like you, you know."

"But I—" she began.

Only Grady wouldn't listen now, and she couldn't blame him. She had jumped to the wrong, the worst possible, conclusion about him.

"Besides," he said, "broadcasting that decision isn't the point of Gam-Anon or any twelve-step program. This problem is *mine*. I own it. I'll beat it. I hope Larry will too." He paused again. "The night you left me I made a pile of all the playing cards in the house, then burned them. A symbolic gesture, I know, but—"

"Grady, I'm terribly sor—"

Again, he cut off her apology. "I'd really hoped that after my being ill, and after the other day upstairs with you, we'd finally turned the corner. Too bad I was wrong. Just like you, Theresa." Then he turned and, still holding her keys, walked toward the door.

"Grady, wait."

But he didn't stop. He spoke over his shoulder, his tone sad. "You know, Ethan and I made this deal not long ago. If we worked hard enough, we could show you and Chloe how we felt about our relationships. But I could never work hard enough for you, could I? I don't know how to make you understand or believe in me. God knows, I've tried. And hell, maybe this is the next step for *me*." He had his hand on the doorknob. "You still don't trust me, Tess. And I don't know what else I can do to prove you should."

His tone was proud. Yet, even more, resigned.

Frankly, my dear, I don't give a damn.

Rhett Butler's classic movie good-bye echoed inside Tess along with Grady's message like a death knell. Far worse than their divorce. Stricken by his actual words, knowing what it had cost him to even say them, Tess could only stand there at the door. And watch him leave.

❧ 14 ❧

"I. AM. FINISHED," Tess heard Meredith say.

As Merry swept into the office, Tess did a double take. Instead of the long face and glum mood that would mirror hers this morning, and which Tess had come to expect from Merry in the past weeks, she looked rested and happy. Or at least at peace with the decision she'd obviously made.

"You left Frank?"

"How could I leave him?" Merry dumped her tote bag on the desk with a satisfying thump. "As you pointed out he was living in my house. Past tense."

"You kicked him out?"

"With pleasure. But not until I took back the credit cards he was authorized to use. And made him write me a check for last month's utilities."

Tess sank down on her desk chair. She still felt saddened by Grady's abrupt departure last night, and his intent to give up on their relationship after all this time. Sometime before dawn, her car had mysteriously shown up in her driveway. Without Grady. Perversely, she wanted him to crawl back, to keep trying to win her over. Crazy, but true.

"Sooner or later," Merry went on, "I'll meet someone else."

Tess agreed. "I know this hurts but I'm proud of you." She hesitated, unwilling to probe what must be a sore spot. Like Grady for Tess. It seemed better to comfort Merry this morning than to dwell on her own mistaken suspicions of her ex. "I don't mean to pry, but what was the final straw?"

"Kentucky. The bed and breakfast inn where we should have had a hot time between the sheets—but didn't."

Tess winced. "I shouldn't have suggested that."

"Not your fault. It was Frank's—or mine in the first place for thinking he could change. Ha," she said. "Then there was that No-Tell motel we moved to with high definition TV. I guess they had to offer something except a trysting place for the locals. I took those extra days off in the hope we could still connect. But wait," she went on, "there's more. Last night Frank walked into *my* living room with his latest toy. A huge flat screen, no less, when what we really needed was a new garbage disposal."

"Unbelievable," Tess murmured.

"As if I'd want that TV hanging in my living room instead of my Picasso."

"You don't own a Picasso."

Merry had her own brand of logic. "I might. Someday. Then where would I put it? Can you believe? He bought the TV on credit, some kind of no money down, no payments for a year, no interest deal. Too bad he couldn't 'afford' to buy me dinner in Bardstown at that romantic little restaurant with the fireplace." She paused. "I made him write me another check to cover the television set."

"Frank has money?"

"The check will probably bounce," Merry admitted, "but at least I made the gesture. If you know a good lawyer, I might need one."

Tess half smiled. "I take it you refused to accept delivery on the TV."

"I took one look at that humungous box, Tess, and I swear I saw red. What other proof did I need? Frank was too busy shouting at every sporting event on cable with the announcers blaring through his surround sound speakers to pay attention to *us*. He never heard a word I said about our relationship!"

"His hearing's probably gone." Tess felt her role was to make soothing comments while Merry got this off her chest.

She laughed a little. "All at once, I tell you, I had this superhuman strength. I dragged that sucker through the house, out to the garage, and dumped the box at the curb. With any luck the screen shattered." Her face glowed with triumph. "Then I told him to get his sorry butt out of my house." She grinned. "I winged him with half a dozen remotes before he could back his old beater car out of my driveway."

"Good riddance," Tess murmured.

"I always knew you didn't like him. I should have listened."

"I didn't want to say too much when you cared about him."

Merry snorted. "How could I ever be in love with such a jerk? I must have been stricken with some weird virus or something. How else can I explain squandering years of my life—precious years—being the woman he relied on? When all along I should have been asking 'what about me'?"

"I've set a bad example," Tess said, feeling guilty. "How could you work here at The Go-To Girl and not be the person other people come to with their problems?"

"That's not always bad, is it?"

"Not in business," Tess agreed.

Until Grady had walked out last night, even her ex had depended on her. Maybe, considering the wreck she'd made of her personal life, she should find a different way to deal with her family and friends.

At least Merry had taken control of her problem.

Tess gave her a quick hug. In another minute Merry had gathered herself and was making fresh coffee in the crowded corner where they kept the machine. Tess marched toward her cluttered desk. After making such a decision about her life, Merry deserved a reward.

Tess picked up the phone. "This place has outlived its usefulness," she announced, searching through her contacts for the number she wanted. "I'm calling a Realtor. With luck Sybil Shallowford can find us bigger quarters. What do you think?" she asked. "Two rooms or three?"

Merry's eyes lit up, and Tess noticed that her whole appearance had already changed. As if to sweep Frank completely from her life, she'd abandoned her usual eye-catching skirts and often scandalous tops. Today Merry wore tasteful pumps, a tailored dark skirt, and a classic silk shirt with a gorgeous emerald green camisole underneath that matched her eyes. "Three," she answered. "One for your office, one for mine, and one for the reception area."

"We'll need someone to man the phones," Tess agreed. The concession didn't even scare her that much. "Once we get a few corporate accounts we'll be able to specialize. A new focus—"

But Merry cut her off with a grin. "Who *are* you? And what have you done with Tess O'Neill?"

Tess waved a hand. "No, you were right. It's time to make some changes here. As soon as we rent the new offices—how about in Hyde Park?—with more room and lots of light, maybe overlooking the square near all those great restaurants, we'll buy new furniture. It's you and me now."

Merry turned from the coffee maker, her eyes as big as the

new world into which Tess had just plunged them. This decision hadn't been that hard to make after all.

"Does that mean you've done more than take off your wedding ring? You've kicked Grady to the curb too?" A small frown formed between Merry's eyes. "I thought you still loved—"

Tess tightened her lips against a renewed flash of pain.

"Actually, Grady kicked me."

"You can't be serious. He adores—"

"Not anymore," Tess said then couldn't go on. She punched in a phone number. She wouldn't ruin Merry's mood today, or her pleasure in being right about their office space if not about Grady.

"Sybil," she said when the call connected. "I know we're meeting at the house later, but what do you have for rent in commercial real estate?" Tess might as well kill two birds with one stone. "My partner and I need something wonderful. With character. Not too expensive."

From the other side of the desk Merry mouthed the single word. *Partner?*

"Yes," Tess explained, "for The Go-To Girls."

At least, after she told Sybil no about the house, she would have a new office, if not a home of her own.

"Creative financing."

Sybil had been waiting on the front porch of the house-to-die-for when Tess arrived. Sybil wore a gorgeous lime-green linen dress that made her blue eyes look teal, and she held a portfolio, apparently ready to write an offer. Tess's heart sank.

She'd left Merry practically dancing around the office on Fields Ertel Road, only to battle her way through traffic on

Montgomery going north past the strip mall where she'd adopted the kittens, and—frazzled a bit more—drew up at the curb in exactly the neighborhood near the park where she wanted to live. A pipe dream now.

How could she tell Sybil there'd be no deal on this house? The office rental suddenly seemed to Tess like a bandage for a gaping wound.

"Sybil, I'm sorry but there's no need for me to tour the house again. I wanted to tell you in person."

The Realtor knew a crumbling sale when she saw one.

"Don't be hasty. After you've looked around, we'll sit down and go over the figures. This is a very good value, Tess."

Unable to resist, Tess followed her into the house and was smitten all over again by its light, its airy colors. Her mouth began to water. Oooh, that fireplace. This was the ultimate shopping experience. The biggest investment in most people's lives, certainly in hers. The one thing Tess wanted so badly she could taste it like a rich Italian wedding cake. A replacement—and even better—for the home she'd once lost with Grady. The home she'd never had with Larry and her mother.

"Oh, Sybil," she murmured, at a loss for words after that.

"Is there anything better than the chance to poke through someone else's house?" Sybil sent her a knowing smile. "It's why I became a Realtor."

I thought it was because you needed something to occupy your time.

Tess hadn't spoken Emery's view aloud—had she?—but Sybil answered.

"Emery believes I'm unable to get through the day without his guidance. Silly man." She bobbled the folder, spilling a stack of blank forms onto the floor. "Oh! He's right about one thing. I do have a tendency to trip over myself."

Tess helped her scoop up the papers. "So does my daughter-in-law."

"That would be Chloe." For a second Sybil's voice cooled. "The dear girl did give me a shock when she spilled the beans about your part in buying my anniversary gift. I was actually tempted to return the diamond." She flashed the stunning ring in Tess's face. "Then I realized I had the perfect weapon to keep Emery in line. Perhaps for the rest of his life. Do you know where I was while you were in Mexico?"

Tess shook her head.

"I didn't return your calls because I was—we were—on a cruise through the Panama Canal. *Emery's* surprise. Well, that, and because he knew I was still the tiniest bit peeved with you. But for this trip he didn't even use a travel agent." She smiled. "Believe me, that was just a down payment." Like Larry's gambling debts, Tess thought. "It will be a cold day in the deep, deep South before that man is completely forgiven."

Tess couldn't help but laugh. Sybil did, too.

"I may be accident-prone, or mad. But I'm not without my resources." She led Tess into the dining room where they sat at the table.

Tess decided Sybil was a very interesting person.

In the next moment she knew she was also a shrewd business woman.

"You can rest your mind about new office space. I know just the place." She paused. "Now, let's talk about your personal finances. How much money do you have?"

Tess laughed again but her heart hurt.

"Thanks to some 'creative debt,' I'm not in a position to buy right now even at this price point." Sad, just when she'd learned from Grady that her father had finally come to his senses and might, indeed, begin to take care of himself.

Maybe once she helped Ethan and Chloe with their marriage, found some way to apologize to Grady...and after her house fund took an upward swing...

"Nonsense." Sybil didn't take no for an answer. "I need real numbers."

From her Prada handbag, she withdrew her cell phone then accessed its calculator. Tess supplied what figures she could off the top of her head, and Sybil's gel-manicured nails tapped the keys. Then she turned the display to show Tess the total.

"True, you're a little 'light,' but I'm confident we can get you approved. Your business gives you good standing in the community." She waved a hand, the flash of her Tiffany diamond all but blinding Tess. "And about the list price, I'm an excellent negotiator. Just ask Emery."

A male voice spoke from the entryway. "The bank won't know what hit them." The front door had opened, and Emery walked in as if Sybil had summoned him through telepathy. "Stop talking about me, girls."

Sybil's face flushed. Her blue eyes warmed. After three decades of marriage she was obviously still crazy about her husband. And vice versa.

"Darling, we're *women*—and you're supposed to be in surgery now."

"Canceled. My patient has pneumonia. We'll reschedule." He strolled into the dining room, bent down to kiss Sybil then nodded at Tess. "What did I tell you, Terry? The sellers here are relocating to Florida. They've become what Sybil calls 'highly motivated,' which means they're giving away this house." He smiled. "Works for you, doesn't it?"

"Not quite," Tess said, still not daring to hope.

"Tess has buyer's remorse," Sybil told him. "She's gotten ahead of herself."

Emery patted Tess's hand. "Sybil will take care of that."

She had to admit the new price on this house was good, yet she needed to leave, to regroup—not to get her hopes up that Sybil could work her magic to lower it further—and try to forget the look on Grady's face last night.

The rest of the items on today's to-do list flew through her mind like a bunch of bats from a cave. Most important would be her meeting with a corporate CEO's assistant, which might provide Tess with a major new client. She envisioned hundreds of Christmas employee gifts, retirement watches, fine wines for visiting foreign colleagues. If she and Merry concentrated on finding a few such accounts, as Tess had said, their business would really flourish. Maybe then she could reconsider buying a house, if not this one.

But Emery and Sybil wouldn't let her go. "This is your lucky day," he insisted, but to Tess it didn't feel that lucky. He sat next to her. "You tell Terry what I have to offer?"

She glanced at Sybil. Was he trying to flirt with her right in front of his wife? *He's the biggest player in town...* Wasn't that what Grady had said? But Sybil had him in the palm of her hand. And Grady had been wrong about him.

"Honestly, Emery. Her name is Tess." Sybil winked at her. "This man has been in deep water for thirty years. I'd make it difficult for him now if I were you."

Tess had no idea what they were talking about. The couple had a communications system all their own. They also seemed to have a good marriage that had somehow survived his infamous flirtations, and now Sybil had given him another chance. They looked like honeymooners. If that wasn't possible for Tess and Grady, she was still happy for them.

"I have a job for Ethan," Emery suddenly announced. "My manager is leaving, and Ethan has a degree in business, doesn't he? The practice needs someone good with numbers."

When Tess remained speechless, he said, "Isn't that what you want? It will get him out from under his father's thumb and away from O'Neill's less than sterling reputation."

Tess had frozen. Her quick mental defense of Grady went unspoken. *From what I could see in Cabo, he's doing fine.* And how much of Grady's "reputation" stemmed, as he had said, from Emery's attempts to make sure it stayed ruined? Grady wouldn't be pleased to lose Ethan, especially to Emery. Which was an understatement.

"Too many hours at work has put a strain on Ethan's marriage," she finally said, "but I don't remember asking you to find him another job."

"You mentioned your concerns."

Sybil spoke up. "Emery and I have three daughters. They're grown now, but he can't seem to stop playing Papa. You might as well give in, Tess. He's determined to see to your welfare."

So that explained the various greeting cards he'd sent. Emery glanced her way as if to warn Tess not to bring that up. Or their one lunch together. For a moment she felt tempted to expose him, but Sybil probably knew more than she'd let on.

"This would be a good opportunity for Ethan," Tess agreed. *And Grady will hate me for it. Forever.* "But I know you and my ex-husband aren't on good terms."

Emery smiled. "O'Neill and I did butt heads a few years ago."

"Taking Ethan away from him now would be payback," she pointed out. Her comments didn't trouble Emery, though, and Tess had been worried ever since Ethan joined Grady's firm. This would be their son's chance to stand on his own. True, that first job had made it possible for Ethan and Chloe to buy a home, yet it had also been Ethan's choice to obsess over his smart phone and damage their relationship.

"Sometimes you have to take a risk," Emery said. "That's what I do every time I pick up a scalpel. But because of my training and experience, it's a calculated risk."

"The same," Sybil observed, "could be said of marriage."

Oh, yes. Sybil knew all about Emery. She meant *their* marriage, and Emery meant Ethan's career, but they could have been talking about Tess and Grady.

Emery rose. "Think about it, Terry. If Ethan's interested, we'll talk."

"In the meantime, I'll be speaking with the bank," Sybil added. "Let's sound them out before we do the paperwork. Between us, Emery and I will straighten out your life."

Taking risks has always been too easy for you, Tess had told Grady.

He supposed that was true. As true as the fact that Tess avoided all risk. And sure enough, in forty-six years he'd done more than his share of gambling, played one too many hands of poker. He'd lost Tess. So how did he explain walking out on her this time? Losing her all over again when for four years what he'd wanted more than his next breath was to win her back?

Grady's mood remained glum. Ethan's disapproval when he'd helped his father return Tess's car hadn't helped. By the time his brothers phoned during his personal unhappy hour for another of their two-against-one calls, he was spoiling for a fight. He didn't need a beer to set him off.

"Hey, bro. How's the old tool belt hangin'?" Logan the Lawyer asked.

Brice the Banker laughed. "Put up any ticky-tacky developments lately?"

Ha-ha.

"Ethan and I will be doing some commercial building

soon," he finally said. "You know, low-rise brick jobs for all you bankers," then couldn't resist taking another jab of his own. "Foreclosed on any widows and orphans this week, Brice?" His attention turned to Logan. "Sent any innocent men to prison?"

Silence.

They weren't used to Grady defending himself, or attacking them, but his scene with Tess was too fresh in his mind. He needed an outlet.

"What's your problem?" Brice asked. "I take time from my busy schedule to see how my little brother's doing, and you take a punch at me."

"Virtual punch," Grady muttered, gripping the phone, his free hand balled into a tight fist. If Brice had been standing in Grady's living room right now, Grady would have decked him. "I'm not your 'little brother.' That would be Logan. I'm the middle guy, remember?"

"Always seem like the baby to me," Logan put in.

"Why?" Grady's tone sharpened. "Because I only have a high school diploma instead of a fancy law degree? Or an MBA? Because I make my living with my brawn, not my brain? At least I don't bill hours I never put in, and I never charge twenty-seven per cent credit card interest."

Brice paused. "What the hell's got into you?"

"Tess." Her name came out before he even thought it. Grady stared at himself in the mirror above the sofa and saw a white-faced man with sorrowful brown eyes. "You two," he added.

"Oh, boy. Guess the ex came after you, huh? What does she want now?" Logan hesitated. "If you need legal advice, for you I can work pro bono."

Gee, thanks. "It's not that," he said.

"Then what? You need a loan, buddy?" Brice was quick to

offer his services. "I can fax you the forms. Fudge things a little. I imagine your credit's not that good."

"My credit's...fine. Believe it or not, I can add." He threw in more sarcasm. "I actually balanced my checkbook last month."

"Nobody's better than you, bro, with numbers. On a deck of cards."

Grady felt the last of his temper snap. Sibling jabs were one thing, but all his life he'd been the loser, the family screw-up. Like Chloe, he realized. They hid their own talents because other people—supposedly competent people—expected them to fail. Only he wasn't failing now. He and Ethan had parlayed the Mexico conference into more work in the States than they'd dreamed of having. At the moment several new contracts lay on his desk, one from a high-tech firm in Columbus that needed a new office complex. With the money that brought in, he'd be debt-free. He could help Tess.

Why did he let his brothers talk to him this way? Why did he apologize for himself? The way Chloe had done too?

"Do me a favor," he said. "Don't call me again until you can show me some support. O'Neill Construction is on its way to becoming a premier builder in the Cincinnati area and beyond." He paused. "That three-bedroom condo in Vail belong to you outright, Brice? How about the fancy new townhouse you bought in Philly, Logan?"

"Mortgaged," they both said at once. "But hey, no problem."

"Good for you." Grady held one finger above the End button. "Good for me," he said and hung up.

For a long moment he stared at the dead phone with a slight sense of loss. It seemed unlikely that his brothers would ever be his closest friends, but they were still family.

Like Ethan and Chloe and Dilly.

Oh, Brice and Logan would eventually call again. But from now on, he would handle them—and demand their respect.

Hold his head high.

Hold his own, like Chloe did now.

He would stop putting himself down.

His mood lifted at last. Until the night before he'd never been a quitter. That was what bothered him more than Tess's mistaken impression about Gam-Anon. He knew her well. By now, her soft heart would be forming an apology.

Well, so could he, if not in words.

Hell, yes, he did believe in himself. Grady might not be the best thinker, but he knew when to act. The notion that had popped into his head was a guy idea, but it was all he had. And it just might work.

What would Tess do if she felt stressed?

She'd go shopping.

Not a bad idea, and Grady knew just what he needed to buy. Had to buy. In order to win her back he needed to ante up, to take one more risk. Go for broke.

Chloe had asked Tess to meet her at the mall that afternoon. Now at six forty-five, having accomplished her mission there, she stood in front of the mirror in Tess's bedroom to check her reflection once more in the glass. She loved the new dress she'd bought with Tess's help, another stylish wrap in a bold geometric design with vivid colors. It was so unlike her usual bland big shirt and baggy pants she could scarcely believe the image she saw of her womanly figure and shapely legs in strappy sandals with three-inch heels.

Chloe smiled. She was a new person.

She hoped Ethan would like her improved style.

Still, dressing well for their date wasn't her first concern. With one last look in the mirror and a final fluff of her normally lank hair—she'd treated herself to a salon visit before shopping—she started downstairs.

Ethan was waiting at the bottom. He'd let himself in to Tess's house, which shouldn't surprise her. As her son he often did.

When he saw her his eyes widened, and he tugged at his tie. He'd dressed up as well for tonight's peace-making dinner in a dark suit, pale blue shirt, and an expensive-looking navy and gold-figured tie that Chloe had never seen before. Usually she saw him in work clothes, often grimy after a day on the job at O'Neill Construction. How long had it been since they'd made an effort for each other? Impressed, she gave him a brilliant smile.

"Wow. Don't you look handsome?"

Ethan didn't speak for another few seconds. He just stared. "Something's... different," he said at last. "The dress, of course. But I've never seen you show cleavage—outside our bedroom." His eyes intent, he studied her again. "But no, it's not that. Or the new hairstyle." Then his features brightened, and he smiled, his gaze even warmer. "I know. You didn't stumble on the stairs."

Chloe stared back. What a lunkhead.

"That's all you can say? This dress, my shoes and hair, these streaks of color, cost everything I earned working for Tess," she told him.

"Chloe, I'm teasing. You look spectacular."

All right. That was better.

"But none of that matters," she said. "It's only appearance. *I'm* different and I like it."

LEIGH RIKER

He took a few steps toward her, his smile on the mouth she loved slowly fading.

"I didn't say I don't like it. I like it too much. Not," he added hastily, "that I didn't like the way you looked before. Hidden treasure. You were like a sexy gift in a plain brown wrapper."

She bit her lip. He hadn't chosen the perfect image. Maybe she should turn around, go back upstairs, and wait in Tess's room until he slammed the front door and left her alone again.

The notion didn't appeal. Being alone, living here, no longer seemed necessary.

But then, neither did giving in to the less-than-satisfying life she'd led before with Ethan. The second he dared to pull out his phone she would—

Then Chloe noticed what was different tonight about Ethan too. He hadn't yet reached into his beautiful suit for that darned device. Her look sharpened but she couldn't detect the slightest bulge under his jacket.

Was it possible...?

Watching her closely, Ethan held his breath. He could see Chloe's gaze searching, but she wouldn't find what she sought. Finally, maybe he'd done something right with her by sheer instinct.

"If you're looking for my iPhone, you might as well give up."

Her gaze widened. "It's not in the car or on Tess's porch railing either?"

"No, I left it at home." He made a rash but necessary decision. "If you want, I'll even throw it out. Hard as that would be to do business."

Chloe looked stunned. "I understand it's important for

your work. I'm proud of you, Ethan." She hesitated. "But that's you, not me. At the same time we bought the house and you were doing really well with Grady, I was standing still."

"You're a terrific mother. A wonderful wife," he insisted.

"Thank you. I think you're the perfect husband for me. But I need more."

"More?" He'd give her the moon and stars if he could. He'd work his ass off if only she'd come back to him, but before he could say so, Chloe went on.

"More for *me*," she explained.

He sighed. "I suppose I deserve that. Chloe, baby, I'm sorry. I got so caught up in trying to get ahead, in helping Dad, in proving to you that I'm a good provider for you and Dilly—" He stopped and glanced around.

What he wanted to say next couldn't be said in front of his mother or Dilly, who tended to eavesdrop, but the whole house was quiet.

Chloe followed his gaze. "Tess and Dilly went to McDonald's for dinner. Dilly insisted on taking the cats after they came home from the vet. She claims they love Happy Meals."

He cracked a smile. "She meant *she* loves them."

Chloe grinned. They always connected about Dilly. "It's a good way for her to get one and a half cheeseburgers instead of just one. The kittens share the other half of a second meal."

"So, then we're alone."

She looked toward the living room mantel and the clock. She moistened her lips, making the gloss she'd applied tonight shimmer even more. "For another few minutes," she murmured.

Ethan glanced up the stairs. "I'm tempted to forget our dinner date. I'd like to stay right here—Chloe, don't you know? I can hardly keep my hands off you."

"We haven't settled anything," she reminded him.

But he didn't care. She looked tempted—tempting—and he wanted his wife. Now. Here.

"Do we have to talk our marriage to death?" he said then regretted using the last word. "I love you, Chloe. That's all that matters to me."

Which didn't seem to sway her as much as he hoped it would.

"Grady loves Tess, too. That doesn't mean there aren't problems to be overcome." She looked again at his jacket as if to spy a hidden cell phone.

Ethan half smiled. "Not there, but you're welcome to look. And touch."

As if she agreed, and he was about to be put out of his misery, Chloe drew him from the hall into the living room. She shut the French doors behind them.

His heart began to thud with anticipation until she said, "A few points first: One, I love you too, Ethan. I loved you the minute I first saw you. I loved you the whole time I was staying here with Tess."

Hope exploded in his chest. "Was?"

"I'll love you until...I don't exist anymore." She took a breath, her gaze holding his. "Helping you through school then the first months of working for your dad was my privilege. I didn't mind quitting college. I wouldn't swap you or Dilly for the world," she went on, "but now I also love myself. That's what changed."

Ethan took her hands. "What's not to love?"

"Part of the Chloe I used to be," she told him. "I've taken a few falls," she admitted, "down more than one flight of steps. I made more than a few mistakes. But now I know what it is I want." She thought for a moment. "It wasn't until Grady got sick that I discovered that. I'm good with Tess's cats, Ethan—I've always been good with animals." At times, he knew, her family pets had been her only companions. "And now I want to finish school."

"You should. You could become a vet tech," he suggested, but Chloe only gave him a smile that looked an awful lot to him like pity.

"See? You still don't understand. Ethan, I want to go to veterinary college to become a *doctor*. Dr. Chloe O'Neill, DVM." He heard the pride in her voice, the unleashed passion.

She was right, but Ethan felt clueless. Man, when she changed, she really changed. His mind couldn't quite catch up with her yet.

"I know how hard you work to take care of me and Dilly. The problem was never really your iPhone," she said, "or your iPad. It was *me*. Inside myself I didn't believe I could do anything as worthwhile."

He felt a swift surge of anger. "Good thing your father's not here. For what he did to you, I'd be real tempted to push his nose right down his throat."

"It's not his fault either. He didn't intend to hurt me or my self-image."

Ethan frowned. "But he did, Chloe. I don't care how good his intentions might have been. The result damaged you."

"Even so, I'm grown-up now. The choice is mine whether to live with his criticisms ringing in my ears or to decide who I am for myself. You know what? Once I make a stand with him, I think I'll get his respect. Ethan, you can't protect me from him, from my own clumsiness or anything else."

His mouth tightened. "Maybe not. But I can sure help you finish school. I can see to it that you get to become a vet."

Chloe squeezed his hand. "You can help—as I helped you —but you can't do it for me. I need to take this chance for myself."

Before he could respond, he heard a car in the drive and

seconds later Dilly's voice rang out. His dreams of taking Chloe upstairs faded away. The next moments would be crucial. If he didn't comprehend her need to make her own way in the world, to do something that fulfilled her dreams along with his, he would truly lose her.

"I can do this, Ethan." Her words rushed, Chloe moved into his embrace. "If we love each other enough, we can do anything. Together and separately."

He had just pulled her closer when the door swung open. Dilly dashed in, talking a mile a minute.

"Mommy!" Wearing a white tee, miniature camouflage-patterned skirt and bright orange Crocs, she broke off to stare at Ethan. "What are you doing here, Daddy? Me and Grammy are going to name the kitties!" She flung herself at Ethan's knees. "You can help."

"I can help," he said, his heart full, his gaze still connected with Chloe's above their daughter's head, "but that decision's all yours."

He meant the cats but Chloe's future, too. As his mother stepped into the house with the animal carrier, Chloe said, "You've taken such good care of me, Ethan. You're just like Tess."

Ethan felt as if he'd been hit in the head with a steel I-beam. God, she was right. And he did understand. What he had to say was too important to keep until later even when his mother and Dilly would also hear the words that came straight from his heart.

"I do see," he said. "Ever since we met, since I started to love you, I've made it hard for you to grow. I've tried to shelter you from life itself. I've all but smothered you when what you need, other than my love, is to fly." Of course he and Dilly needed Chloe. She also needed them but not to save her from some silly accident. She needed him—both of them—to be the wind beneath her wings.

Chloe laughed. "Oh, Ethan. You do get it!"

"You're right." He tried to lower his voice, but Dilly clung tight to his middle and the breath wheezed from his lungs with the words that he knew would change the rest of his life, too. "I've been an enabler," Ethan said, "just like Mom."

❧ 15 ❦

GAPING IN SHOCK AT ETHAN, Tess stood on the threshold of her living room. All day she hadn't had a chance to breathe. She'd run from her meeting with the CEO's assistant to the mall to shop with Chloe, then out to supper with Dilly and the cats. Oh, and somewhere in between she'd looked at the new suite of rental offices in Hyde Park where she and Merry as The Go-To Girls might take up residence.

Everything seemed to be in limbo. If Sybil couldn't get the rent reduced on the office suite, Tess couldn't sign the lease. Her corporate presentation had gone well, but they would "get back" to her. Maybe Tess's portfolio with the glowing letters from clients, photos of the varied gifts she'd bought for a myriad of occasions wouldn't be enough in the end. And then there was the house. Sybil's "creative financing" hadn't yet borne fruit. The first bank she'd talked to said a flat no.

Tess felt utterly adrift. She still had to tell Ethan about Emery's job offer, which she dreaded. And what about Grady? She would apologize to him soon, but if he couldn't forgive her for jumping to conclusions about gambling...

"Mom," Ethan said helplessly. He set Dilly aside then left

Chloe in the living room and followed Tess back into the hall. Still holding the cat carrier, she also held herself apart, stiff with hurt. Inside the mesh-windowed container, the two kittens howled.

"I'm sorry," she said. "I never meant to...I was only trying to...You and Chloe were in such trouble when all I wanted was for you to be happy."

Chloe joined them in the entry hall. "Tess, what Ethan wants to say is that we all love you."

"Me too, Grammy." Behind her mother, Dilly gazed up at Tess. "Why are your eyes watery?"

Tess looked down at her. "Sweetie, it's been a long day. I'm just tired."

"But you're not old," Dilly said, remembering another conversation.

"Tonight," Tess murmured, "I'm not that sure."

Ethan sent Dilly upstairs so the adults could talk, then took the carrier from Tess and set it on the floor. "Chloe, thanks for reminding Mom that we love her, but just like you I can speak for myself." Inside their crate the cats cried harder, as if to express Tess's pain, but no one moved to free them. "I only meant that you hold us all up, Mom, like I did with Chloe. That's over. Now we have to stop depending on you to intervene, to help solve everything."

They did love her, and oh, how she loved them. But in the past few days her whole life had fallen apart again.

Ethan was right. For most of her life—first with Larry, then with Grady—she'd been the person they all came to with their problems. But had she really helped? Or, as it appeared, had she merely helped everyone else continue with some harmful behavior?

And when the going got tough for Tess, who did she have to rely on?

Ethan forced a smile. "I want *you* to be happy. I know

what I think would make you happy, but it's not me who has to live with that choice. It's you."

She couldn't miss his meaning. "I doubt your father will have me now."

She saw that familiar flash of yearning in his eyes. "You never know—"

"—what you can do until you try," Chloe finished, beaming.

Tess gave a shaky laugh. "You both sound like a Hallmark card."

For a few seconds she held onto the feeling of hope that washed through her. Could she try again with Grady? This was the worst possible moment to mention Emery's offer but, still, she had to tell Ethan. And chance alienating Grady forever.

"Ethan, I saw Emery Shallowford today," she said. "He has a job for you."

"Shallowford?" Ethan echoed. "What job?"

She tried to explain but could sense Ethan's growing impatience. He didn't seem pleased about the offer.

"If Dad finds out you had a part in this—"

"I realize that. I'm thinking about you, about your family."

"Are you?" He frowned. This wasn't going well at all. *Mom, we'll deal with this ourselves,* she remembered Ethan saying at the hospital. "I've been in the middle between you two since long before you walked out on Dad. I know you felt you had to then, but if I take the Shallowford job, sure, I might benefit. But you have to know I'd also break Dad's heart. I'd feel like a traitor."

"But you and Chloe...that cell phone..."

When Chloe had come to stay with her, Tess's first impulse had been to help even when, at the same time, she'd wondered how to save someone else's marriage.

Yet, as Ethan had pointed out, and just as he and Chloe had tried to fix Tess, that wasn't up to her.

It never had been, with Larry, too. And Tess's mother.

Chloe stepped closer to Ethan. She laid a hand on his arm. Her voice was normally husky, but now even more so when she spoke. "Ethan, you don't need to sacrifice this opportunity for me. If that's what you want, *I'll* understand."

He didn't hesitate. "I don't want another job. Dad and I work great together." He swiped a hand around the nape of his neck, like Grady. "How could I leave him?" Then he softened his tone. "Chloe, I do need the iPhone for work, but I can stop doing the thumb tango so much. Dad and I are now O'Neill & Son Construction," he announced. "With our new contracts we can hire more people and won't need to work as many hours. We can concentrate more on our personal lives. For me with you," he said, "and Dilly." He looked pointedly at Tess. "You and Dad can focus on each other."

Turning away, Tess glanced at the front door. Through its side window she saw a familiar truck pull up at the curb, and before she could gather her defenses again Grady climbed out. He started up the walk, whistling.

Tess's pulse leaped. "Did you call your father?"

"No," Ethan said, following her gaze. "Looks like he's here, though." When Tess looked at him, he added, "I swear. I never said a word."

He was grinning. So was Chloe who had one more thing to say.

"Let's borrow Tess's office, Ethan. I want to make a phone call...to my father. And—oh, Tess, I forgot to tell you when we were shopping. Last night on your computer a turkey platter finally showed up on eBay! I ordered it. I'm still looking for the Haviland piece for you, though."

"No hurry, Chloe," Tess murmured. "Thanks."

"Never mind Mom's office, Chloe. We'll call your dad

later. Come here, Dill," Ethan called up the stairs and, with barely a pause, she clambered down the steps to them, having obviously been eavesdropping. "We'd better make ourselves scarce here. Mommy and I will take you with us to dinner, a night on the town."

Chloe laughed. "Dinner with you two sounds perfect."

"I already ate," Dilly said with a solemn look at both her parents.

"You can have dessert."

"But what about the kitties?"

Before Ethan steered her toward the door, he bent down to release the latch on the cat carrier, but for another moment they didn't emerge. "The cats are on their own."

"No, they're not, Daddy. They're mine, too. I call them Pinky and Blue."

Her favorite colors. "We'll talk about that," Tess said.

Ethan and Chloe and Dilly had no sooner kissed Tess goodbye and left her to her fate when Grady rang the bell. On their way out, they paused to greet him.

Then finally, they were in Ethan's car, pulling away. The little family she loved so much.

Grady stepped into the house and, as if he'd given them their cue, Big Boy and Little Girl pushed open the carrier door then exploded into the hall. For once Grady held his ground. "Sit," he said but neither kitten obeyed.

"Sorry," Tess told him, "but cats make their own rules."

She had a tender spot for them, particularly while they recovered from surgery. She and Dilly would have to negotiate about those permanent names. She stepped back to let Grady walk past her, but he stopped and watched the kittens scamper off toward the kitchen to see what might be waiting in their bowls. Then he stared at Tess.

"Did I interrupt something here?"

"Ethan is a very perceptive young man," she said. "He told

Chloe he's enabled her to stay stuck in that clumsy routine. He didn't realize she needs to succeed at something beyond being Dilly's mother or his wife." She paused. "Two roles that are so important to Chloe, I know. They'll ensure that Dilly is always the beautiful, capable person we know and love. But Chloe is, too, and I'm so glad she finally realizes that."

His tone sounded thick. "They'll be okay, Tess."

This was where they still connected now, in their caring for family.

But Tess cared about Grady, too, in a very different, thoroughly feminine, way. Everyone else had accepted that—except, for a long time, Tess. It had taken her until Cabo and then Grady's stay in the hospital to know that in her heart. Might as well make her last pitch of the day now before she lost the rest of her fragile nerve.

"They'll be more than okay, Grady. Emery Shallowford is another example," she said. "He thought Sybil's career in real estate would 'keep her out of trouble.' Can you believe that? But just like Chloe, she's a competent person. I think Emery sees that now."

"What are you trying to say, Tess?"

She took a deep breath. "That all my life I've been just what Ethan said tonight: an enabler. It's classic in families dealing with addiction, and after my mother died I made it easy for my dad to keep playing the ponies or the slots. For years I made it easy for you to play 'just one more hand of poker.'"

From childhood Tess's mother had provided a poor example; she'd scraped money together to cover Larry's gambling debts, like Tess later with Grady. And more recently, with her father. Her mother had been forced to leave every temporary home in which they'd ever lived, just as Tess had eventually lost her house with Grady. Unlike Tess, however, her mother had stayed in that addictive environment until the end—and maybe it had even killed her. At forty-four Tess could hardly keep blaming Larry or Grady.

"You couldn't have stopped us then, Tess."

"No, but not long ago I also made it easy for Chloe to stay here with me instead of working out her problems with Ethan. You said so, and I was wrong."

"I shouldn't have played poker in the first place," Grady admitted. "Then I couldn't stop." He hesitated. "This isn't easy for me to say either, but just as Chloe did with her dad, I let my brothers influence who I was, what I could or couldn't do with my life, instead of telling them to go to hell if they can't accept me as I am. Or as I want to be." He half smiled. "Actually, I did tell them. Haven't heard from them since."

"You will," Tess assured him. Brice and Logan's taunts had always made her suffer for Grady, but underneath she sensed they loved him. Since he'd finally drawn his boundary, they would have to change their approach. Like Chloe's father. And, she hoped, Larry. But what about Tess?

"I figure the enabling should end with this generation. Right now. You've pulled yourself out of a very dark place, Grady, and I know that's going to last."

His gaze softened. "You're a good woman."

"Yes, I am, but you know what? There are all kinds of addictions. You and Larry with gambling. Ethan with his phone, which doesn't seem quite as serious until I remember that he risked losing Chloe. Even Emery's silly flirtations hurt Sybil in the past but must have made him feel like a bigger man." She added, "Then there was Frank with his remote control, Merry who stayed too long in a bad situation. And there's also me."

Grady groaned. "You mean shopping."

"What if I couldn't stop spending my own money or yours rather than someone else's for my business? You were right in Cabo. It could happen."

"I was only trying to make a point, Tess."

"Then we agree." But did she dare to stop standing in her own way and take the risk to change herself? Could she get another chance with Grady? He hadn't said he would forgive her; but he hadn't said he wouldn't.

Tess had to try. And all at once she knew how. She reached into her pocket then unfolded a computer printout, a picture of the house she'd seen with Sybil and wanted so badly. With luck, Tess might find her own "creative financing." Not only for herself.

"If you can forgive me," she said, "maybe we can agree on something else."

If you want a house, he'd once said in that edgy tone, *we'll buy one.*

She waited while he scanned the listing, murmured things like "hmm, a fireplace," and then "ah, three baths," before he carefully refolded the sheet then handed it back to Tess. "Not a bad-sized lot," he said, not looking at her.

She cleared her throat. "What do you think?"

He looked noncommittal, almost blank. "The price is right."

"You know I want a home of my own," she said. "For four years I've dreamed of that. But more important, Grady, I want a home with you." With the hardest part over, her voice grew stronger. "If we share a mortgage, we can swing it." Her enthusiasm surged. The worst he could say was no. "You could move out of that apartment and I could stop renting here—"

"A business deal, Tess?"

Her spirits sank then rose again. "No, a very personal one. If I wanted a business deal, I'd let Sybil keep working her financial magic—or find me another house. Knowing Sybil, I'm sure she could." She tried again. "But, Grady, you said our divorce was a mistake. I think so, too."

"Why?" But she saw a smile flirt at the corners of that mouth she loved.

"You're teasing me again." Or was he about to walk out on her for good?

"Go ahead. I dare you. Say it, babe."

For a long moment, still holding the computer printout of the house, Tess froze. Because of Larry and her mother, she'd always felt afraid to take a risk. Any risk. That she'd ever had the courage to start The Go-To-Girl was a miracle. Yet she'd already offered Merry a partnership then chanced Grady saying no to the house, and to her.

What had Emery said? *Every time I pick up a scalpel, it's a calculated risk.* And Tess was all in now.

In fact, her position and Grady's seemed to be reversed. No longer quite so afraid, Tess had weighed her options and tossed more chips into the pot. At the same time Grady, no longer reckless, was holding his cards close to his chest. They were like LG and BB, one kitten reticent, the other bold. But with their surgeries behind them, the cats would both mellow. *Change*.

Life required taking a risk at times—like Emery, based on his experience—and, in this case for Tess, on love. She didn't hesitate another instant. It was time to give Grady back her trust, the greatest gift she had to offer.

The next words burst from her, as if she'd somehow contained them for four long years. "Grady, in the twenty-plus years we already had, there were some wonderful times." She had tried to sustain them, even to rewrite and improve their history with her If Onlys. Maybe one day she'd tell Grady all about them, but Tess didn't need fantasy now. Reality promised to be even better.

Like Grady. His warm brown eyes, his easy smile, his lean, well-muscled body were still the same, his teasing manner, and his decency. But now, along with the other qualities with which she had fallen in love and that had grown over time, he had already changed, conquered his addiction. He was stronger, more mature. And still, she hoped, all hers. "There can be more good years," she finally said.

"Yeah?" He tilted his head to study her.

"If the Shallowfords have lasted through thirty years of marriage—and a lot more to come—there must be something to this trust business."

His gaze flickered. "You're sure?"

Tess swallowed. "Absolutely."

He was really putting her through the wringer—and she knew exactly what that meant. His teasing was worse than the day she'd convinced him to go with her to Angela Fortini's engagement dinner.

But he'd gone, she reminded herself. He had gone.

And would wonders never cease, Larry had gone to Gam-Anon, too. After she settled things with Grady, she would follow Chloe's example and call to see how her father was doing, offer her support but no more handouts.

With Grady she used one last persuasion. "As someone once said, 'There are people who get divorced, and then there are people who get divorced on paper.'"

"You're saying that's us. The paper people."

"Yes. I am."

He blinked. "If you're absolutely, positively, completely sure, Tess—"

"I'm sure. We both made mistakes, but we do belong together, as you said. I believe in you, Grady. In us."

"Then I guess we just bought ourselves a house." As Tess had done, he reached into his own pocket. "As a token of how I feel, and since we were dirt poor when we got married in that justice of the peace's parlor—"

"I loved our wedding."

"First wedding. So, I should give you this now..."

Tess's eyes filled. What did he mean? Her wedding band? But, no, the ring was upstairs in her dresser drawer. She made sure each morning that it was still there. Instead, Grady pulled a jewelry box from his jacket. Such a familiar, and yet unknown to her, blue box that Tess felt her heart skip a few beats. Tiffany blue.

Grady sobered. "It's about time I made a sound investment."

With that he flipped open the lid on the box and Tess caught her breath at the sudden flash of light. "Oh, Grady. Oh, dear."

He held her gaze with his. "Will you marry me again, Tess?"

"Yes. You know I will."

With shaking fingers, he withdrew the crystal-clear, sparkling diamond ring in a brilliant oval cut. Two carats, if it was one. *Tiffany*. She'd bought Sybil's ring there but never anything this special for herself. Nor had she ever had an engagement ring.

Grady said, "See if it fits."

"This must have cost a fortune."

"Don't worry. I can afford it."

His voice held no edge, though, as it had in Cabo at dinner, and without a qualm Tess met his gaze again, willing him to see her trust, her love. Taking his cue, Grady slipped the ring on her bare third finger, left hand.

"My favorite store," she said, her throat tight as she watched the stone twinkle in the light.

"I know."

Yet it wasn't the expensive diamond that made her sure of him.

"Oh, Grady," she said again. "You had this when you walked in tonight before I even asked you about the house—" Then Tess couldn't go on. He had come prepared.

He smiled at her loss for words. "No, actually, on my way up the walk I had this piece of coal I'd found at a job site. Crushed it in my hand like an old beer can—and voila, a diamond." He was grinning, that same silly grin he'd worn in the hospital when his brain didn't work. It worked now, though. It worked just fine, which was nothing new. "Seriously, this hunk of pressed carbon cost me more than several months' pay and worth every penny."

Tess couldn't wait any longer to start her new life—their life. She flung her arms around his neck then hung on tight. The real risk for her wasn't with Grady; it never had been. The gamble was with Tess. This time—for all time—she was going to bet on herself.

That decision—and the odds in her favor—seemed easy now.

"I love you, Grady O'Neill. I've always loved you."

"I love you too, Saint Theresa." He ran his hands down her arms and then over her ribcage to rest lightly on her hips. "Tess Trueheart." He angled his face toward hers and kissed her. Once, twice, a third time before they came up for air. "Tess," he murmured against her lips. "So what do you say ? Sex with your ex?"

"My ex-ex now," Tess told him.

Grady laughed. "You'll have to wait for the wedding band."

"It's in my drawer. I thought you had a no-return policy."

"Yep. But you can't wear it until the ceremony. Again."

Anyone could change, she knew now, any*thing*—except in one case. Forget Grady? Never. No wonder she hadn't removed her wedding ring for so long, and temporarily at that. It was a symbol of their commitment, past, present, and future.

Grady had been her first love.

He would be her last love.

Her only love.

When the going got tough, as of course it could, it was Grady she would rely on. Just as he would be there for her, she would always be there for him. Tess was still smiling into the warm curve of his neck when he carried her—his very own limited edition Go-To Girl—upstairs to bed where they sealed the deal.

Tess felt absolutely certain. The best was yet to be.

ABOUT THE AUTHOR

Award-winning, *USA Today* best-selling author Leigh Riker grew up with her nose in a book. She later began her career by writing short stories, but with her first novel she found her true fictional "home," and to this day her passion for writing romance and women's fiction remains as strong as ever.

When not writing, or thinking about writing, she loves to spend time with family, read, travel, and watch movies that make her laugh and cry.

After living in various places, she is now at home in the Southwest where she is (of course) working on a new novel.

facebook.com/leighrikerauthor.com
twitter.com/lbrwriter
pinterest.com/pinterest.Leighriker

ALSO BY LEIGH RIKER

Morning Rain

Unforgettable

Tears of Jade

Just One of Those Things

Oh, Susannah

Danny Boy

Strapless

Change of Life

If I Loved You

Man of the Family

Lost and Found Family

The Reluctant Rancher (book #1, Kansas Cowboys)

Last Chance Cowboy (book #2)

Cowboy on Call (book #3)

Her Cowboy Sheriff (book#4)

The Rancher's Second Chance (book#5)

Twins Under the Tree (book#6)

The Cowboy's Secret Baby (book #7, July 2020)

Mistletoe Cowboy (book #8, November 2020)